A Rancher's Revenge

Also by Monty R. Garner

Buckshot

Card Jordan Series

Card, Kill Them All

Card, Man of Justice

Card, Taking Care of Business

Card, Day of Reckoning

Card, Duty Calls

Card, Unleashed

Card, A Test of Faith

Sawyer McCade Series

Life After War

Take No Prisoners

A Rancher's Revenge

Sawyer McCade
Book 3

Monty R. Garner

WOLFPACK
PUBLISHING
— EST 2013 —

A Rancher's Revenge

Chapter One

The hot Kansas sun beat down on the lone figure in a pasture that extended far beyond the horizon. The man removed his hat and wiped his forehead and face with his handkerchief. Sawyer McCade knew next to nothing about cattle ranching. He sat on his majestic black horse, Raven, and looked over his herd, wondering what he'd gotten himself into. Ranching was a new trade for him, and nothing like his former training as a soldier who killed the enemy without mercy. But Sawyer's days of killing men were over, and that was one of the reasons he had resigned as sheriff of Allen County three weeks earlier.

His job as sheriff had put him into situations with drunks, thieves, rapists, and murderers. There had to be law and order, but he wasn't the man who wanted to do it for a living. He wanted a simple life, one where he didn't have to worry about getting shot in the back or having to kill someone. His sister Nancy was his new business partner, and she was another reason for getting away from violence. They were each other's only family

1

now, and he felt an obligation as her brother to help and protect her especially since she is expecting?

He knew enough about cows to realize that he needed to find someone with experience to help him move the cattle from the Turner place to the new McCade ranch. He shook his head and smiled. Sawyer McCade, a rancher.

Sawyer had just bought this herd of shorthorn cattle off of Faith Robbins, Chip Turner's daughter. A friend, county commissioner John McDaniel, facilitated the sale. John knew most of the farmers and ranchers in and around Iola, Kansas, since it was the county seat, and he was an elected official. Hopefully he would be an excellent source of finding cowboys who could help Sawyer move the herd.

Sawyer turned his mount toward Iola, where John had his office in the newly built courthouse.

Sawyer's plan was to get this small herd onto his land and start a breeding program with the cattle that had come with the twelve hundred and eighty acres he and his sister had recently purchased. Nancy had made a deal to acquire two sections of land in addition to the section she owned and the section that she and Sawyer had inherited from their parents. She'd also bought the livestock on the property—one hundred and sixty-five head of mixed-breed cattle. The four sections together, all 2,540 acres, was their new ranch.

The cattle that came with the property, along with these eighty head he had purchased from Faith, would be the start of a brand-new breeding program. Sawyer also expected his friends from Texas to bring him twelve hundred head of longhorn cattle. They were on their way up through Indian Territory and would arrive soon. Once all their cattle were gathered on their new ranch, Sawyer and Nancy would also need to hire some full-time cowboys.

Sawyer stopped at the county courthouse and had just entered the building when he saw John coming down the hallway toward him.

"Hello John. Do you have a minute to talk?" asked Sawyer.

"Sure, I'm finished for the day and have nothing important to do. What's on your mind?"

"I need to hire some men to help me get those cows I bought from the Turner farm over to my place. Do you know of any wranglers who might be willing to give me a hand in moving them?"

John ran his hand over his chin as he thought. "I bet you can ask Lawrence Mullins if he and his boys will assist you. He's got four sons, and they're all good cowboys. His spread is two miles west of the Turner place and two south. Ride over there and tell him that I sent you. I'm sure he'll help."

"Thanks John, I'll go there now."

Sawyer had left his horse ground-tied outside the courthouse. He'd spent a considerable amount of time training his horse and knew the big black would still be right where he'd left him. When Sawyer got back outside, he whistled and the horse walked to him, bobbing his head.

Sawyer reached into his pocket, brought out a piece of hard candy, and Raven ate it out of the palm of his hand. Sawyer had given his horse the name Raven not long after he'd bought the animal. Most people feared the horse because they thought Raven was a biter. Sawyer still smiled at the fact that the black horse often took his hand in his mouth like he was going to bite it, but never did. It was Raven's way of telling his owner he liked him. The horse liked Sawyer so much that he wouldn't let anyone else groom or ride him. Sawyer rubbed his horse's head and neck as he went around the animal to mount from the right side.

He set off for the Mullins' place. If they could help him with the cattle, that would give him six hands, counting himself. That should be sufficient to move the small herd.

Less than thirty minutes later, Lawrence Mullins's ranch headquarters came into view, and Sawyer recognized the archway over the lane leading to the house. It consisted of three small wagon wheels hanging from the arch-shaped timber over the entrance.

On one side of the lane was a plowed field, on the other was pastureland.

Sawyer's pa had brought him here many years ago to buy a milk cow from the Mullins family. He could tell by the look of the home and outbuildings that the owners kept the place in tip-top shape. They had painted all the buildings and even whitewashed the fence post and boards on the corral to protect the wood from the elements.

Sawyer rode up to the house's front porch and dismounted, where he was met by two of the Mullins boys. "Howdy, I'm Sawyer McCade. John McDaniel sent me out here to talk to your pa."

"I'm Larry Mullins, it's nice to meet you, Sawyer. We've heard a lot about you." Larry stepped off the porch, and he and Sawyer shook hands.

The other young man also came up to Sawyer to shake hands. "I'm Jeffery."

"It's my pleasure meeting you men," replied Sawyer.

"Our pa is in the house. You can follow us inside." Jeffery went to the screen door and held it open for Sawyer and Larry.

Sawyer touched the brim of his hat as he passed by Jeffery.

The boys took Sawyer to the back of the house, where Lawrence, his wife, and two other sons sat at the kitchen table, each with a cup of coffee and a bowl of cobbler.

"Come on in and have a seat," said Lawrence, motioning to an empty chair.

"Thanks," said Sawyer, and sat down. "I'm Sawyer McCade, and John McDaniel sent me out here. I bought all of Chip Turner's cows and need help getting them to my ranch east of Humboldt. Could I get you and your boys to help me with that?"

Lawrence took a sip of his coffee. "Excuse my manners. Would you like a cup of coffee and a bowl of cobbler?"

"A cup of coffee would be great."

Lawrence looked at one of the boys seated at the table. "Samuel, would you get our guest a cup of coffee?"

"Sure, Pa," said the young man, and he went to the stove.

"Sawyer, this beautiful lady is my wife. Her name is Ruby, and that is our other son, Billy," said Lawrence, pointing to the boy still sitting at the table. "I assume you've already met Larry and Jeffery."

"Yes, sir, we've met. Mrs. Ruby, it's nice meeting you," said Sawyer.

She smiled and nodded her head, then looked at Larry and Jeffrey who were still standing in the doorway. "Boys, find a place to sit. This involves you also."

Lawrence took a sip of coffee and said to Sawyer, "Larry is the ramrod of my place now, and I let him make most of the decisions." He pointed to his son. "Go ahead, son, and talk to Sawyer about his cattle."

Larry nodded at his father, then looked to their guest. "Sawyer, how many head of cattle do you want to move?"

"There are eighty head total, and that includes the young stock," said Sawyer.

"I assume you'll also help us move them?" asked Larry.

"Yes, I certainly will. But you should know up front that I'm not a cowboy. I know nothing about herding cattle."

"That's fine, we'll teach you," said Larry, and the others laughed.

Larry turned to his pa. "I think we can move them tomorrow. It'll take us most of the day and maybe a few hours the following day."

Lawrence nodded. "Sawyer, are the cows running on open range?"

"No, they're in a pasture with a split-rail fence around most of it," said Sawyer.

"Is there a holding pen or a smaller pasture that we can move the cattle on today? That way, we can show up in the morning and head them down the road to your land," said Lawrence.

"I think there's a small pasture on the south side of the house that will work," replied Sawyer.

"That'll be good. You boys saddle up and go with

Sawyer to move those cows. Also, make sure we can use the road to drive them tomorrow," said Lawrence.

"There are roads from the Turner ranch to my place," said Sawyer.

"Good, then get the cattle to the smaller pen today, and we'll all meet you there right after daylight tomorrow," said Lawrence.

Chapter Two

Sawyer and the four Mullins brothers made their way up the lane to the Turner ranch that afternoon. This September day was hot and muggy, with just a hint of a south breeze. Sawyer stopped his horse and leaned over and opened the wooden gate to let them into the pasture west of the house. He eased his mount through the opening and said, "There's another gate about a hundred yards up the lane that opens into the big pasture to the east. We'll have to drive the cattle from the big pasture through that opening and down this lane. From here we'll drive them through this gate and into the holding pasture."

"Sawyer, I bet there's another gate behind the house where they can go from one pasture across to the other," said Larry. "Folks usually make it easy to move cattle around."

"I don't remember seeing one, but you could be right."

"Billy, you and Samuel go behind the house and see

if you can find an opening. We'll stay here in case we need to close up this gate," said Larry.

The two young cowboys took off, and in about five minutes, Billy returned. "We found the gate, and it's a double, so we won't have any trouble moving the cows through it into the holding meadow."

Sawyer leaned over the black horse's neck and began to close the gate he had previously opened. Samuel came around the house at a dead run and Sawyer had just finished shutting the gate when the young man brought his horse to a stop.

Breathing hard, the boy said, "There are three armed men back there with the cows, and they don't look friendly!"

"Okay, take a deep breath and settle down. Do you know who they are?" asked Sawyer.

"No, sir, but they all pulled their guns when they saw me. I turned tail and came back here as fast as I could," said Samuel.

"Fine, I'll go see what this is about. Y'all stay back out of the way. If things go bad and there's shooting, you hightail it out of here," said Sawyer.

Only Larry and Jeffery wore guns. The other two had no weapons at all, not even rifles. Sawyer swung Raven around, removed the pistol from his shoulder holster, and held it in his left hand. He pulled the pistol from the holster on his hip and kept it along with the bridle reins in his right hand. He trotted his horse around the house and started for the pasture when he saw the men trying to herd his cattle.

Sawyer heard horses behind him and turned his head to see Larry and Jeffery joining him.

"Sawyer, we've got your back," said Larry.

"Thanks, Larry, spread out and don't stay bunched up. We make a good target if we're together," said Sawyer.

The suspected cattle thieves stopped moving the cows when they saw Sawyer, Larry, and Jeffery, and started riding toward Sawyer with their hands close to their guns. Sawyer turned to the Mullins boys. "Stay here for now."

Sawyer continued on near the men another ten feet and stopped when he was within twenty feet of them. He stopped his horse and let go of the bridle reins. "Howdy, what're you fellers doing out here with my cattle?"

"These ain't your cows. I'm Lester Turner, and these cows belong to me now that Chip is dead. Who might you be, anyway?"

"Well Lester, I hate to bring you bad news, but Chip's daughter, Faith Robbins, inherited everything, including these cows, and she did it legally through the county judge. It just so happens that I bought this herd off her, and I intend to take them to my place," said Sawyer.

"Mister, I don't give a hoot what the judge says or if you paid for these cows. Me and my boys are taking them to my place today," said Lester as he moved his hand closer to his gun.

Sawyer smiled at the man. "You and your brother had a lot in common, didn't you? Both of you are over-bearing and try to ride roughshod over everyone. I'm Sawyer McCade, the man who killed your brother and his murdering boy. If you want to make a play on me, then pull those hoglegs and die right here." Sawyer brought up both his guns and pointed them at the Turners.

Lester went wide-eyed, and beads of sweat popped out on his forehead. The two boys with him put their hands on their saddle horns, not wanting to fight.

"Don't worry about these other two, Mr. Sawyer. We got them dead to rights," said Larry from off to his right.

Sawyer grinned and said, "Lester, are you dumb enough to pull on me, or are you smart enough to turn tail and leave us be?"

"I think my boys and I will go home. You and I will meet again another day," said Lester.

"That doesn't work for me. I'm not one to wait for someone to shoot me in the back. We settle this right here today," said Sawyer. "You can go for that gun, and I'll kill you in front of your boys, or you can give me your word that it's over between you and me, and you call it quits. The choice is yours. What's it going to be?"

Lester sat on his horse and stared at Sawyer before he moved his hand from his gun back to his saddle horn. "I reckon it's over between me and you. You have my word on it."

"Okay then. You and your boys go on home, and we'll start moving my cows, unless you want to stay and help," said Sawyer.

"Are you for real? After what just happened, you'll take our help?" asked Lester.

"Sure, you told me it was over, and I believe you. And now if y'all want to help, that's fine by me."

"I think we should go home and get our chores done. You have more than enough help to move these cows. They're pretty tame and will trail easy," said Lester.

Sawyer shifted in the saddle. "If you fellers are ever over around Humboldt, look me up and I'll buy you a mug of chalk."

Lester touched the brim of his hat, and he and his boys took off.

Chapter Three

Larry took a deep breath and hollered out once the Turners were out of sight. "Samuel! Billy! Come on to the back of the house. The fun is over, and it's time to get busy."

Sawyer and Jeffery rode to the double gates and opened them without dismounting. The double gates were designed for a man on horseback to be able to open the lever, making it easy to swing them open without dismounting.

Larry led the way as they rode where the cattle were grazing. "We'll ride around to the east of the herd and spread out in a half circle. As we advance on the cows, they'll start moving toward the gates to the west. Sawyer, you stay with Billy at the rear and work the drag. Just do what he does."

Next, Larry turned his attention to his other brothers. "Samuel and Jeffery, you work the swing position, and I'll take the lead. As the cattle get close to the gate, Billy, you and Sawyer ease up while the rest of us get them bunched and started through the opening. After

13

the lead cows enter the other pasture, you and Sawyer can push them forward."

Not knowing exactly what Larry had meant by all that, Sawyer said to Billy, "You tell me what to do and I'll follow your orders."

"Yes, sir, I can do that. Stay close to me and you'll learn quick."

The cowboys got in position at the rear of the herd. All of the wranglers started hollering and used their ropes to slap the older cows. The herd moved slowly forward. Samuel and Jeffery took up positions on each side of the group so no cows or calves could run off. Larry stayed with Billy and Sawyer as they worked their horses at the rear to keep the cattle moving.

As the cattle made for the opening, Larry headed to the front of the herd and ensured the animals were lined up so they could go through the gate. A big older bull tried to run at Larry's horse when he got too close, but a rope to the bull's head stopped that.

When the herd leaders had made it through the gate and into the small pasture, they left the main bunch and started grazing on the tall grass. Sawyer and Billy pushed the last cows through the opening while Samuel and Jeffery closed the gate behind them.

The men left the holding meadow and rode to the water well behind the Turner house. They dismounted, and Billy drew a bucket of water so everyone could get a cool drink.

Sawyer removed a dipper from a nail driven into one of the crossbars over the well that housed the pulley and rope. He took the first drink from the bucket, then handed the dipper to the next cowboy and said, "Those cows didn't give us any trouble at all. That went well."

"Yes it did. They're used to men on horses, and that helps. That was a close call with those cowboys though. For a while there I thought we might have to shoot it out, but fortunately, Lester Turner had better sense than his dead brother did," said Larry. "We knew Chip Turner, and he was not a nice man. Pa bought a couple of young bulls off him once, but he wouldn't go around the man after that."

"Well, that's water under the bridge now," said Sawyer. "Let's mount up and head on home."

"That sounds good to me," said Jeffery as they got back in the saddle.

The five men rode together for the first two miles, but Sawyer continued west as the four brothers turned south to go home.

"I'll see you right after daylight tomorrow," said Sawyer in parting.

"We'll be there. You have a good evening," said Larry.

Sawyer rode to Nancy Lou's house and put his horse in an empty stall inside the barn. He went ahead and fed him some oats and rubbed him down before starting to the house.

The two sections of land that Sawyer and Nancy purchased each had a house. He planned to move into one, and she would take the other so they could be close together. Sawyer hired contractors who had started working on his sister's house first, since she was with child. They planned to be finished in a few days, and then they'd start renovating the one he planned to live in. Nancy planned on selling the house she was currently living in plus the acre of land it sat on. She and her late husband had bought it, but now that she was widowed, she wanted to be closer to her brother. Nancy thought she was seven months pregnant and wanted her baby close to its Uncle Sawyer.

His sister was standing at the back door when he left the barn and started to the house. "Did you find someone to help move those cows off the Turner place?" she asked.

"Yep, Lawrence Mullins and his four boys will help me tomorrow. The boys and I went over there this afternoon and moved the herd to a small pasture so we could get started first thing in the morning."

"That's good news. Speaking of good news, I was in Humboldt today, and Mr. Hoffman from the telegraph office gave me this message for you." She handed Sawyer a slip of folded paper.

He unfolded it and read the message. "What day of the month is today?" he asked. Sawyer read the message again to make sure he'd gotten it right the first time.

"It's all going to work out perfectly. Abigail is finally getting here, and your new house should be ready to move into in a few days," said Nancy.

Sawyer had met Abigail when he was in Clarksville, Texas, to gather wild longhorn cattle. He had been smitten by her beauty, charm, and playful nature. It had been love at first sight for the ex-soldier and future cowboy. Her blue eyes had pierced his heart when he looked into them right before they'd kissed that first time. They had spent a little time together, but then Nancy had asked for his help, and he came home to eliminate the criminals in Humboldt—a terrible bunch who'd murdered his parents and Nancy's husband. After becoming sheriff of Allen County, he sent Abigail a love letter asking her to come to Kansas so they could start a life together.

The plan was for Abigail to stay at Nancy's house and help during the last months of the pregnancy, giving Sawyer time to get his house remodeled and Abigail time to plan their wedding.

Nancy grinned from ear to ear. "She's coming in on the stage in two days. I suggest you get those cows home tomorrow, then bathe and get gussied up for your girlfriend's arrival."

"You're right. We must get those cows moved tomorrow, and I'll need to check on the carpenters at your house to make sure they're on schedule. If they are, I'll go to Humboldt early and hire some men with wagons to move your things to the new house. I don't want you working hard and hurting the baby," said Sawyer.

"Brother, it'll be fine. You don't worry about movers. I hired Elmer Wren to move my things when I was in town today. You only need to worry about getting those cows home and cleaning up for your lady."

"I must look a mess and probably smell like my horse. Come on, let's go eat. Tomorrow will be a long day and I need to look at my Sunday go-to-meeting clothes in case they need washing."

As they shared a delicious meal, Nancy said, "I looked at your clothes today and washed your white shirt."

"Thank you, sister, I appreciate that."

They lingered at the table and talked, neither of them in a hurry to do the dishes.

Sawyer took a sip of coffee and set the cup back on the saucer. "I had a run-in with Chip Turner's brother today. He thought he could take the cattle to his place. We agreed that they belong to you and me."

"I take it you didn't shoot anyone?" asked Nancy, laughing.

"Yeah, it went well. But if you want me to, the next time I have a misunderstanding with someone, I can shoot them."

Nancy got up from the table. "Go ahead, just don't tell me about it."

Sawyer stood up and hugged his sister. "I'm going to turn in. Good night."

Chapter Four

Sawyer showed up at the Turner place before the Mullins men arrived. He sat on his horse, looking over the cows. Some were eating grass while others had lain down and were chewing their cud.

Sawyer had a difficult time getting to sleep the night before. He kept thinking about Abigail's arrival and how he wanted to welcome her. He could wear that new dress jacket he'd bought a few weeks ago, over a clean white shirt. But the jacket might be too much for this weather. It was the first of September and still hotter than blue blazes, although it was expected to start cooling off by the middle of the month.

He hoped his friends and former army buddies, Cowboy, Hooter, Harold, and Ronnie, would arrive in Wichita soon with his cattle from Texas. They should be more than halfway to his new ranch by now. The weather had been good, and there had been enough rain to fill the water holes, so the cattle had plenty to drink along the dusty trail.

Sawyer heard the Mullins men coming before he

saw them and stayed where he was until they arrived at his location.

"Good morning," he said.

"Howdy, Sawyer," said Lawrence. "Iffin it's all right with you, I'll let Larry make the assignments and be the straw boss on this drive."

"That's fine by me. Like I told you yesterday, I don't know anything about cows."

Larry removed his hat and wiped the sweat off his forehead before he said, "Pa, you ride point and watch that old bull over there by himself. He doesn't like to be crowded none at all. Bill, Sawyer, and Samuel will ride drag until the cattle get used to the road. Me and Jeffery will ride swing. If we start having too many cows wanting to leave the group, some of you working drag will have to help. Are there any questions?"

"Yep. Will we stay on this road all the way, or do we have to turn off it somewhere?" asked Lawrence.

"We turn onto the road that goes east out of Humboldt. We'll be on it for a mile or so until we arrive at my place," said Sawyer.

"Okay. When we get close to that crossroads, you can spread the word," said Larry.

"I'll open that gate we saw when we arrived, and we can get going," said Lawrence, and he took off for the front of the property.

The others went into the pasture and started getting the cattle up and moving them toward where Lawrence sat on his horse in the middle of the road to the north of the gate. He was there so the cattle would turn south and go down the road.

The old bull that had run at Larry's horse the previous day was the first animal through the gate.

Lawrence sat on his horse on the north side of the road, and the bull turned south, and the rest of the cows and calves followed. When the drag riders were on the road, Lawrence took off and got in front of the bull so he would get used to the horse and follow along.

Larry and Jeffery didn't have to chase many cows. Hardly any wanted to leave the herd. Every once in a while, the two brothers had to stop one from eating grass alongside the road, but that was rare.

Two miles into the drive, the cattle were strung out on the road, moving at a steady pace. Lawrence left the front and rode to the rear, where Sawyer and Billy were covered in dust. "If you want to push them a little, that'll be fine. It seems like they're trailing well and staying on the road. If you can make them go faster, you boys might be able to get on each side and get out of some of this dust."

"Come on, Billy, let's move them on out," said Sawyer, and urged his horse closer to the trailing cattle so he could hit them with his rope. It took the cattle a few minutes before the ones leading the drive were pushed to go quicker. By the time the entire herd was moving at almost a run, Sawyer and Billy took swing positions, allowing them to be free of the dust from the cow's hooves.

After three more miles, the animals were tired and slowed to a walk. Sawyer and Billy kept their position, but occasionally one of them had to ride to the rear of the herd to let the animals know their keepers were still there.

Sawyer rode to the front so he could talk to Lawrence. "We have to turn east at the next road. Then we go one mile, and that'll be my place."

"Once we turn east, you ride on ahead and open the gate. You can get in the road to help me make them go into the pasture."

"Okay. I better get back to the rear and help Billy," said Sawyer.

The herd turned east with help from Larry and Jeffery on the road, and the cows followed the leaders. Sawyer waited until they were a half mile from his place and then rode past the herd to open the gate. After that, he got in the middle of the road and as Lawrence arrived, the two of them turned the lead bull and cows into the pasture. A pond was about a quarter of a mile into the pasture, and that was where the old bull took the herd.

"Let me get the gate back up and we'll go to the house for a cool drink of water," said Sawyer.

"That's the best idea that you've had today," said Billy. Dirt and dust covered his clothes and face.

The cowboys spread out across the pasture as they rode to the house. Deep down inside, Sawyer was proud of what he had learned that day about cattle and couldn't wait to get the herd from Texas onto his and Nancy Lou's land.

Chapter Five

"Sawyer, would you pour a bucket of water over my head, and I'll do the same for you? We're covered in dust, and I hate the feel of it on my face," said Billy.

"Heck, yes, I will. I think the rookie and the youngest got the worst jobs this time," said Sawyer. He picked up the bucket of water and poured it on Billy's head as the boy leaned forward. Billy stood back up and shook his head from side to side, getting the water out of his long hair.

"Give me a minute to get another bucket," said Sawyer. "I'll pour it slower this time and you can clean your face." When Billy had rinsed off most of the dust, Sawyer leaned over, and Billy poured water on him. Sawyer rubbed his face. It only took one bucket for him to clean up.

"Now that you two are a little more presentable, let's sit down and discuss a few things," said Lawrence.

"What's on your mind?" asked Sawyer.

"Since you don't know diddly-squat about raising cattle, I suggest you hire someone to help you," said

Lawrence as he took a chunk of tobacco out of a small satchel he kept in his shirt pocket. "I happen to know a man who's a good cowhand and a family man. He has a son that's about Billy's age who can also help around the ranch. A good helper can greatly benefit you and your sister."

"I've been thinking about that, but I don't know anyone who might be interested or how much to pay them," said Sawyer.

"The man I know is named Edward Monks. He has a wife and three kids. I suspect that if you were to offer them a house to live in and pay him forty a month, they would take you up on your proposal," said Lawrence.

"I'll have to talk to Nancy Lou about this. She plans to move into one of the houses we bought and sell her old house and one acre of land. If she agrees to hire Monks, maybe she can keep her place and let his family move in," said Sawyer. "Where do they currently live so I can talk to them?"

"I hate to tell you this because I know it'll upset you, but they live in a little rundown shack on Harold Jones's farm. They're good, God-fearing, hard-working folks and need a better place to raise their family." Lawrence spit tobacco juice on the ground. "If you and Nancy would consider hiring Edward, I'd appreciate it."

"I tell you what," said Sawyer. "Let's go talk to my sister, and if she agrees, then you and I can talk to Edward and his wife."

Lawrence turned to his kids. "You boys go on home, and I'll meet you there after I finish up with Sawyer."

"Come on, fellers," said Larry. "We still have chores to do at home before supper."

Sawyer and Lawrence mounted and headed out to Nancy's place. As they rode by the newly remodeled house she was going to move into, Sawyer pulled back on the reins of his horse.

"We need to stop here. I see Nancy's horse tied under that bois d'arc tree."

The two men tied their mounts in the shade, and his sister came out of the house as they went up the front steps.

"I saw you all go by with the cows. I assume that the drive went as planned," Nancy said.

"Moving the cattle went great. I'm glad we caught you—me and Lawrence have a proposal on something that's important. Lawrence is acquainted with a family that needs work, and the man of the house knows cattle. His son would be able to help as a cowhand. Let's offer the man a job helping with the cattle and let his family move into your house after you bring your things here."

"I'm sure we need the help, since you and I know nothing about cows. The men from town will be at my old house tomorrow with wagons to move some of my things here," said Nancy. "Lawrence, what is this man's name?"

"It's Edward Monks, and his wife is Lilly," replied Lawrence. "They have three kids. Roy is the oldest at maybe fifteen, and then there are two girls, Malinda and Beverly."

"I know that family, they came into the bank a few times while I managed it. I fully agree we should offer them a job. I think we offer them seventy-five a month, and that includes the boy's pay," said Nancy. "Sawyer, they need to know that the pay includes both men, not just Edward."

"Lawrence and I will go to their place now and make them an offer. Do you think your old house will be available for them to move into by the day after tomorrow?"

"Yes, I do," said Nancy. "I'm not bringing everything over here. Some furnishings, like tables, chairs, and beds, was left here by the previous owner, and I'm going to use it. My old house is full of things that I won't need here. We should be able to equip both houses."

"So I can offer them the job at seventy-five a month and a fully furnished house to live in?" asked Sawyer.

"Yes, that's correct," said Nancy. "I'll also leave some provisions such as potatoes, canned vegetables, and the garden is planted with greens and peas."

"That sounds perfect. Lawrence and I are going to talk to Edward now," said Sawyer. "I'll see you later."

Sawyer and Lawrence started off the porch and Nancy said, "Brother, can we buy a two-seater carriage? Getting on a horse while pregnant is beginning to be a problem, and I'm still a couple of months away from giving birth."

"I think that's a great idea," replied Sawyer. "I'll go into Humboldt when I'm finished with the Monks and see if there's one that I can buy."

"Thanks, Sawyer. It was good seeing you again, Lawrence."

"Likewise, Mrs. Nancy." Lawrence touched the brim of his hat.

Sawyer and Lawrence rode to the shack where the Monks lived. Edward and the kids sat outside under a shade tree, and Edward walked up to the two men as they dismounted.

"Hello, Edward," said Lawrence. "This is Sawyer McCade, and he's here to talk to you and Lilly."

Edward stuck out his hand to Sawyer. After shaking both men's hands, he told the kids to get their ma. While they waited for Lilly to come outside, the three men sat down in rickety chairs in the shade. Edward was in his late thirties or early forties, and Sawyer could tell by the wrinkles on his face that he had worked in the wind and sun for years. The man shaved his head as well as his face, giving him an unforgettable appearance.

Lilly and the three kids came outside to join the men. None of the children had on shoes, and neither did Lilly. She was only about five feet four with a slender frame. She wore a dress that had been mended many times, or so Sawyer guessed based on the number of patches sewn onto the fabric. She seemed a little apprehensive, and Sawyer knew he needed to make her feel at ease.

Roy was tall and skinny, with peach fuzz beginning to grow on his young face. He didn't shave his head, but his hair was cut short, and Sawyer suspected Lilly cut it with scissors. Both girls had long, stringy blonde hair and favored their mother.

After seeing the shack they lived in and the way they were dressed, Sawyer was glad he and Nancy could offer this family a better place to live and enough pay for Edward to support his family. It made his heart feel good to know he'd be helping them, and this family would be assisting him and his sister.

Sawyer stood up and stuck out his hand. "Hello Mrs. Lilly, I'm Sawyer McCade. Have a seat. I have something important to talk over with your family."

Sawyer continued to stand, and when everyone was seated, he said, "My sister Nancy Lou and I are going into the ranching business. We need the help of someone who knows cattle, and Edward, Lawrence recommended you to us. We want to offer your family a nice place to live, and we can pay you seventy-five dollars a month. Currently, we have a little over two hundred head of cattle. We also have twelve hundred head of longhorns coming up from Texas. They should be arriving soon."

Edward stood up and looked at his wife. "Lilly, what do you think about his proposal?"

Lilly looked at Sawyer. "Where's this house?"

"It's Nancy's old place. She's moving into the remodeled residence on the land we bought from Mr. Tomlinson. She said your place is furnished and she's leaving some provisions there too," said Sawyer. "This offer is for the whole family, but the pay is for the men's work. We'll pay extra if Lilly and the girls need to help out."

Lilly looked at Edward. "I'm all in, if you're good with it. Maybe we can go see our new house before supper. I'm so ready to leave this shack and have a real house to live in."

Sawyer stuck out his hand and shook Edward's and Lily's hands. "It'll be fine if you want to come by today, or you can come tomorrow. I'm glad to have y'all on board. I know nothing about cattle, so I'll be depending on your judgment."

"Don't you worry none, I know enough to keep the cattle healthy and fat," said Edward.

Lawrence got up and shook hands with everyone. "I must be going. It'll be suppertime soon."

"Thanks again, Lawrence," said Sawyer. "I'm in your debt."

"I'm just glad to help. That's what neighbors do," said Lawrence. He mounted and rode off to his ranch.

Sawyer talked for a few more minutes with the Monks before he left with the understanding that Edward would come to the ranch tomorrow and look over Nancy's old house, land, and cattle.

Chapter Six

Sawyer rode away from the Monks's shack with a sense of pride and humility about hiring Edward and Roy to work for them and be part of their extended ranch family. And Lilly and the girls would be a massive help to Nancy Lou as she entered the last months of her pregnancy.

He remembered what his sister had said about a carriage and rode into Humboldt to see if he could buy one. His first stop was at the livery on the south side of town.

"Howdy Elmer, do you know of any two-seater carriages for sale?" he asked the young man out front.

The hostler thought for a few seconds. "I'm not sure, but I think there are two or three at the wagon yard next to the blacksmith shop."

"If you don't mind, would you feed my horse while I check? I'll walk to the wagon yard."

"Yes sir, that is if he doesn't try to bite me," said Elmer. He took Raven's reins and led him inside the barn.

"Don't put your hand close to his mouth and he won't try to gnaw on it," said Sawyer, and left.

Sawyer walked along the dirt street toward the wagon yard, and as he passed the Star Saloon, three men came out the batwing doors and almost collided with him.

"Watch where you're going, mister," said one of the men.

"My apologies, it won't happen again," said Sawyer, and kept strolling toward his destination.

"You better walk away. We don't cotton to strangers running into us," said another of the men.

Sawyer stopped and thought about turning around to teach the three men a lesson, but decided it wasn't worth the trouble. He continued to his destination.

The loud sound of a gunshot stopped Sawyer in his tracks. The bullet had gone into the boardwalk where he felt splinters hit his boots.

"Hey mister, we want to see you dance. Turn around or I'll start shooting again and make you do a little jig for us."

Sawyer reached his right hand inside his vest and removed his shoulder gun. Without turning to face the three, he said, "You men are making a deadly mistake messing with me. I don't dance. But if you want to tangle, I'll oblige you."

"John, put a couple of bullets in those boots and I bet he'll dance for us," said another of the men in a slurred voice.

Two more shots were fired and hit the boardwalk. Small splinters of wood hit Sawyer's legs.

"Dance or I'll keep shooting until one hits you in

the foot," said the one who had answered as John, laughing.

Sawyer let the man shoot one more bullet before he turned around with his gun in his hand. Sawyer aimed at the man holding the smoking gun and fired. The bullet hit the top of the man's foot and went right through. The drunk hollered out in pain and dropped his gun onto the wooden walkway.

Sawyer pointed his gun in the general direction of the other two. "You two shuck those sidearms or I'll leave you lying on the ground."

The man he shot in the foot hopped to a porch post, wincing in pain. Blood spattered the boardwalk and more seeped out the hole in the top of his boot.

"You didn't have to shoot me. I was only funning with you, mister," said John.

"My name is Sawyer McCade and I'm only funning with you also. The next time you decide to have some fun with me, you might ought to think twice before you do it." Sawyer holstered his gun and walked away. He was proud of the fact that he hadn't gotten angry and killed the three men. Hopefully, they learned a lesson and wouldn't repeat their mistake.

Two blocks north of where the skirmish took place, he met Sheriff Martin. "Hello Sawyer. Did you hear those shots a minute ago?"

"Yes, I think some drunk cowboy shot himself in the foot out front of the Star Saloon."

"Okay, I better go check it out. I'll talk to you another time," said the sheriff, and he started walking briskly toward the saloon.

Sawyer continued to the wagon yard and was

greeted by a woman in britches, a man's shirt, and a floppy brim hat.

"Good morning, Sawyer. What can I help you with?" she asked.

"Hello April. I'm looking to buy a two-seater carriage."

"I have two for sale, right this way."

Sawyer followed her to two buggies that were parked along the side of the building. One had a canopy, and the other had an open top. Sawyer walked around the one with the canopy. "Has this one had the hubs packed and all the maintenance done on it?" he asked.

"Yes, it's ready to be used, and I guarantee it for a month," April said.

"How much do you want for me to buy it outright?"

"Do you need a harness and a horse?"

"Yeah, I do. How much for everything?"

April pulled a snuff tin out of her pants pocket and tapped some into her bottom lip. "I'll take nine hundred for everything."

"I want a good quality horse for that price," said Sawyer.

She spit snuff juice on the ground. "I guarantee the horse as well as the equipment. Do you want me to get the horse harnessed up and ready to go?"

"Please do. I'll go to the bank and get your money."

"I'll get right on it. You take your time."

Sawyer went to the bank and withdrew the money to pay the woman for the carriage, gear, and horse. He returned to the wagon yard, and the carriage was out front, ready for him to drive it away.

"April, I appreciate you getting everything ready.

Nancy will be pleased that she doesn't have to ride a horse anymore."

"It's my pleasure, and if you need anything else, come see me."

Sawyer gave April her money, tipped his hat to her, and climbed into the driver's seat. He drove directly to the livery stable to collect his horse.

Elmer had Raven tied to the hitch rail out front when Sawyer arrived. The man came out of the barn, shaking his head. "I swear that horse of yours tries to bite more than any animal I have ever seen. Every time I get close to him, he tries to eat my hand."

"Elmer, let me show you something," said Sawyer, and went to his horse. "Come here, and don't jerk away." Sawyer took hold of the man's hand and put it close to his horse's head. The horse reached his head forward and took Elmer's hand into his mouth. Sawyer said, "See, he doesn't bite. That's his way of showing that he likes you."

"Well, I'll be doggone. All this time, I thought he was a biter."

"Yeah, well, you keep this to yourself. I don't want anyone else to know it. I'm telling you since you help care for him and he likes you."

"Yes sir, I'll keep quiet, that's for sure."

"Thanks, I best be goin'." Sawyer tied his horse to the rear of the carriage. "I'll be seeing you."

"You come back anytime," said Elmer. "By the way, that's a sharp-looking buggy you bought."

"I'm sure Nancy will enjoy using it more than I will. Here's your money for taking care of my horse," said Sawyer. "You take care now and thanks again."

He climbed into the driver's seat and gathered up

the reins. The horse took off at a good pace and Sawyer was tickled that he had come through in getting the carriage. Now he and Nancy could use it whenever they wanted and would no longer have to deal with the rough-riding buckboard she owned.

Since it was a two-seater, it could hold at least four adults and maybe more passengers, if they were children. He decided to use it to pick up Abigail from the stage station the following day. He might need to purchase another one after he and Abigail got married, but that was something they could discuss in the future.

Chapter Seven

The buggy was considerably more comfortable than Nancy's buckboard wagon that she kept at her farm. Nancy would like her new carriage—she could even ride into town to buy groceries since there was a box on the back for luggage or whatnot.

He smiled and got a funny sensation in the pit of his stomach when he thought of the young woman he had met in Clarksville, Texas, earlier in the year. He felt that they were made for each other, especially on the night he'd walked her home from work and she kissed him on the lips in front of her house. Sawyer ran his tongue over his lips as if he could still taste her after all this time. He was beginning to get anxious to see the beautiful, brown-haired, blue-eyed woman who had a smile that made him weak in the knees. He couldn't wait to hold her in his arms, look into those eyes, and gaze into her heart. There was still a lot that they both needed to tell each other. He wanted to know about her childhood and her family, and where she was born and raised.

His daydreaming about seeing Abigail occupied his thoughts for at least half his trip home. Then he turned his attention to the men bringing his cattle up from Clarksville. It had been four weeks since they'd left Texas, according to the last update he'd received they should be arriving in Wichita soon.

He decided to send Abe Jordan a telegram tomorrow when he was in Humboldt to meet the stage. Abe was his contact about the cattle, although Sawyer doubted he would know where the drovers were unless there had been trouble along the trail and they'd gotten word back to him. But if that were the case, Abe would have probably sent him a telegram.

Sawyer started up the lane to Nancy's house and saw men loading clothing and furniture into several wagons. So today was moving day for his sister after all.

Nancy came outside and waved at her brother as she walked to meet him. Her arms cradled her baby bump.

"I love the carriage! And I see you bought a horse to pull it with," she said.

"I was able to purchase everything at one good price. I'll leave the horse hooked up and you can drive it to your new house when the movers are loaded," said Sawyer.

"Brother, would you ride ahead and make sure the carpenters have finished the inside work? We should leave here within the next hour."

"Sure. I'm surprised to see you all packed up here—I didn't think you were moving until tomorrow."

"Since I'm mostly just taking personal items and clothes, I decided to go ahead today."

"That's fine by me. I'll get my horse and head on out. Sis, be careful driving the buggy."

"I will. You turn it around and park it under that oak tree to your left. The shade will keep the seat from getting too hot."

"Okay, and I'll put out a bucket of water for the horse."

Sawyer took off when he had the horse and buggy taken care of. When he arrived at Nancy's new house, the carpenters were loading their wagon with tools and spare lumber.

When Nancy and Sawyer had purchased the two sections of land from Mr. Tomlinson, the properties each had their own house and barn. Sawyer had hired Owen Potter to remodel both houses.

"Howdy Owen, how's it going with the remodel?" asked Sawyer.

"We're finished with this one for now. I still have a little painting to do on the outside, but the hardware store is out of the color Nancy wanted."

"That sounds good enough to me. I assume you'll get started on my house tomorrow?"

"Some of my men have already been there for a few days, and the rest of us will get started today."

"Fantastic, I'm going inside to see which room I'll sleep in until you finish my place."

Sawyer shook hands with Owen again and went inside Nancy's house. It looked very nice, and he could see that Nancy had put her personal touch on the kitchen by the way it was laid out. The cupboard, sink, and worktable were all on one wall so she could easily access supplies. The stove was beside several shelves where she could keep pots and pans.

He went through each room in the house, and they all looked very inviting. In his sister's bedroom was a crib. Sawyer looked at it briefly and considered that soon he'd become an uncle and perhaps even a father figure to his niece or nephew. He smiled at the thought of having a baby in the family, and what a joy it would be to see new life brought into this world. It was a welcome contrast to all the death he had seen the past three-and-a-half years.

His thoughts were interrupted by the sound of wagons coming up to the house. He went out on the front porch and went to meet her as she parked the carriage.

"Well, what do you think of your new buggy?" he asked.

"I love it compared to our wagon. It rides so much smoother, and I'm sure the baby loves it too," she said, laughing and patting her stomach.

"Let me help you down so you can show the men where to put everything and I'll take the horses to the corral and park the carriage in the barn."

Sawyer helped his sister get down so she wouldn't fall and hurt the baby or herself since her belly was already huge.

When she was safely on the ground, she asked, "Did you hire the Monks family to work for us?"

"I did, and they're going to look at your old house today and see what they need to bring. They were tickled with the pay and at having a real house to live in."

"Good. Why don't you leave the horse hooked to the buggy, and in a little while, we can ride back to my old house. Hopefully I can talk to the family."

"That sounds like a swell idea. You go ahead and do whatever you need, and I'll be inside directly."

The men unloaded the wagon and took everything into the house. Sawyer unsaddled Raven and while the horse ate oats, Sawyer used a cur comb on him.

When he was done, Sawyer went inside and found where Nancy had instructed the men to put his clothes and his bed. He removed the clothing from the bed and put them away in the wardrobe and the dresser. Nancy was paying the movers when he returned to the kitchen.

The movers went outside and were loading up their two-wheel dolly and tools when Nancy said from inside the kitchen, "Let's go back to my old place and see if the Monks are there."

"Okay, I'll get the buggy and pick you up at the front steps," said Sawyer.

"I'll walk with you. I need all the exercise I can get. This baby is getting so big I'm afraid I won't have the energy to do much the closer the big day gets."

"The good thing is Abigail arrives tomorrow. She'll be available to help around the house, and with the baby when it gets here. The oldest Monks girl, I believe her name is Malinda, can also work around the house cleaning and cooking," said Sawyer.

Once they were seated in the carriage with Sawyer at the reins, they took off to Nancy's old house.

They had only traveled a short distance when Sawyer looked at his sister. "Do you reckon you're about ready to give birth to that baby? It has to be getting mighty big by the look of your belly."

"I thought it would be another month or so, but I'm unsure. It's grown so much in the past month, one would think it's almost time," said Nancy.

Chapter Eight

A rundown wagon with a broken sideboard sat in the yard as Nancy and Sawyer rode up the lane to the house. The wagon had two swayback nags harnessed to it. They both stood on three legs, like they were tired.

"Sawyer, we did the right thing by hiring this family to work with us. If what they live in looks anything like that wagon and those horses, I'm sure it's a move up."

"Trust me, it is, and they appreciate the jobs."

The two girls came out of the house and stood in the yard with their hands over their eyes, shielding the sun so they could see who was approaching the house.

"Hello girls," said Sawyer. "Come over here and meet my sister."

"Hi, Mr. Sawyer," said Malinda as she walked to the buggy and stuck out her hand to Nancy. "I'm Malinda and this is my sister, Beverly. She's twelve and I'm thirteen."

"Hi girls, it's nice to meet the both of you," said Nancy.

"Bev, go get Mama and Pa," said Malinda.

41

As the girl started to the house, Edward and Lilly came out the door. Nancy slid over to the edge of the buggy seat so she could get out, but Lilly said, "Nancy, you stay seated. You're in no shape to be getting in and out of buggies. We'll come to you."

"It's no bother. Sawyer can help me," said Nancy.

Lilly came up to the side of the buggy and reached over the front wheel until she could put her hand on Nancy's stomach. "I've had three kids and helped deliver around twenty more, and you're within four weeks of delivery. You need to take it as easy as you can until then."

"I'll try. I'm used to being active and caring for myself. What do you think of the house?"

"Oh my goodness, it's really nice! I can't wait to live here," said Lilly.

"That's good, because you can move in whenever you want to. I have everything that I need already at my other house. There's a wagon in the barn and two horses in the pen. Feel free to use them when you're ready to bring your belongings over."

"Oh yes, ma'am, thank you so much. We may start moving our things here today and finish in the morning. Is there anything the girls and I can do for you at your house?" asked Lilly.

"No, not right now. Sawyer's girlfriend is coming in on the stage tomorrow, and she'll stay with me and help out for a while. But I'll let you know if something comes up and I need more help," said Nancy.

Sawyer took Edward by the arm and walked away from the ladies. "Let's get away from the womenfolk so we can talk."

"Is something wrong?" asked Edward.

"Oh no, I just wanted to let you know that we don't have any cattle on this place right now. Nancy had some milo and field corn planted out back, which might need harvesting soon so we can use it for feed this winter. Look it over and see what we need to do. The other three places are a mile down the road. We have four sections in a row. This is the first section where y'all will live. Nancy lives in the house in the second section. I'll live in the house on the third section, and there is nothing but grass and weeds on the fourth section. That's our parent's old place where the house and barn were burned down when they were killed."

"Yeah, I remember hearing about your parents. I sure am sorry about that."

"Thanks, we're trying to put it behind us."

They stood in silence for a moment before Edward asked, "Where are the cows located?"

"They're in the first two sections. There's a little over two hundred head there now, but I have another twelve hundred head of longhorns coming up from Texas as we speak."

Edward frowned. "I don't think we should put those longhorns with the cattle that are already here. We should keep them by themselves until colder weather kills some of the ticks on them. If you can buy some sulfur, that would be good to put on those cattle before they even get here. It helps make those nasty ticks fall off the cows as they come up on the trail. It's a known fact that Texas longhorns have been bringing tick fever into Kansas, and the government is considering turning them back at the border because of it."

"That's a good idea, but I don't know where I can buy large amounts of sulfur."

"I'd inquire at the feed store or hardware store in Humboldt; they'll tell you," said Edward.

"I'll check with them when I go to town. We have plenty of pasture to keep the cattle separated for a while. I may need to go meet up with the herd and bypass Wichita in case the government decides to do something," said Sawyer in a worried tone. "I wish I could find a holding pen somewhere along the way that we could use as a place to douse the cattle with sulfur."

"The few times I saw it used, we put it along their backs, and that was enough to do the trick. It seems the ticks don't like the smell of the stuff."

"I have to agree with the ticks. Sulfur sure doesn't smell good to me either. We were around it some during the war," said Sawyer.

"When we get moved in and situated, I'll start looking each place over and make suggestions on what I think you should do," said Edward.

"I have a better idea. You look the places over, and whatever you think we should do, just go ahead and do it. I trust your judgment. I have to be in Humboldt tomorrow to meet the stage. You and Roy will need something to ride, so I'll make a deal at the livery stable for two horses and riding gear. You'll have to go into town and pick them up. I'll also arrange to pay for your first order of provisions at the mercantile, and Lilly and the girls can pick out what you'll need."

"Thanks, Sawyer. That really helps us a lot and I am sure grateful to you and Nancy."

"It's no trouble at all. Well, I best be getting my sister home so she can rest. Maybe we'll see each other tomorrow in town," said Sawyer.

"Maybe so," said Edward.

Sawyer returned to the carriage. "Sister, we need to get going so these nice folks can start moving."

"It was so nice talking to you all," said Nancy. "Now remember, I'm just down the road if you want to visit."

"I sure will," said Lilly. "I think we'll get busy and start moving in today."

Sawyer waved at the girls and turned the carriage around. He and Nancy headed for home.

"I'm so glad that we have them living so close, with the baby coming and all," said Nancy. "Lilly is a midwife, and the girls can help with the daily chores until I get back on my feet."

"You use them however you see fit," said Sawyer. "Just remember to pay them for their time."

Chapter Nine

The following morning, Sawyer was up at daylight, anxious to get the day started and ride into town so he could get some business done before Abigail arrived on the stage. This would be the first time he had seen her in months, and he was excited to hold her in his arms again.

After putting on his britches, he entered the kitchen and placed wood in the cookstove, then set the coffee pot that he had filled with water the night before on it to heat. It would be a good idea to shave and bathe before Nancy got up. An oval-shaped tin bathtub hung on the wall off the back porch. He took the tub down, grabbed two buckets, and headed to the well. Those first two buckets of water went on the cookstove to heat up. When he had four buckets of cool water in the tub, he put two more buckets on to heat while he put coffee grounds in the pot and moved it off the hot stove top so the grounds would settle. When the coffee was ready, he took a cup and went into his room. There he got his straight razor and shaving mug and stood in front of the mirror to shave off a week's growth of whiskers.

By the time he finished shaving and returned to the kitchen, the water on the stove was heated. He had plenty of time to wash his hair and get clean before Nancy woke up. In fact, he was bathed and even had bacon frying by the time she came into the kitchen to get her morning coffee.

"What time did you get up?" she asked while rubbing the sleep from her eyes.

"About daylight. I've already had a bath and I'm ready to start my day. How are you feeling?"

"I'm doing just fine and excited to meet Abigail today. What time do you want to go into town?"

"I'm going to Humboldt in a little while. I have some errands to run before the stage arrives around ten o'clock. I want to make a deal on a couple of horses at the livery for the Monks and set them up with credit at the store for provisions. And I need to telegram Abe Jordan in Texas to see if he's heard anything from the drovers bringing us our cattle. By my estimations, they should be close to Cowtown by now."

"If you harness up the horse to the carriage before you leave, you can ride on into town on Raven, and I'll be along when it's closer to ten. I want to be there with you when Abigail arrives."

"I can do that."

"Thanks, brother, that way I can take my time and not have to rush."

Sawyer wanted to talk about what their sleeping arrangements would be once Abigail arrived. He sat at the table with another cup of coffee and talked to Nancy Lou about his plans. Abigail could have his room, and he would move his things to the spare bedroom that didn't have a bed in it yet, or he could go on to his house and make do until the carpenters were finished.

"I'm sure she won't mind taking the spare bedroom," said Nancy. "When do you expect the cattle from Texas?" she asked.

"I don't know. I'm beginning to worry some. I've had a bad feeling lately that something is wrong with the drive. When I send a telegram to Abe Jordan, I'll also send one to the cattle buyers in Wichita. Hopefully, I can get news of where they are."

"You know it's a long way from Texas to here. I'm sure everything is okay, and you're just being overly watchful."

"Yeah, maybe you're right. In any case, I best be going. I have a lot to do in town before the stage arrives."

"I'll be along directly with the carriage," said Nancy, and she hugged her brother.

Sawyer went into his room and put on the gun and holster he wore on his hip, which happened to be the same Colt Dragoon he had brought home from the war. He already had the shoulder rig on and wanted the other gun too, but he wasn't sure why. It was a gut feeling that forewarned him to strap on the extra gun. Or maybe it was because he'd let his fears be known about his Texas friends, and now the possibility felt more real that something was wrong. He still had a second Dragoon and a .36-caliber in his drawer, but decided he didn't need them today.

It would get scorching hot later in the day, which made the ride into town in the cool of morning even more pleasant. Sweat had already started to form on his body, but it wasn't all from the day's heat. He was nervous to see Abigail. She was beautiful, and he still felt like the most blessed man to have met her. She was the final missing piece of his new life, and now he could truly put the war behind him.

His first stop was at the livery stable, where Raven was left to get fed and watered. Sawyer purchased two horses for Edward and Roy. He considered buying one for Abigail but decided to wait in case she wanted to pick one out herself. He realized from the short time that he'd known her, that she was a little headstrong, but at the time he thought it came from being a waitress and having to put up with jabs from her customers.

As he walked to the telegraph office, he thought about where else he would send inquiries other than to Abe and the buyers in Wichita. He didn't know anyone who lived along the cattle trail or in Indian Territory, for that matter, so contacting anyone down there was out of the question.

When Sawyer entered the small agency, the telegraph clerk was alone in the office.

"Hello Sawyer. What can I do for you?" asked the clerk.

"Mr. Hoffman, I want to send a couple of telegrams. The first one is to Abe Jordan in Clarksville, Texas, and others are to the cattle buyers in Wichita," said Sawyer.

"You've sent some to the Jordan feller in the past, so I know where that one should go. Do you know which buyers in Wichita you want to write to?"

"No, sir, I don't know any of their names."

"Give me a few minutes, I've got their names here

somewhere." Mr. Hoffman went through a stack of papers and pulled three out. "I have a Haney Wilson, Delbert Johnstone, and William Crawford."

"That's great." Sawyer handed him a slip of paper that he had written on. "Send this same message to each of those three men while I fill out the one for Abe."

Sawyer paid for the messages and left while Mr. Hoffman pecked on the telegraph key. The mercantile was his next stop, where he set up an account for the Monks to buy groceries.

A quick glance at his pocket watch indicated that the stage would be coming into town shortly. Once he was on the boardwalk, he looked down the street toward the stage station and wondered where his sister was, since he didn't see her carriage. He smiled and shook his head. Nerves and anticipation were getting to him. Nancy would be in town with plenty of time before the stage arrived.

Raven should be finished eating by now and tied in the shade outside the livery, so he walked there to get his horse. He took Raven with him so he would be close to the stage station. He was left by the water trough in front of the hardware store, right next door to the stage office.

Sawyer figured he still had plenty of time until the stage arrived and went inside the hardware store. The owner came out from behind the counter.

"Good morning, Sawyer. How may I help you?" asked the man.

"Hello Robert. Me and my sister are going into ranching, and we've hired Edward Monks to be our ranch foreman. I was hoping we could set up an account so he can come in and get what he needs in the way of tools and such."

"Absolutely. You tell him to come in anytime he needs anything, and we'll put it on your tab."

"I'd like to itemize each purchase and have him sign for it, if you don't mind. You know my sister likes everything on the up-and-up."

"Yep, I know she does, and I can't blame her."

"Do you know where I can buy a large amount of sulfur?" asked Sawyer.

"What are you calling a large amount?" asked Robert.

"I'm thinking three hundred pounds."

"That's a lot, but I'm sure you can get that much at Wichita Seed and Fertilizer Company. They sell a lot of fertilizer that contains sulfur."

"Thanks a lot." Sawyer heard pounding horse hooves and men hollering. "I'm sorry, but I have to go meet the stage."

He hurried to the door, and the stage was already stopped by the time he got outside. The stage door swung open and there stood Abigail, just as beautiful as he remembered. He started to walk to her when the three men he had encountered on the boardwalk the day before started to the stage from the other direction. Two of the men were side by side and the man Sawyer had shot in the foot was following along, limping. They arrived at the stage before Sawyer and were about to approach his beautiful Abigail. The injured man stayed back about eight feet and held onto a porch post, standing with his leg bent so he didn't have to put weight on his hurt foot.

Abigail was on the stage step so she could see better

with the side of her hand against her forehead to shield the sun and didn't pay any attention to the strange men. She looked past them and smiled when she saw Sawyer and said, "Hello darling."

One of the two men, who removed his hat and ran his fingers through his oily hair, replied, "Well hello, pretty lady. Take our hands and we'll help you down." They extended their arms to her and one of them bowed.

Sawyer had walked up behind them by this point and reached out with both hands to smack the men's heads together. They both dropped to the boardwalk, unconscious. He looked back at the third man, who was already trying to go back the way he had come.

Sawyer reached his arm out to his future bride. "Miss Abigail, you come on down. Those two decided to take a nap."

She took his hand, climbed down the stage steps, and walked between the unmoving men. Abigail leaned into Sawyer, put her arms around his neck, and their lips met.

When the kiss was over, she said, "Sawyer, I've been dreaming of this day for a long time, and I don't care if the entire town sees me and you showing our affection."

"Abigail, I've been dreaming about this moment too, and I want you to know that you can kiss me anytime, anywhere you want." He put his arms around her and drew her to him and kissed her. If anyone had been watching close enough, they would've seen the teardrop that rolled down his cheek from happiness.

The townsfolk that had gathered to meet the stage applauded for them, since everyone in town loved him for what he'd done to get rid of the criminals who had taken over four months ago.

Sawyer broke the kiss as Nancy Lou approached them, clapping. "Hello Abigail, I'm Nancy. It's so nice to finally meet you." She reached out and gave Abigail a hug. When Nancy let go of her, Sawyer put his arm around his fiancée's shoulders.

"Nancy, I'm so glad to meet you and I just know we will become close. I can hardly wait to help out with your baby. By the looks of your belly, it won't be long."

"No it won't. Come on, let's start walking while Sawyer gets your luggage."

Chapter Ten

Sawyer loaded Abigail's trunk into the small bed of the carriage and put her two bags in the back seat. "Both of you ride in the front, and I'll ride alongside the buggy on my horse," said Sawyer.

As they went down the main street of Humboldt, the good people looked with curiosity at the young woman who was with Sawyer and Nancy. Sawyer focused on the road, but let his eyes wander occasionally to see who was watching. There were no secrets in a small town, especially when everyone knew him and his sister.

"Abigail, I'm so glad you're finally here so you can get my brother under control," said Nancy, giggling.

"Judging by the way he took care of those two men at the stage, I would say I may never get him totally under my control," replied Abigail, laughing also.

"I'm sorry, but I didn't see what happened at the stage. I did see two men on the ground, but didn't know Sawyer was involved," said Nancy.

"Those two decided to help me off the stage and my

54

loving man didn't appreciate their generosity," said Abigail. She laughed and looked up at Sawyer.

"That's right, you two go ahead and gang up on poor me, but when that little one gets here, he or she will take my side," said Sawyer.

The three talked and had fun on the way to Nancy Lou's place. When they got there, Sawyer unloaded Abigail's luggage and took it into her room while Nancy showed their new guest around the house.

Sawyer found the women in the backyard looking at the chickens scurrying around, eating bugs and looking for scraps. "Brother, if you'll catch a couple of young pullets, I'll fry them for dinner," said Nancy.

"That sounds good, but I think I'll get your squirrel gun and shoot a couple of them in the head. That's much easier than trying to catch them."

"Come on, Abigail, we'll go heat water so Sawyer can scald the chickens and pick the feathers off."

"Sure, but I'll come back out and help Sawyer when the water is boiling. I don't want him doing all the work," said Abigail.

Sawyer started toward the house but slowed down long enough to put his arm around Abigail and they walked together to the back door. "If you don't mind, hand me a couple of buckets and I'll draw some water," said Sawyer.

"Of course. I'll be right back." She entered the house, and Nancy approached Sawyer and spoke quietly. "Brother, you did good. I really like her."

Sawyer smiled and took Nancy's hand to help her up the steps to the back door. As soon as Nancy was inside, Abigail came back out and handed Sawyer the two buckets he had requested.

Sawyer filled the buckets, took them to the kitchen, and put them on the hot stove. It would heat while the women cut up potatoes to fry. Next he went into the living room, where the rifle he wanted to use was leaning against the wall behind the front door. He checked to ensure it was loaded and made his way back out to the chicken pen.

He took careful aim and shot a young rooster in the head. The remaining chickens scattered and ran off at the sound of the gunshot. He had to go around the house's west side to shoot a second chicken.

Sawyer reloaded the gun and put it back in the house, then went to the chickens to make sure they bled out completely before he scalded them and plucked the feathers.

Abigail came to the back door. "Darling, would you come and get the buckets?"

"Sure. I'll just get one for now. It may do both birds."

He set the bucket down on the ground by the porch and put one of the chickens in it for a few seconds. He only wanted to loosen the feathers and not cook the meat. Abigail came out the back door, took the bird from him, and began to pluck it. Feathers went everywhere, including all over her dress. Sawyer started on the second chicken, and when he had a handful of feathers, he pitched them at Abigail. She, in turn, did the same, and they both laughed as they covered each other with feathers.

While Nancy and Abigail cooked dinner, Sawyer worked in the barn, putting up the carriage and tending to the horses. He was walking back to the house when he saw a rider approaching and went to the front of the house to wait until the unknown man stopped his horse in front of the hitch post by the porch.

"My name is Walter, and Mr. Hoffman, the telegraph operator, sent me out here with a message for Sawyer McCade."

"I'm Sawyer. Thanks for coming all the way out here." Sawyer took the folded piece of paper from the man. "Here is a couple of dollars for your time." He handed the man two silver dollars.

"Much obliged. I can wait, if you want to send a reply."

Sawyer unfolded the paper and read the message.

A herd came two days ago, and the owner said they had trouble with renegade Apaches about thirty miles north of the Cimarron River. The ramrod heard gunfire to the east and was sure there was another herd having trouble nearby.

Haney Wilson, Cattle Buyer.

"You can ride on back to town. I don't have a message to send at this time."

"I'll be on my way then. Thanks again for the money."

Sawyer stood trying to make sense of the message. The thought of his friends in trouble got his dander up.

Abigail came to the front door. "Come on in and wash up. Dinner is ready."

He walked up the steps and passed the telegram to Abigail without saying anything.

She read it and asked, "I assume this is about our Texas cowboy friends bringing your herd to you?"

"Yeah, I've been kind of worried about them lately."

"Sawyer it may not be our friends who are in trouble, and I pray that it's not." She handed the telegram back.

"What's the matter?" asked Nancy Lou as they came into the kitchen with worried looks on their faces.

Sawyer handed her the message and took a seat. He filled his plate, and she passed the paper back to him.

"Let's eat and we can discuss this after dinner," said Nancy.

"I agree. We need to think about this and not let it interfere with our first meal together with Abigail," said Sawyer.

When dinner was over and the three were having coffee afterward, Nancy spoke up. "Do you need to go to Cowtown and see if you can find out more?"

"I don't know. I really hate to go now that my sweetheart is here. I want to spend time with her," said Sawyer, looking at the blushing Abigail.

Abigail reached out and took one of Sawyer's hands in hers. "Those cattle are important to all of us, but those men with them are more important. Most of them grew up with me in Clarksville, and I sure don't want anything bad to happen to them. If they're in trouble, you have to go see what happened. I also think you should take some help in case the outlaws are still fighting with Cowboy, Ronnie, Harold, and Hooter."

"She's right, you know," said Nancy. "Those men could need help. We'll be fine here until you get back. I know how to use a gun, and the Monks are nearby."

Sawyer was perturbed about the whole situation. "I know the cattle and my friends are important, but so is mine and Abigail's relationship. I hoped to spend a lot of time with her and get married soon. We have some catching up to do and we're not certain the drovers in trouble are Cowboy and his men. All we know is that the other herders encountered renegades and heard the gunfire to the east."

Abigail got up and went to Sawyer. She sat down in his lap and put her arms around his neck. "Sawyer, you and I have the rest of our lives together. A few days apart won't make me love you any less. This is something you have to do, whether you want to or not. I love you and want to spend the rest of my life with you, but these are our friends, and I'm sure they would come to your aid if you needed them."

Sawyer sighed. "Deep down in my heart, I know you're right. But darling, you need to understand something. I'm trying hard to put the war behind me. I was taught skills that most men will never have. I've killed more men in the war than I can remember, and I quit the sheriff's position so I could get away from fighting and killing. Now this has come up, and if I go after the herd, I'm back doing what I have been trying to escape."

Nancy Lou started weeping. "Sawyer, I'm aware of what you are capable of, and I remember what you did to rid Humboldt of the murderers who killed our parents and my husband, Richard. You did what you had to do, and now is no different. We need those cows in order to survive, and you need your friends. If you turn your back on them, it will haunt you for the rest of your life."

Sawyer put his arms around Abigail's waist. "Give me another kiss, and then let me get up and pack. If I leave today, I can be in Cowtown by tomorrow night. I'm sure I can hire a few men there to help me out."

"Go gather up what you need, and Abigail and I

will put you a grub sack together that will bind you over for a couple of days," said Nancy.

"I'm packing light, so don't load me down with a lot of food."

Sawyer went to his room and strapped the .36-caliber pistol behind his back. He secured the other Colt Dragoon on his left hip so he could cross draw. A flour sack in the bottom drawer of his nightstand kept his extra gunpowder, balls, and wadding, and he pulled it out to take with him. Now he had four guns, plus his Henry repeating rifle. With only one change of clothes and the bedroll out in the barn, he was now equipped for war.

The armed warrior exited his bedroom and walked to the kitchen, where Nancy and Abigail were still putting provisions together for him. "I have a coffee pot and small skillet out in the barn," he told them. "I'm going after my horse and will bring the cooking utensils back."

Abigail stopped what she was doing and said, "I'll go to the barn with you."

Sawyer smiled at her and reached out his hand. She took it, and they walked to the barn holding on to each other. When they were inside and out of sight from Nancy, she put her arms around his neck, and they stood and kissed for a long while.

"Sawyer, I love you and you had better come back in one piece."

"I love you too, and I promise to return to you."

Chapter Eleven

Abigail walked alongside Sawyer as he led Raven out of the barn and stopped behind the house at the back porch where Nancy had set two flour sacks full of provisions.

"You have enough food to get you to Wichita. If we hear anything from the telegraph clerk in Humboldt, I'll have him forward the message to you there. If you must go into Indian Territory looking for the herd, please send us a telegram," said Nancy. "I love you, brother, and you should be extra careful."

"I love you too, sister, and I'll let the both of you know what I have to do when I get more information."

Sawyer turned to Abigail. "You'll need to check on the carpenters working on our house. Have them remodel everything how you want it, it's up to you."

She sniffed and wiped the tears from her eyes. He took her into his arms and gave her one last kiss. "I shall return."

After mounting up and heading down the lane to the road, he never looked back at the two women because of the tears that were running down his face. The sad feeling that gripped his heart was from having to leave them, and from the distress knowing he would probably have to kill more men before he returned home.

Raven loped all the way to Humboldt and slowed down as they hit Main Street. Sawyer stopped at a water trough, only two buildings from the telegraph office. He dropped the reins to the ground and went to see if Mr. Hoffman had any more messages for him.

A lady stood at the counter writing on a scrap of paper. Sawyer waited until she had finished her business before he said, "Hello Mr. Hoffman. Do I have any messages?"

"No, I only had that one I sent to your house."

"I'm on my way to Wichita. If you get any more for me, you can send them there."

"I sure will. You be careful."

Sawyer nodded and left the building. He mounted up and headed to the river crossing. Once across the bridge, he urged his horse to go faster, and Raven took him down the road toward Cowtown at a fast lope. Sawyer had time to think about what he might have to do, and he made the conscious decision to once again be the soldier and scout that had managed to stay alive during the Civil War. He would shoot first and worry about the consequences later.

If he had to deal with renegade Indians, there would be no time to be timid or meek. During the war, most of the looting and killing of innocent people on homesteads had been done by leaders with warped minds. They killed for the fun of it, and the men who followed them stole and killed as ordered. As far as he was concerned, that was not war, but cruelty and murder. Those bands of soldiers were nothing less than gangs or renegades of ex-Confederate bushwhackers. Some even had Indian members. Some were made up of terrible white men, and others had raiding parties that included Mexicans who terrorized and murdered travelers.

Sawyer didn't want to tire his horse out, so he loped him for a few miles, then slowed down to a walk to let Raven catch his wind. The weather was still hot, and Sawyer was covered in sweat. Every so often he made sure to sip water from his canteen.

Raven was lathered up, and each time Sawyer saw a pond or a small stream, he let his horse cool down for a few minutes and then let him drink.

When the sun was setting in the west, and it had been a few hours since the last time they'd stopped, Sawyer again started to watch for a water source with nearby shade, so he could stop for something to eat and refill his canteen. His horse also needed water, grass, and rest from the heat.

Raven was walking to cool off when Sawyer spotted a farmhouse about three hundred feet off the road. Flowers lined the front porch, giving the impression that the place was occupied. Someone must have been watering them, or they would've died in the heat.

He started up the path to the house and stopped when he was fifty feet from the front door and called out in a loud voice, but there was no answer. He pulled his gun from its holster and called out again. This time, he saw a man in bib overalls and a woman in a long dress come around from the back of the house.

"Howdy, I'm Sawyer McCade, and I'd like to know

if I could use your water well to fill my canteen and give my horse a drink."

"I've heard of you. You were the sheriff in Allen County who cleaned out that bunch of crooks in Humboldt."

"I was the sheriff, but now I'm trying to ranch."

"You take all the water you need. The well is out back and there is plenty of shade for you and your horse to cool off in."

"Much obliged," said Sawyer. He dismounted and led his horse to the back of the house. The man and woman followed him. "If you don't mind, what are your names?" he asked.

"I'm Luther Van, and this is my wife Sissy. We've been here seven years trying to make a living by raising corn and wheat."

"It's real nice to meet the two of you," said Sawyer as he went to the well and dropped the bucket in the water. There was an old water trough close to the well, and he poured four buckets of water for his horse. He drew another bucket and filled his canteen, pouring the remaining water on his horse's neck. That would help cool him down while he grazed on grass under a tree.

Sawyer sat in the shade with his canteen and one of the grub sacks he'd taken off his saddle. "I hope you folks don't mind if I eat something. It's been a mighty long spell since I had any food."

"You go right ahead. We'd offer you something, but don't usually cook until right before dark. There is still work to be done shucking corn, so we'll be in the barn if you need something," said Luther.

Sawyer nodded as the couple walked off. In his sack, he found fried chicken, biscuits, and some sugar cookies. The food hit the spot and after he had his fill, he refilled the canteen, mounted up, and rode to the barn. "Hello in the barn. Thanks for the water and shade. I have to be going now."

Luther came to the barn door. "You come back by anytime."

Sawyer touched the brim of his hat and turned his horse back toward the road.

It was well after dark before the tired man and horse finally stopped in a grove of cottonwood trees next to a creek to get a few hours of sleep. Before bedding down, Sawyer removed Raven's saddle and rubbed him down with a double handful of grass. He didn't build a fire since the moon gave enough light for him to put down his bedroll and get as comfortable as he could.

The following morning before daylight, it seemed like every muscle and bone in his body ached from sleeping on the ground. He had gotten used to a soft bed since he'd been home from the war, and now he would have to get accustomed to sleeping outside again. There was no need to start a fire for coffee; he could stop at a trading post along the route for a cup. He dug through his grub sack and ate the remaining chicken and biscuits before he saddled his horse and stowed his bedroll and supplies.

Raven was rested up and wanted to run, but Sawyer kept him at a lope for the first few miles. Then he walked him for a spell to catch his wind and cool off before letting him lope again.

The sun was setting in the west when they rode up on Turkey Creek, which he figured was about twenty-four miles from Wichita. Sawyer let Raven get his fill of water from the shallow stream before continuing. A few miles west of the brook, he came to a building that looked like a house, but the sign read, *STORE, owner C.N. James.* There was a total of three houses located in the small settlement along with the store.

Sawyer dismounted and stood for a few seconds, letting his legs get accustomed to bearing weight. He was tired, hot, and hungry. Raven made his way to some green grass by an oak tree and began to graze. Sawyer loosened the gun on his hip and went into the dimly lit store.

The only light in the place was a kerosene lantern hanging on a rope from the ceiling over the counter.

A woman came into the store from the back of the building through a doorway with a quilt hanging over the opening. "Howdy mister, can I help you?"

"Yes ma'am, I would like something to eat, if you have any food, and maybe coffee."

"I have a fresh pot of coffee and cornbread in the oven. I'll go fetch your coffee and when the bread is ready, I'll bring you a plate of beans and pork chops."

"That sounds good. Thank you ma'am."

"You're welcome. You can have a seat over there." She pointed to a small, round table with three chairs.

Sawyer walked to the table, pulled out a chair, and sat. He didn't realize how tired he was until he got comfortable. The long day of riding had made him sleepy.

He heard a sound and looked to the doorway. A man in buckskin britches and no shirt walked in and came to the table with a cup of coffee in each hand.

"You have to excuse my manners, but I been outside working and forgot my shirt when I came in the house.

I'm C.N. James, and you have already met my wife, Lucille." He set the coffee on the table and sat in one of the other chairs.

"Nice to meet you C.N. I'm Sawyer McCade and on my way to Wichita." Sawyer picked up his cup and blew on the hot liquid before he took a sip.

"It's another twenty miles to Wichita if you plan on getting there today. It'll still be going strong until about midnight. That is, if any herds came in lately."

"I'll continue on after I've eaten. I need to get there tonight."

The quilt curtain moved, and Lucille came into the room singing "Amazing Grace" and carrying a plate of food in each hand. "Here you fellers go, dig in while it's hot. I'll be right back with my plate and the cornbread."

Sawyer picked up a pork chop with his hands and took a big bite. By the time he'd swallowed, Lucille was back.

The three of them ate their food and conversed with one another until Sawyer pushed his plate away and finished off his coffee. "Now that was a mighty fine meal. I really appreciate the food. How much do I owe you?"

"That'll be a dollar if you can afford that much," said Lucille. "I'll throw you in another pork chop and a piece of cornbread for the road."

"That won't be necessary." Sawyer pulled two silver dollars from his pants pocket and placed them on the table. "I best be on my way if I plan on making Cowtown by tonight. I'll most likely stop here again on my way home."

"You come back anytime and be careful around those cowboys in Wichita. We know you've seen your share of trouble by the amount of guns you carry, but the boys coming off a trail drive can get rowdy when the liquor gives them courage."

"I'll be careful. Good night, folks."

It was dark when Sawyer rode away from the James' store and urged his horse to go faster.

Chapter Twelve

Sawyer rode up on the Whitewater River a few miles west of the store. It was light enough from the moon for him to find the spot where travelers had been fording the stream. He didn't like to ford rivers and creeks in the dark, but there was just enough moonlight reflecting off the water to see the far bank, and he decided to risk it. Fortunately, the stream only came up to Raven's belly, making the crossing easy.

The twenty miles from the James' store to Wichita seemed to take forever. Sawyer was miserable from the large meal he had eaten. The food gave him gas, and that made his stomach hurt and cramp. Raven was tired, hot, and lathered up from the heat, and needed a proper rest after the long journey they'd been on the past two days.

Sawyer figured they were only a short distance from Wichita, based on the length of time he had traveled since he left C. N's store. There were more houses along the road than before. He could see the dark forms on each side of the road, and every once in a while, lights shone through a few windows.

Raven was tired, and they covered the last two miles at a slower pace. By entering Wichita from the east, they passed by a few more houses with lights on inside. There had to be a livery stable and a hotel nearby, but as he looked at the buildings along the street, he realized this end of the city was more housing than businesses.

A few minutes later, the sound of music drifted along the road. Occasionally, he heard a muffled sound that sounded like a gunshot inside a building.

As he got closer to the central part of town, the streetlamps, along with the light coming out the windows and doors of the saloons and dance halls, made it easier for Sawyer to see. These places stayed open late and provided a place for the cowboys coming in from the trail to blow off steam and spend their money. On his right was a livery stable that was still open, and he turned in that direction.

Two boys, around sixteen years old, came from a shed where he figured they lived, and one reached to take hold of Raven's bridle. "Don't do that unless you want to get your fingers bit off," said Sawyer.

The boy backed up away from the horse. "Thanks, mister. Do you want us to feed your horse and put him in the corral?"

"I want him fed, watered, and combed. But put him in a stall by himself and don't try to ride him or rub his head."

"Yes sir, we'll take mighty good care of him. That'll be three dollars in advance."

Sawyer gave the boy the money and asked, "If some

cowboys came in on the trail a few days ago, where might they be?"

"Most likely at one of the saloons, unless they went broke and hightailed it back to where they come from."

Sawyer stood outside the livery and watched men walk up and down the boardwalk going inside the different dives. He thought about leaving the saloons alone tonight and heading to the hotel for a room. Most likely, the cowboys in the saloons were drunk or close to it by now, and it might cause trouble if he went in to ask questions.

"Hold up a second," he called out to the two boys as they led his horse to the barn. "Where would I find a cattle buyer named Haney Wilson?"

"He could be at his office down at the cattle pens. It's the second set of pens on the west side of the tracks. If he ain't there, then he has a room at the White Hotel," said one boy.

"Where's the White Hotel and where are the cattle pens located?" asked Sawyer.

"The hotel is a few blocks south of here, and the cattle pens are a half mile to the west. You can't miss them for the smell."

"Thanks, I'll be back tomorrow for my horse. Make sure you feed him some oats."

"Oh yes sir. We'll take good care of him."

Sawyer walked south on the boardwalk, but it was so crowded that he veered to the edge of the street so he wouldn't bump into drunks who wanted to fight. A few people did the same as him and walked in the street.

He wanted to check for Haney at the hotel first. If he was already there, it would save him a mile walk to the pens and back.

He counted a total of six drinking holes on his way to the hotel, two on his side of the street, and four on the opposite side. As he walked past the first establishment on his side of the street, music and other sounds like glass breaking, men talking loudly, and laughter filtered out the doorway and open windows.

As he neared the second saloon, the sound of fighting caught his attention. He heard cursing and what sounded like a table or chairs breaking. Sawyer stopped walking just in time to avoid two men who came flying through the bat wing doors with fists swinging at each other. He decided it'd be safer to walk down the center of the street, and as he started that way, one of the men was hit so hard that he stumbled across the boardwalk and out into the street. It looked like he was going to collide with Sawyer until Sawyer took a step backward, and the man fell on the ground at his feet. The other cowboy ran to the man and pulled out a long-blade knife.

"I'm going to cut you really good," he said to the man lying on the ground.

Sawyer grabbed the man's arm and held the knife steady. "Drop the knife. You're not cutting anyone tonight."

The drunk tried to hit Sawyer with his free hand but missed, and a right cross struck the drunk cowboy square on the chin. His eyes rolled back and his knees buckled. Still holding onto Sawyer's arm, the man slumped onto the dirt, unconscious. Sawyer reached down and pried the knife from the man's hand and took it with him as he continued down the street.

When he was a good hundred feet past the saloon

and could see the hotel, he pitched the knife into a water trough and headed into the hotel.

The hotel clerk greeted Sawyer as he made his way into the lobby. "Good evening, sir."

"I'm looking for Haney Wilson. Would he happen to be in his room?"

"Mr. Wilson eats a very late supper and is in the dining area having his meal. If you go down this hall and through the doors on the left, you'll find him."

"I'm afraid I've never met the man. Can you describe him to me?"

"He's the only man in there. You can't miss him."

"Much obliged," said Sawyer, walking to the dining room door.

The clerk was correct—there was only one man having his evening meal. He wore a wide-brim beaver hat, striped britches, and a dress jacket over a white shirt. He looked to be in his fifties, with hair that was short on the sides. His face was clean-shaven.

Sawyer felt a little out of place in the same clothes he'd been wearing for the past three days. He also hadn't shaved in a while. But there was no time to be modest now. "Excuse me, are you Haney Wilson?"

Haney was finishing his supper and sopping the last of the food from his plate with half of a biscuit. The man put down his fork and moved his right hand closer to his gun. "That's right, I'm Haney. What can I do for you?"

"I'm Sawyer McCade from over in Humboldt. You replied to a telegram of mine a couple of days ago. I'd like to get as much information as possible about the trouble on the cattle trail through Indian Territory you heard about. I have a herd of cattle coming up from

Texas that's overdue. I'm afraid for the safety of the cowboys and the herd."

"Have a seat." Haney called out to a woman wiping off tables on the other side of the room. "Bessy, bring my friend a cup of coffee, please."

"Thanks," said Sawyer, and he sat down.

"I've heard from two trail bosses that there is trouble north of the Cimarron River and west of a trading store called Alfred's. Both men said they could hear sporadic gunfire to the east, and one of them even saw a herd of longhorns bunched up in the direction of the gunfire. They said they got their own herds out of there as fast as possible before anyone tried to engage them in the ruckus."

"Did they see any of the men with the cows?" asked Sawyer.

"I don't know. They didn't mention seeing anyone. Jeb Carlson was the last person I talked to about it when I bought his herd two days ago. He said that he spoke to some locals on the trail, and they told him to be watchful for renegade Apache's riding with some white men across the prairie between Fort Sill and the Kansas border. Supposedly, they had been attacking some homesteads and smaller herds traveling through the area."

"How long will it take me to get to where those men saw the bunched-up cattle?" asked Sawyer.

"It's around a hundred miles, give or take a few. Are you planning on going down there by yourself?"

"I'd like to take some fighting men with me if I can. Do you know anyone that might hire out to go with me to get my cattle and men?" Sawyer took a swallow of his coffee.

When he finished the last bite of his food, Haney put both hands around his coffee mug. "I know most of the men here in town. We can go by the saloons and assemble a crew, if you so desire. How many men do you plan to take with you?"

"I want to travel fast, so I think just four plus me. I can buy us extra horses so we can change out around midday. I'm pretty sure we can make it there within two days if we ride hard," said Sawyer.

Haney stood up and took one last swallow of coffee. "Come on, let's go hire you some cowboys."

Sawyer got up from his chair. "Do you have time for me to register at the desk for a room first? A soft bed tonight will do wonders for me. I need to get some good rest before heading into the Indian Territory."

"Absolutely. Sabastian should be at the counter at this time of night. We'll get you checked in quickly."

The clerk was still at the desk going through a small stack of receipts when they entered the lobby.

"Sabastian," said Haney, "put my friend in a room for the night."

"Yes sir," said the clerk, and he handed Sawyer a key.

"You'll be in room five at the top of the stairs and that will be four dollars for one night." He turned the ledger book around so Sawyer could sign his name. With the room paid for, Sawyer and Haney left and walked up the street.

"We'll start at the Silver Saddle Saloon," said Haney. "I see you came armed. Can you use those guns you have on?"

"Yep, I can use them."

Chapter Thirteen

Sawyer followed Haney to the Silver Saddle and they went in. The bar was constructed of planks sitting on top of whiskey barrels. The place stunk of stale beer, vomit, and tobacco smoke.

Haney went to the counter, but Sawyer stood inside the doorway, giving his eyes time to adjust to the dim, smoke-filled room. He also wanted to look around to see if he saw anyone he knew, but he didn't recognize any of the patrons. He approached the counter, where the barkeep was talking to Haney. The man pointed to a table at which sat five men drinking whiskey.

Haney waited until Sawyer was next to him before he leaned in close and said, "We'll go to that table and talk to those men. You might want me to start the conversation, and then you can chime in."

"That's fine by me," said Sawyer, following along to the table.

"Hello boys," Haney said.

The men looked up. One of them raised his glass

and said, "Evening, Haney. I figured you had already turned in for the night."

"No, not yet Billy Bob, but it's getting close to my bedtime. I hope you're enjoying your stay in town," said Haney.

Billy Bob nodded. "You want a drink?"

Haney smiled. "Not tonight. I came by to introduce you to my friend Sawyer McCade. He's concerned that his men and cattle are in trouble north of the Cimmaron River and west of Alfred's Store. He's looking to hire a few men to go with him into Indian Territory, get his cattle, and drive them to Humboldt, Kansas. Do you know anyone who might be interested in helping him out?"

A lanky cowboy sitting at the table and wearing a bright red bandana tied around his neck spoke up. "You should buy us a round of drinks while we ponder on it."

Sawyer stepped in closer to the table. "I ain't here to buy whiskey. I'm here to hire cowboys who will ride with me to rescue my friends and get my cattle home. If any of you want the work, I'll pay fifty dollars to each man, and if you want a job afterward, we can discuss it."

The oldest looking of the five men, who was most likely in his late thirties, spoke. "I'm in! The name's Luke Dickson. When do we leave?"

"I need to get there fast, so we leave at first light. I'll buy each rider a spare horse so we can swap out around midday. I want to be there in two days if we can," said Sawyer.

Luke put his glass up to his lips and drained the stout liquor. "Well, are any of the rest of you going?"

The other men at the table drained their glasses also.

"I'm Jesse Southard, and I'm in," said the lanky cowboy with the bandana.

"I'm Barney Jackson," said another of the men. He stood up and stuck out his hand to shake. Sawyer noticed the man was missing the thumb on his right hand.

"Nice to meet you, Barney."

The last man to stand said his name was Austin Grant. He sported a beard that was so long, it came down to the top button of his shirt.

The fifth man, who Haney had called Billy Bob, said, "I've already taken a job, so I won't be going."

"Sit back down, men, and make room for our boss. We have some things to work out tonight," said Luke.

Haney patted Sawyer on the back. "I'll be on my way and let you plan your trip. It was nice meeting you, Sawyer."

"Thanks Haney. I appreciate all you've done. I'll see you on my way back," said Sawyer. He pulled a chair over from one of the other tables where only two men sat.

One of the men at the table smarted off. "You can put that chair right back where you got it from, mister."

Sawyer turned to the man. "Look, I'm not hunting trouble. No one is using this chair, so I'll sit in it."

The man pushed away from the table, and as he did, Sawyer pulled his gun and cocked the hammer in the firing position. "Mister, are you willing to die over a chair?"

"No, I don't believe I am. You go ahead and use it as long as you want."

"Thanks, I appreciate it," said Sawyer, and he moved the chair around the table so he could watch the man he'd drawn on while making plans with his new hires.

"Do you have a pack horse to carry the grub?" asked Luke.

"No, I thought we could carry it on the spare horses. I want us to travel light and not bring any unnecessary supplies," said Sawyer.

"If your men have been waylaid and are holed up fighting, I'm sure they are running short on supplies," said Barney. "They probably have plenty of beef to eat, but things like coffee and beans would be useful. I'd even bet they're getting low on ammunition by now, and some may even be wounded."

Sawyer sat and thought about what Barney said. He had a good point.

"If you want," continued Barney, "me and Jesse can round up all the supplies for the trip. The mercantile stays open until eleven at night. Thay don't want to miss a sale to the traveling herds going through."

"I would sure appreciate that. Luke, would you and Austin help me at the livery to get the riding horses and another two to carry the provisions we need?" asked Sawyer.

"Sure thing. We have our mounts down the street at House Livery, and they have a pen full of horses for sale. Come on, Austin, let's get busy before House closes for the night," said Luke.

Sawyer, Luke, and Austin walked the three blocks to the livery and arrived just in time. Buford House, the livery owner, was closing up for the night.

"Buford we'd like to buy six horses from you," called out Luke.

Buford stopped closing the barn door and hurried over to the men. "Well now, I ain't never turned down the sale of some mangy horses. What kind are you of a mind to buy?"

Sawyer spoke up. "Four of them have to be good, solid cow ponies, and the other two can be pack animals with pack saddles. We have a far piece to go, and they need to have the stamina for a long trip."

"I have just the animals for you. Come on out back and we'll put ropes on them and lead them over here so you can see them in a better light," said Buford.

Luke and Austin took their time examining the horses. They were able to pick out four suitable strong mounts for riding. They also chose two packhorses that were sturdy and could be ridden if needed.

Sawyer paid Buford and he and his men put all six horses in a small pen by themselves so they would be easy to get to in the morning.

Luke looked at his pocket watch and said, "Austin and I will go to the mercantile store and see if we can help Barney and Jesse with the provisions. The store will close soon."

"Okay," said Sawyer.

Sawyer stayed at the livery and asked the hostler if he knew where the Wichita Feed and Seed was located.

"Yep, it's on the north side of town, about a mile from here. Terrance Rogers owns it, but it's closed right now."

"Thanks. Maybe I can get there in the morning before we leave."

When Sawyer entered the store, Luke and Austin

were hard at work stacking their supplies close to the door.

The men had bought a twenty-five-pound sack of beans and a sack of potatoes.

"You reckon we'll need all this food?" asked Sawyer.

"The beans and such is for your cowboys, in case they have run out of provisions. Plus, we'll need food on the way back," said Luke.

"Okay, but I don't want to overload the pack animals." Sawyer walked to the counter and saw they had also picked out several boxes of ammunition. That would be awful heavy on the pack horses too. "Barney, you may want to distribute the ammo to each man, so the pack animals don't have to carry it."

"Yeah, you're probably right. I think we have everything to get us there and hopefully back," said Barney.

"I've already talked to the store owner and we can leave our purchases inside the building for the night," said Jesse.

"Fine, let's finish up here and go get some sleep," said Sawyer. "We'll meet at that café a few doors south of here for breakfast at daylight."

"Fine by us," said Luke. "Come on fellers, let's go turn in."

It was almost midnight when Sawyer and his men finished up, and he finally got to his room. He took off his guns and boots, lay down on the bed, and went to sleep.

The horrors of war overtook his dreams and caused him to recall his days of fighting. The bloody memories of killing men in battle got to him, and in the middle of the night, he bolted upright, opened his eyes, and reached for one of his pistols out of habit.

It had been seven months since the war ended, and he'd tried hard to put the killing and mayhem behind him. But the lingering visions of death still interrupted his dreams at times.

The lack of information he had concerning his friends and his cattle had probably triggered the nightmares. He felt in his heart that he would have to kill again to rescue the herd and the men. Starting in the morning, he must become the former soldier self again if he and his men were to have any chance of surviving.

The old Sawyer had ice water running through his veins. Just the thought of reverting back to that man, and not having any compassion for the men he would face in battle, made him shiver.

But then the vision of his future wife flashed before him, and he smiled. She was the woman he wanted to marry and spend the rest of his life with. The cattle he was going after were essential to his and Abigail's future, and the future of his sister and her baby. He thought about what he would do to the renegade criminals once he located his herd. Men were going to die by their guns for the crimes they had committed.

Sleep finally overtook the young man, and he was able to get some rest before he awoke right before daylight. It was still dark when he dropped off his travel bag at the livery stable where he had put Raven. The light was on in the café, and it was time for a steaming cup of coffee.

Chapter Fourteen

Sawyer was the first of his crew to arrive at the café for breakfast. The waitress placed his cup of coffee on the table as the four cowboys entered the chow hall.

"Do you all want coffee?" she asked.

"That's right, darling," said Jesse. "We all want coffee, hot and black."

The woman smiled and headed for the door to the kitchen. She came back with four mugs and put them down for each man. "I'll bring you boys a pot of coffee and leave it on the table. We have ham and eggs with biscuits and gravy today."

"That sounds really good," said Sawyer.

"I'll go tell the cook and get that coffee pot," said the waitress.

While they ate their meal, Sawyer told his new cowhands what Haney had said about where his men and cattle might be. He also gave them all the information he had on the renegade Apaches that were attacking people in the area.

Luke ate without interrupting Sawyer. When his

boss had finished talking, Luke said, "We're familiar with that general location. It's mostly rolling hills covered with grass and scrub brush. There are gullies in the valleys from years of runoff, and you've also got buffalo wallows scattered across the grasslands. I believe we can be there by late tomorrow, if we can cross the streams without difficulty."

"I'm not so sure we can be there tomorrow," said Barney. "We have to contend with two pack horses and four other horses. They could sure slow us down."

Luke sat there a few seconds mulling over what Barney said. "I have a suggestion. Sawyer, how do you feel about this? Me and you can ride ahead with two spare horses, and the other three can follow up with the rest of the ponies. We can set up camp tonight and they can get there later with the provisions."

Sawyer shook his head. "We should stay together. We're stronger in numbers in case we encounter trouble along the way."

While they continued to talk and drink coffee, the door opened, and Haney came in.

Sawyer motioned to a chair. "Have a seat and I'll buy your breakfast." He waved to the waitress. "Please bring Haney a plate of food."

The cattle buyer sat down and took off his hat. "I have more information for you. I was at my headquarters before daylight, and a rider from a herd that is passing by came to the office with a message from a man by the name of Ronnie. Ronnie asked them to notify you that they're north of the Cimarron River and need help. He said you could find them, whatever that means."

"I fought with Ronnie during the war, and he

knows that I'm a trained scout," said Sawyer and took another bite of food.

"At least you know it's your men now, and you can plan out how to rescue them," said Haney.

The waitress came by and refilled their coffee cups while they ate.

Sawyer finished his plate and pushed it away. "I want to get started as soon as possible, but I have one thing to do before we leave. Luke, if you'll be in charge of getting us ready to ride, I'll go finish my business."

"I guess since we're done, we'll all go to the livery after our horses," said Luke. "Barney, you and Austin take the pack animals with you and start loading the provisions. Me and Jesse will put halters and lead ropes on the spare ponies."

Sawyer paid for their meal while Luke and his men headed to the livery stable. Sawyer walked to the stable where Raven spent the night. His horse was saddled and tied out front.

He mounted up and headed north at a trot and hoped the Wichita Seed and Fertilizer store was already open.

There wasn't any activity going on outside the business, but he ground-tied his horse and walked up the steps to the front door anyway. It was unlocked, and he went inside. The room smelled like molasses and leather.

An elderly man wearing bib overalls and a leather apron greeted him.

"Good morning, stranger. What can I do for you?"

"I'm Sawyer McCade from over in Allen County. I have a herd of longhorns coming up from Texas, and I need to dust them with sulfur to get rid of ticks before we get into Kansas. I was told you might have enough here for us to purchase."

"I do have sulfur in stock. Do you know how much you'll need?"

"Three hundred pounds ought to be enough."

"How soon do you need it?"

"That I don't rightly know, maybe a week from today," said Sawyer.

"I assume you have a wagon to haul that much in?"

"No, but I was hoping I could pay you to deliver it. We also need a place to apply it to the cattle," said Sawyer. "Do you know of any place that would work?"

"I have a suggestion for you. There are some abandoned cattle pens in Crowley County, just north of the Kansas border. You can use those old pens. Any ticks that fall off won't bother anyone since the pens are south of the Arkansas River, and that's not a populated area."

"Are the pens hard to find?" asked Sawyer.

"No, most cowboys know where they're at. If you give me a couple of days' notice, I can have one of my men bring the sulfur to you."

"Okay, I'll give you two days' notice," said Sawyer. "I really appreciate you doing this for me."

"I'm glad you're getting rid of those darn ticks before you bring the cattle into Kansas. We don't need our livestock to get sick over a bunch of longhorns. I'll send along a bill with my driver when he brings the sulfur to the pens."

Sawyer stuck out his hand to seal the deal. "Thanks again. I best be on my way."

Chapter Fifteen

Sawyer arrived at the livery stable ten minutes later. The men had already been to the store and loaded the provisions on the two pack horses and their mounts and were ready to go.

"I need to tell you the plan when we head the cattle into Kansas," said Sawyer. "I've made arrangements with the Wichita Seed and Fertilizer store to deliver a load of sulfur to the old loading pens down by the Kansas border. He said you men would most likely know where they are. I want to apply the dust to the longhorn cattle so the ticks will fall off and hopefully kill them."

"That's a good idea," said Luke.

"I know where those pens are located," said Jesse and some of the others nodded in agreement.

"Good! You men know more about where we need to go than I do," said Sawyer. "I think one of you should take the lead and get us on our way."

"I know the way to Alfred's Store in the Nation," said Jesse. "I'm not sure if I'm welcome anymore, because the last time I was there, me and old Alfred's daughter were romantic."

Sawyer laughed. "I guess we'll just have to take our chances. We have a long, hard ride before we get there, so you move on out, and we'll follow you."

"Boss man I'd feel better if you rode up front with Jesse," said Luke. "I've heard how good you are in a fight, and we sure don't want to be surprised by thieves or outlaws. The part of the Territory that we have to travel through is unclaimed land, and ain't no telling what or who we may encounter along the way."

"Okay," said Sawyer.

"I'm hoping we can take the lead ropes off the spare horses after we go a few miles and they will herd along with us," said Barney.

"We'll see," said Luke. "Jesse, lead out."

The four cowboys and the one fighter headed south down the street, letting their mounts walk until they came to the Arkansas River. Jesse found a shallow spot and rode across first, and when all the horses were on the south bank, the riders urged their mounts to lope down the dirt road leading toward Indian Territory.

By three in the afternoon, the mounts were tired, and it was time to change them out for the spare horses. Sawyer raised his arm and motioned for the men to slow down. They watched for a good place to water their horses, and when they found one, they'd make a quick camp to change horses and eat some food.

As they walked their horses, Jesse said, "We are close to a place they call South Haven. There isn't much there, but we can get food and fresh water for our canteens."

"We'll continue a little farther, but if we don't find

it in the next hour, we'll have to stop someplace else," said Sawyer.

The trail, which most people would call a road because it was wide enough for a wagon or two horses side by side, curved to the east. Sawyer and Jesse were the first around the bend, and the first ones to put eyes on the settlement. There was little to be seen in the way of houses or businesses. The sign on the front of the largest building let travelers know that it served as a mercantile, saloon, and café.

Sawyer stopped his horse and sat looking at four horses tied to the hitch rail in front of the place. He had a bad feeling down in his gut about who they belonged to and thought about riding on by.

"What's the matter?" asked Jesse.

"I'm a little worried about the men who own those mounts," said Sawyer.

"What do you want to do? Stop or keep going?" asked Jesse.

Sawyer reached down and took the safety strap off the gun on his right hip and also from the one on his left side, which was in a cross draw. "I've never backed away from a fight and don't intend to now. You wait here until the others catch up. I'll ride on in and check out the place."

Jesse removed the strap of his gun. "I'm going in with you. I ride for the brand, and that means I back your play."

Sawyer nodded at the young cowboy, urged his horse to go forward, and said, "You follow my lead and let your eyes adjust to the light when we step inside. Keep your gun hand free—don't pick up anything with your right hand."

The rest of the crew came riding up about the time the two men were off their horses and standing in front of the building. Jesse looked at Sawyer. "Luke is mighty good in a fight, if you want to take him with us."

Luke moved his horse in beside Sawyer's. "What seems to be the trouble, boss?"

"I'm not sure, but these horses give me a bad feeling about the men riding them. We may be walking into trouble," said Sawyer. "Each of those animals has a different brand, and by the look of their gear, I would have to say their riders never treat the leather. These men don't even cur comb their horses."

Luke pulled his gun from his holster and made sure it was fully loaded. He kept it in his hand and sternly looked at Sawyer. "How do you want to play this out, boss?"

Sawyer waited until all four men were near enough to hear his instructions. "I'll go in first. Luke and Jesse, when you come in, spread to each side of me, then we'll play it by ear and see what they do," said Sawyer. "Barney, you and Austin come in a few moments after us but sit in a different location than the rest. Make sure you don't sit where you might hit each other in a crossfire."

Barney and Austin made sure their guns were loaded and ready for action as well.

Sawyer paused for a second at the door, then entered the building. It was lit better than he'd expected. The proprietor had hung lanterns all around the large room so people could see the goods he sold. To the left of the door were aisles of clothing, fabric, blankets, and quilts, all stacked on shelves and tables. Down the center of the store were rows of shelves carrying an assortment of canned goods and other food items.

To the right, against the west wall, was a bar made from a log that had been split in half and smoothed down. It sat on top of sawhorses that had once been used for carpentry work. Between Sawyer and the bar were six tables, each with four chairs. Sitting at one of the tables were four men who hadn't seen a barber or a bathtub in months. Their greasy hair was down to their shoulders and there was no telling what might be hidden in there.

Four empty bowls sat on their table, along with a whiskey bottle that was three-fourths empty, plus four glasses. Two men had their pistols on the table like they were expecting trouble, or maybe trying to convince someone they were men to be feared.

Behind the makeshift counter stood a man wearing a soiled apron over his shirt and britches. He looked to be middle-aged, but the thing that caught Sawyer's attention was the scar along one side of his face.

"Howdy, strangers, come on in and have a seat. My name is Aiden O'Connor and I own this store. I have whiskey and some chalk that is mighty tasty," said the man, and he motioned at a table. "If you are hankering for food, there's some delicious beans with ham in the kitchen that I can get you. Two bits a plate."

Sawyer motioned with his left hand for Luke and Jesse to sit at the table to their left while he walked to the counter and stood so he could see the four hard cases drinking their liquor.

Barney and Austin came inside and walked past Luke and Jesse's table. They sat down at the two tables closest to the counter. The four men were now located between their table and the one that Luke and Jesse sat at.

One of the four men got up, walked to the door, and went outside. When he re-entered the store a few seconds later, he pulled his gun from its holster and sat at a different table with his gun in plain sight. "Are those ponies out there for sale?" he asked, pointing to Luke.

Sawyer turned his back to the men drinking whiskey and reached inside his vest to remove his shoulder pistol, keeping it hidden from view. He looked at the store owner and mouthed the words, "Keep quiet."

The man who had gone outside raised his voice. "I asked a question, and I reckon someone better answer before I get my dander up."

Sawyer turned slightly so he could address the man. "Those are my horses. They're not for sale, and you fellers ain't going to take them."

The two men with their guns on the table reached out for their whiskey glasses. Sawyer watched as they picked them up and took a drink.

Sawyer cocked back the hammer on his shoulder pistol and waited on the men at the table to put their glasses down. Sure enough, they set them back down on the table and reached for their guns. Before Sawyer could turn and raise his weapon, a burst of lead from Sawyer's crew was already hitting the four men.

Luke, Jesse, Barney, and Austin filled the bandits with holes in a crossfire.

"Hold your fire," shouted Sawyer. The powder smoke had filled the room and all four of the men were down, bleeding on the dirt floor. "Let's check and make sure they're dead." He put his toe to one of the men and pushed.

Luke said, "Boss, I believe they are all deceased."

Sawyer turned to the store owner, who stood behind the counter, looking white as a sheet and about ready to pass out. A door at the back of the store slammed, and Sawyer and his men turned toward the sound with their guns drawn. A middle-aged woman and a young girl had entered the store.

"Hold up, don't shoot!" shouted Aiden. "That's my wife and daughter."

"Sorry, ma'am, we don't mean you any harm," said Sawyer. He put his gun in its holster, as did his men. "We'll have some of that chalk and five bowls of food. Me and my men will drag these corpses outside while you get our food and drink," said Sawyer.

Luke said, "Jesse, you and Austin go get a couple of ropes off the horses. We'll tie the ropes to their legs, drag the bodies outside, and use the horses to pull them away from the building."

"If it's not too much trouble, would you drag them under that big oak tree on the south side of the building? I'll dig graves for them over there," said Aiden.

"Yep, we can do that," said Sawyer. "You can keep all their belongings and the horses for the trouble. What's your name? I don't remember."

"My name is Aiden O'Connor," said the shopkeeper.

"Who were those ruffians?" asked Sawyer.

Aidan frowned. "I don't know their names, but I say good riddance to the trash you just killed. They sometimes come through here from the Indian Territory to buy guns and ammunition that they sell to the Indians."

"I see," said Sawyer.

When Sawyer and his men had disposed of the bodies, their food and drink were ready. Sawyer was the first to finish eating and asked the store owner, "How much farther is it before we get into Indian Territory?"

"It's a day's ride from here. If you ride south about five miles, you'll find a road that'll turn east. Take it until you come to another road going south and it will take you all the way into the Nations and across the Cimarron River."

"Luke, have the men swap out our mounts and let's get going again. We still have a few hours of daylight left, and I'd like to put more distance behind us today."

A few minutes later, Sawyer and his men went outside to swap their saddles to the extra horses.

Sawyer adjusted the girth strap on his second horse and asked Jesse, "What did you see those men do to make y'all start shooting?"

"A few months back, I saw the one in the buffalo vest gun down a man in a saloon in Cowtown. He shot the poor soul for bumping his table," said Jesse. "He up and pulled his gun and shot the man in the back. After that, he got up, laughed at the dead man, and left the saloon. Then he just rode off. Today I figured it was time to start the ball rolling before they had time to grab their guns."

"I reckon you were right in shooting them before they hurt or killed one of us," said Sawyer.

Chapter Sixteen

Sawyer watched Aiden search the four corpses while he and his men finished swapping their saddles and gear to the spare horses. Aiden's wife came outside with two buckets for her husband to put the bounty in. He filled up both pails with guns, money, knives, tobacco, and other items. He handed the buckets to his wife, and she took them back to the store while he continued to search. She returned with the buckets emptied and started filling them with the rest of the bounty.

The black horse that belonged to Sawyer wasn't happy that his owner was getting on another mount. Raven reared up and tried to hit the other animal with his front hooves. Sawyer got off the spare horse and calmed Raven down by rubbing between his ears and talking calmly to him. The horse put his mouth on Sawyer's arm to let him know it was okay. Sawyer mounted the other horse, but Raven stayed right beside them.

"Well, I'll be dad-burned," said Luke. "Your horse

shows affection by taking your arm in his mouth without biting it?"

"Yep. Most people think he's a biter, and he might be, to anyone but me," said Sawyer. "Come on, men, let's go."

Aiden and his wife stopped what they were doing and waved at the cowboys as they rode away.

"I think that family at the store are right glad we came by. There ain't no telling what they'll make off that dead scum," said Barney.

"Yeah, I'm just glad it's them going through the dead men's pockets," said Austin.

"Those fellers smelled mighty nasty when they were alive and no telling how bad they stink now that they're dead," said Jesse.

Since everyone had fresh mounts, the cowboys put the miles behind them. They rode into the evening until the sun was beginning to go down and the day's heat was diminishing.

"I've been this way before on a cattle drive," said Luke. "There should be a good place to camp for the night up ahead. Back in the day, drovers took their cattle through here on the way to Cowtown. There may be a store and a few other businesses up ahead too."

Sure enough, several miles later they came upon a store on one side of the road and a tent saloon on the other side. There were some wooden buildings and most of them looked unoccupied and abandoned.

Luke stopped and the rest of the men followed suit. "I like to take a drink of rotgut as much as the next feller, but we need to stay away from the saloon this trip."

"I agree with Luke," said Sawyer.

"How about we see if that store can feed us tonight? That way we won't have to get food and utensils out of the packs," said Barney. "We can leave everything secured on the pack saddles when we take them off the horses."

"That's a good idea," said Sawyer. "I'll see if they can rustle us up some food while you find us a campsite."

"If my memory hasn't failed me, there might still be a corral about a quarter of a mile south," said Luke. "We can put the horses in there for the night."

"Y'all go on that way and check it out, and I'll meet you back here in a little while," said Sawyer. He rode over to the front of the store and dismounted.

The small store had little in the way of provisions, from what Sawyer could see when he went inside to look around. It did have a good supply of blankets, hides, and cooking utensils, which was strange to him since most of the items were things a person already had at their house. Maybe these items were used to trade with the Indians from a place like Indian Territory.

"Hello, anyone here?" he called out.

"Yes sir, I'll be right with you," said a voice from the back of the building. Sawyer was looking at items on the shelves when a man came into the store. He had blood on his shirt and britches. He sported a mustache and long hair jutted out from under a flop hat that had seen better days. The man spit tobacco juice onto the dirt floor. It looked as if the man had something packed into his right cheek, and Sawyer figured it was a big glob of cotton boll twist.

Sawyer decided to not mention anything about food

after seeing the man. There was no way he'd eat anything this dirty man cooked.

"I was wondering if you had any guns and ammunition for sale," asked Sawyer.

"Oh, no sir. I don't have any weapons for sale at all," said the man.

"Okay, thanks, I'll be on my way." Sawyer walked to the door. Three gunshots came from what sounded like a quarter mile to the south. He ran to his horse and took off in the direction his men had gone. It only took a few minutes to cover the distance to the pen. Dense forest surrounded the corral on three sides, and the only clear area was between the road and split-rail fence. The horses were in the pen and to the west of the enclosure stood his men, surrounding a corpse on the ground.

"What was the shooting about?" asked Sawyer when he came to a stop.

"This feller came out of the trees and fired two shots at us. Austin fired back and put his lights out," said Luke. "If I was a betting man, I'd say he was part of that bunch we ran into at South Haven."

"You say he came out of those trees?" Sawyer pointed to the west.

"Yep, right through here," said Luke as he walked to a narrow trail that led into the woodland.

"Hold up, Luke," said Sawyer. "I'll follow his trail and see what's back there that's so important he needed to come out and shoot at y'all."

Jesse came forward with his gun in his hand. "I'll come with you."

Sawyer raised his hand to stop the young cowboy but then thought differently. Jesse had already proved his fighting ability back at Aiden's store. "Okay, but you stay to my left about thirty feet and be as quiet as possible. I don't want to spook anyone if others are in there."

Sawyer walked into the trees and stayed on the narrow trail. He walked a few feet and raised his hand to stop Jesse. His days as an army scout were coming back to him. He had been taught to rely on his senses and pay close attention to sounds, smells, and his sight. Especially changes to the environment, such as broken twigs or boot tracks in the soil.

Fifty yards inside the timberland, he noticed places where small saplings had been cut. Scanning farther down the trail, it looked like someone had made a makeshift corral out of the small trees. Sawyer circled his left hand over his head, instructing Jesse to go wider and come in from the south.

Sawyer left the trail but stayed close to it to look for more signs on the ground. Fresh horse dung was in the corral, and boot tracks in the soft ground nearby led west. What was to the west?

Jesse was out of sight now, and Sawyer kept advancing. He crouched down as low as he could and proceeded past the corral. Another twenty feet, and he saw Jesse off to his left, motioning with his hand and putting up one finger. Sawyer nodded at him and continued until he saw a grass-covered clearing. In the center was a campfire that had a tripod for cooking set up over an unlit fire. Two tents and a lean-to set up for additional shelter were backed up to the tree line, and a trail could be seen going west. Two horses with hobbled front legs grazed just off the trail, west of the tents.

Sawyer waited a few minutes, looking the camp over before proceeding. Jesse had held up one finger, so he knew only one person was in the camp. Were they in one of the tents or hiding in the trees, waiting to shoot?

The answer came out of one of the tents. It was a woman who look like she had been ridden hard and put up wet. She was barefoot and dressed in a dirty men's shirt and britches that were two sizes too big for her, tied at the waist with a length of rope. She carried a pan of water that she poured out on the ground.

"We have you dead to rights. Stop where you're at, and you won't get hurt," shouted Sawyer.

The woman dropped the pan and turned back toward the tent when Jesse stepped out from behind a tree off to her left and said, "Don't move a muscle, or I'll shoot you."

Sawyer rushed into the opening with his gun drawn. "Sit down on the ground and keep your hands where I can see them. Jesse, come on in and search the tents."

Jesse looked in the first tent and then went to the second one. "Sawyer, you might want to see this," he said, holding the flap open.

Chapter Seventeen

"Ma'am, you stay where you're at and don't try to run off. I'll put a bullet in you if you try to escape," said Sawyer. He walked to the tent, where Jesse held the flap open for him. "You keep an eye on her while I look inside."

"I sure will. You ain't going to believe what's inside there."

Sawyer had to wait until his eyes adjusted to the dim light before he could see. Two blankets were laid on the ground, covered in rifles, boxes of ammunition, and knives. He walked a little farther into the tent and saw a dozen pistols and a six-inch expandable spyglass. The spyglass was something he had a use for, so he picked it up. The glass lenses on each end were in good shape. He extended the tube all the way out and turned to the opening to test the telescope.

Sawyer pushed the sections back together and brought the spyglass outside with him. "The store owner at South Haven suspected that those men we killed were selling weapons to the renegades," Sawyer told Jess. "I reckon he was right. I'm going to question that woman and see if I can get some answers. I must warn you that I may have to use force to get the truth out of her."

"You do what you have to do," said Jesse.

Sawyer looked around the camp and saw a length of rope coiled up between the two tents. He picked up the rope and started tying one end into a hangman's noose. When he finished, he handed the rope to Jesse. "Take this over to that tree and throw the knot over that big limb."

"Are you going to hang her right here?" asked Jesse.

"If I have to. Now go do what I ask," said Sawyer.

Holding another piece of rope, Sawyer walked toward the woman.

"Give me your hands or I'll have to hold you down while I tie you up," said Sawyer.

"Mister, please don't tie me up. I'll tell you whatever you want. Please, I don't want to die. Those men kidnapped me and made me come with them," said the frightened woman.

Sawyer stood looking down at her for a few seconds. Even though he knew better, the new Sawyer had compassion for the woman. But the old Sawyer realized that she could be a danger to him if she had a weapon.

He walked around her and took hold of her left hand, bringing it behind her back. He tied the rope to it. She tried to jerk free, but Jesse walked in front of her and went down on one knee to put both his arms around the woman, pinning her hands to her side.

"You sit still, and I'll let you go when he has you tied up," said Jesse.

"Get off of me!" she screamed, trying to wiggle free.

Sawyer secured both hands. "You can let her go."

Jesse let go of her and stood up.

"Here is the way this is going to work," said Sawyer. "If you're truthful with your answers, we'll let you go. If you lie to me, I'm going to hang you by that rope over there."

"I done said that I'll answer your questions," spit out the woman.

"What's your name?"

"Bertha. It's Bertha Roy, and those men stole me from my home down on the North Canadian River."

"What do you mean by they stole you?"

"Hambone killed my husband and made me come with them. He makes me cook and share his bed. I hate that man."

"Why do they have all those guns in the tent?"

"Are you that dumb?" she asked. "They sell them to the renegade Indians and their white scum friends."

"Do you know if they buy guns from the store just up the road a piece?" asked Sawyer.

"Oh yeah, that shopkeeper sells guns, ammo, blankets, and food that Hambone and his men take into Indian Territory. Can you untie me? I swear not to run. My wrists are hurting something fierce."

"Okay. I'll untie you, but you better not try anything. Is that clear?" asked Sawyer.

Jesse pulled his gun and pointed it at Bertha.

"How many men does this Hambone feller have working with him?" asked Sawyer.

"There's five, counting him. Hambone and three men went after pack horses to carry these guns down to the Nation. They also sell the horses to the Indians on each trip."

"For your information, we killed four men at South Haven. We shot a fifth one by the old corral through those trees. As far as I'm concerned, you're a free woman. If you have a horse, you can head on back home if you want."

She sat looking at Sawyer for a few seconds. "I ain't got no home to go back to. They killed my man and burned the shack we lived in. I have no desire to go back there. I have shelter and food here, so I'll stay put until something better comes along."

"That's fine by us. Come on, Jesse, let's go."

They hadn't walked far when Sawyer turned back around. "Bertha, can you read and write?"

"Yes sir, I went to school up to the fifth grade."

"How would you like to be a store owner?"

"I'd like that a lot."

"Do you have a horse that you can ride?" asked Sawyer.

"There's two horses grazing in those trees over there." She pointed west at the hobbled horses.

"Get your ponies loaded up with all your possessions and as many of them rifles that you can carry. I'll be back directly, and we'll talk some more," said Sawyer.

Sawyer and Jesse walked back down the trail to meet the other cowboys waiting for them at the old corral.

"Boss, what are you going to do?" asked Jesse.

"I'm going back to that store and teach that feller a lesson for selling guns to the Indians. Then I'll come back here and tell Bertha she can take over the store," said Sawyer.

"You do have a kind heart inside you after all. I thought you were going to hang her a little while ago."

"Nah, I wouldn't have done it. I just needed her to tell us the truth."

Chapter Eighteen

Sawyer and Jesse walked into the camp that Luke and Barney were setting up. A small fire was lit, and a pot of water was heating up for coffee while the other cowboys took the saddles off the pack horses.

"Where's Austin?" asked Jesse, looking around.

"He's dragging that corpse off, so we don't have to listen to the coyotes tonight or smell it in the morning," said Luke.

Sawyer went to his horse and mounted up. "Jesse, you can fill them in on what we found. I'll be back later."

Sawyer stopped his horse when he was within a hundred yards of the store. His mind wandered back to the days when he served in the army. Wounded men, lying in pools of their own blood. Corpses scattered across the countryside with missing arms or legs. Guts exposed to the flies and buzzards that swarmed to the smell of rotting flesh.

Then the thought of his friends, trying to protect themselves from renegade Indians who used guns bought from the store up ahead. It made Sawyer's blood boil. He'd had his suspicions when he saw the merchandise in the shop an hour earlier.

It was time to dismount and advance on foot, so he'd have the element of surprise on his side. The stench of wood smoke was in the air, but he didn't see anything coming from the store's smokestack.

With gun in hand, the determined cowboy entered the store and looked around before walking through the rows of merchandise stacked on the floor and on several homemade tables. A hunter could not be too careful when he was stalking his prey.

The storekeeper was probably out back somewhere, doing no telling what. He'd had blood on him an hour ago, so Sawyer thought he might be processing a deer or some other animal.

When he was twenty feet out the back door, Sawyer stopped and looked around. The carcass of a deer hung from a pole suspended between two tree limbs. He took two more steps and heard the faint sound of voices farther east of his location. The smell of smoke had gotten stronger.

As an army scout, he had learned to trust his senses. A scout also remembered that he was at war, and should never give his opponent a fighting chance. Soldiers went into battle determined to destroy the enemy and live through the fight.

Voices and the smell of burning wood meant the store owner wasn't alone. If they were hiding in the forest so no one would see them, Sawyer figured whatever they were up to must be illegal.

Moving like a big cat sneaking up on its prey, Sawyer came to a spot behind a large tree. Now he could see into a small clearing where three men were at work. A whiskey still was cooking up a batch of rotgut. The store owner sat in a chair, peeling apples. One of the other men looked to be in his twenties and had sparse facial hair and blond locks to his shoulders. He wore a pair of bib overalls, no shirt, and sported a gun on his right hip. Sawyer noticed that the man was barefoot as he gathered wood and stacked it by the fire under the mash pot.

The third man, who was much older, was bald and had a long beard. He was also shirtless and had a gun. He too, was barefooted, and stirred something in a large barrel—probably mash.

Taking his time to pull another gun from its holster, Sawyer waited until all three men had turned their backs to him. Then he stepped out from concealment and said, "Hello men."

The store owner turned and when he saw Sawyer, he raised his knife and started to throw it, but the lead balls from both of Sawyer's guns hit him with enough force to topple him over onto the ground.

The older man was bringing up his pistol to fire when Sawyer shot him in the chest. Sawyer didn't wait to see if the man was dead, and instead turned his guns on the young man, who already had his pistol in firing position. The man pulled the trigger, but the hammer fell on an empty cylinder. That was the last mistake he'll ever make. Two balls hit him in the chest, knocking him backward onto the mash pot. The pot turned over, and the man fell onto the fire. Sawyer ran to him, grabbed his leg, and pulled him off the flames. The dead man's overalls had caught fire, but a few handfuls of dirt put it out.

Sawyer hated the smell of burning flesh. In the war, he had experienced that terrible odor more times than he cared to count.

Surveying the area around him more closely revealed two horses tied about fifty feet to the north. The mounts were still saddled, and their reins were connected to a rope tied between two trees. This location out behind the store had been used a lot, based on the amount of horse dung on the ground and the large wood pile and stack of tarps nearby.

Sawyer cut the rope loose from the trees and led the horses back to where the men lay. He was able to tie all three men together and used one of the horses to drag the corpses farther into the woods, where he left them to rot.

Once the bodies were disposed of, he led the two extra ponies to the store and tied them up at the rear of the building. He walked back to the still, picked up a double-bladed axe, and went to work on the metal pots and burners. By the time he was finished, all the equipment to produce rotgut had been destroyed. He was out of breath and sat down long enough to catch his wind before he went after his horse.

Sawyer looked at the store one last time before returning to camp. Bertha could take it over and make a suitable living there, if she wanted to work hard and treat people right. Perhaps a little compassion for a person who had experienced a hard life could lead to them making something of themselves, and it pleased him that he had a little part in it.

Chapter Nineteen

Bertha walked into the camp where Sawyer's men had set up for the night just as Sawyer arrived from his outing to the store. "Bertha, sit down and have a cup of coffee," said Jesse.

"I reckon that I should be going on, if it's okay with the boss," said Bertha and pointed to Sawyer, walking to the fire for coffee.

He poured himself a cup and sat on a log the men had dragged over closer to the flames. "The store and all its contents are yours. I left two horses tied up in the backyard, so you'll need to do something with them when you get there. There may be a horse pen northeast of the building that you can use."

She began to cry. "I can never thank you enough. I want you to know that I'm eternally grateful for you rescuing me and giving me the store."

"I have a few things I want you to do though," said Sawyer. He took a sip of coffee. "I want you to be nice to people and treat them fairly in all your dealings. Don't sell guns to the Indians unless it's to hunt for food. There should be money in the cash box. If there ain't, then it's in the store owner's pockets. I didn't go through his pockets before I dragged him off. His corpse is east about a quarter mile. If you want to search him, you do it early in the morning before the buzzards start eating his flesh."

"You didn't bury him, boss?" asked Jesse.

"Nope, the buzzards and coyotes have to eat also," said Sawyer.

"Thank you so much. You fellers be sure to stop by and see me. The first thing I'm going to do is take a hot bath and put on clean clothes," said Bertha. "I'll be on my way now."

She walked away from the camp, leading her two horses. They were loaded down with guns and other items from the tents that she wanted. Thirty yards up the road, Bertha stopped and hollered out, "Hambone met those Indians and sometimes other white men on the north bank of Black Bear Creek. There's a spring nearby, and an Indian settlement. Be careful—those renegades have a fearsome white leader. Hambone called him Sooty." She turned back to the north and started walking again.

Luke picked up a plate and spooned stew from a pot by the fire. The others did likewise, except for Sawyer. He sat where he was and stared into his cup of coffee for a few minutes, planning out in his mind what he would do if they came across the renegades at Black Bear Creek. When he looked up, his men were watching him. He said, "Tomorrow we ride ready for battle."

"We'll be ready," said Luke. The other men nodded their heads in agreement.

Sawyer set the cup on the ground and helped himself to a plate of food.

Everyone was tired and hungry, and there wasn't any more conversation while they filled their stomachs.

Jesse was the first to finish. "Boss, can I ask you a question?"

Sawyer kept eating with his plate held up close to his chin. He raised his eyes to look at Jesse. With his mouth full, he stuck up one finger, gesturing to hold on until he could talk. He took a few more bites, set his plate on the ground, and picked up his coffee cup.

"Jesse, what's so important that you interrupted my supper?"

"Sorry about that, but I'm confused. You were ready to hang that woman if she didn't tell you the truth. When she did, you had compassion for her. Then you went back and killed that store owner. I'm not saying he didn't have it coming, but you left him for the varmints to feast upon and gave his store to that woman. At South Haven, you walked into that place ready for battle and had us situated so we could catch them in a crossfire. I'm trying to understand what makes you do the things you do, is all."

Sawyer picked up a rag and used it to grip the coffee pot's hot handle. He poured himself some more, and then went to each man to top off their cup. Jesse sat watching. When Sawyer was finished, he sat back down before speaking.

"I scouted for the Confederate army. I was trained by the best, and that training kept me alive for three years. My mentors taught me not to have any compassion for my enemy and to kill them by using any means necessary. In the heat of battle, I did things that normal people wouldn't consider."

He took a sip of coffee. "That store owner and two other men were making rotgut whiskey. They sold it to the Indians, along with those rifles we found. Chances are the renegades who are fighting my friends are using guns that came from that store. Those men got what was coming to them, and I doubt it didn't bother them at all how many people their whiskey and guns destroyed."

Jesse sat nodding his head as Sawyer finished his explanation. "I'm sorry I brought it up," said Jesse. "I can tell it's not something you enjoy talking about."

"Honestly, I thought I had put that old Sawyer to bed for the rest of my life. But I realized that when I decided to go help my friends and get my cattle, it would take the old Sawyer to pull it off. I wanted the killing to be over with and the nightmares to stop, but bad men make the war linger on for me. I intend to get my cattle and friends out of harm's way, whatever it takes. Men, I don't have a problem going after those renegades and their white partners."

Luke stood up and walked over to Sawyer. He stuck out his hand. "Boss, I'm with you all the way. I spent a little time in that war, and I fully understand how you need to operate. And we know what we all have to do. We signed on to help—just point us in the right direction."

"Thanks Luke," said Sawyer.

One by one, the others followed Luke's gesture and shook Sawyer's hand. Jesse went last. He looked Sawyer in the eye and said, "I won't question your tactics again. I've seen you in action, and you're one to ride the river with."

"It's okay, Jesse. I actually feel better talking about it. I want to live a normal life with my future wife and raise a family. I don't know how long I'll carry the war around on my shoulders. I can still see the bloody, mangled bodies scattered over the battlefield. That was what I saw as I rode up to that store and found them cooking up that poison they call whiskey. The rest is history now, and I hope Bertha will make good on her promise about running an honest business."

"So do I," said Jesse, gathering plates to clean.

Chapter Twenty

The wind picked up around four in the morning, and the temperature began to cool off. Sawyer came awake but lay on his bedroll, looking up at the massive clouds moving across the heavens. The smell and feel of moisture was in the air. There would most likely be rain later.

It was time to rouse the others. After a good stretch to work out the kinks from sleeping on the ground, he picked up his boots and turned each one upside down before putting them on so any critter that used them during the night would hopefully fall out.

He went to each man and gently woke them up. "We need to get the supplies loaded and covered with those tarps we bought. It'll rain soon, and we should find someplace to stay dry."

"I reckon we can go into the woods and use those gunrunners' tents, or maybe head to Bertha's store," said Jesse.

Sawyer paused and thought about how much time they could lose if they waited out the storm. It might be minutes, hours, or even the entire day. Time was essential to the survival of his friends. "As bad as I hate to say it, we need to suit up in our rain gear and keep going south. I can't afford rain delays. I'm afraid that any streams we need to cross might get too high to navigate if we wait too long."

"Let's get busy before it starts raining," said Luke. "You men load the pack supplies and get things covered, and Sawyer and I will start saddling up the horses."

The crew had been back on the road heading south for a half hour when it began to sprinkle. The wind blew hard out of the south now, and they had to lower their heads so the rain didn't hit them in the eyes. As they continued, the wind picked up and became more brutal. The horses didn't like traveling into it, since it hit them in the face.

After another half hour, Luke rode up beside Sawyer. "Boss, we need to change directions slightly so we ain't riding directly into the storm. I suggest we turn southwest and ride at an angle across the prairie."

"You lead the way, and we'll follow," said Sawyer, holding his hat so it wouldn't blow off his head.

Luke led the group southwest for a few miles and then turned southeast. Sawyer understood what the second direction change was for. It would put them back on the same trajectory that they had originally been on.

After three hours of rain and wind, the sky began to clear, and the deluge of water decreased to a drizzle. The dirt on the trail had soaked up much of the heavy downpour, creating mud and unstable footing for the horses. Sawyer and his men slowed their pace when they came to places where the ground was nothing but red muck.

The rain finally quit in the early afternoon, and the sun came out. Jesse rode alongside Sawyer and said, "We should be in Indian Territory now, and if my recollection is right, we'll come up to Black Bear Creek later today or in the morning."

"What's after the creek?" asked Sawyer.

"There's a few streams, but nothing as big as Black Bear. The Cimarron River is about thirty or forty miles south, but I'm not sure of the exact distance."

"Bertha said those gunrunners met the Indians close to Black Bear Creek. If possible, I'd like to camp there tonight," said Sawyer.

The sun was doing its job of soaking up the moisture from the soil, and now the men and horses had to contend with hot and humid weather. The mounts had slowed down, tired from working so hard tromping in the mud. The cowboys swapped horses and continued on with the hope of reaching the creek that night.

An hour before dark, they rode up on the creek. Sawyer looked around and chose a campsite on top of a hill about sixty feet away from the water, with abundant grass for their horses as well as trees that could conceal them in case of trouble. Luke, Jesse, and Austin put hobbles on all the horses so they wouldn't wander off, and Barney started supper.

Sawyer set up his bedroll away from the others. He did it partly because he didn't want to hear them snore, but the main reason for sleeping farther away was so he would be in a position to defend them if the camp received any unwanted company.

Thankfully, nothing happened during the night,

and the men were up at dawn packing their ground tarp and bedroll. Luke cooked breakfast while the others saddled the riding horses. They would load the pack saddles after they ate.

Sawyer stood beside a tree with his shoulder against the bark, eating. The ground was too wet to sit on, and everyone had to eat standing up. He finished sopping up the last of his gravy with the remains of a biscuit and when he bent over to pick up his coffee cup, the sound of a rifle shot made him drop to the ground. Bark flew into the air from the tree he had just been leaning against.

"Boss, are you hit?" asked Luke, who had sought cover behind another tree.

"I'm fine," said Sawyer. "I didn't see the shooter, but it sounded like it came from that clump of cedars upstream about forty yards."

Jesse looked around the tree, gripping his pistol. As soon as he was exposed enough for the shooter to see him, another shot rang out, and bark exploded in Jesse's face. He immediately ducked back behind the safety of the tree. "He's in those cedars, all right. I saw a muzzle flash and powder smoke on the north side."

"We ain't going to be able to shoot him from here with our pistols. I'm going to try to sneak out of here and see if I can come in behind him," said Sawyer. "When I'm ready, you men try to keep him occupied with your weapons long enough for me to escape. Aim high so your balls will make it to him."

Sawyer put his hat on a stick and stuck it out from behind the tree. Sure enough, the shooter fired another shot but missed the hat. Sawyer hollered out, "Start shooting in ten seconds. He should be reloading."

Sawyer took off east, going from tree to tree until he couldn't see where his men were. He could hear them shooting, and he also heard a rifle fire three times. Now he knew the shooter had a Henry repeating rifle. That figured, thought Sawyer, especially if he was with the gunrunners or the renegades.

A hundred yards east, he turned north and counted his steps until he reached one hundred and fifty. That should have put him past the cedars, and now he could come in behind the ambusher.

He bent down and kept low as he made his way toward where he thought the shooter might be located. The closer he came to the creek, the thicker the foliage was. He couldn't see who was doing the shooting, and so far it didn't seem that his prey had noticed he was coming.

Sawyer stopped suddenly as a volley of shots rang out. He didn't know if it was his men shooting or if someone was shooting at them. But it could only mean one thing: he was up against more than one person.

He drew the gun at his hip and cocked the hammer back, then removed the pistol from his cross-draw holster. Holding a .44-caliber Colt Dragoon in each hand, he moved in the direction of the sound of the rifle fire. With each step, he was careful not to tread on anything that would make noise, like dry twigs or low tree limbs. He was banking on the element of surprise, which in past years had saved his life more than once.

The hidden shooters fired again, and if he had gone forward only a few more steps, he would have been directly in the line of fire. He'd miscalculated where they were firing from. Slowly and carefully, he turned around and went back the direction he had come until he could walk farther west and get behind the men.

Forty feet to the west, he came to the edge of a small clearing and spotted five horses southwest of his location, tied to limbs farther back in the grove of cedar trees. The clearing looked to be about twenty-five yards wide and continued south all the way to the river's edge.

Movement to the left gave him a glimpse of one of the shooters, who had backed away from his firing location to reload his rifle. The man had a dark complexion, but also hair so blond it looked almost white.

Sawyer crept north until he couldn't see the bushwhackers and then turned west. Going one hundred feet in that direction would get him on the opposite side of the clearing. When he turned to go back in the direction of the men, he stayed clear of their horses in case one of them snorted and warned the shooters he was there. Only one horse had a saddle on it; the other four had circles painted around one eye and markings painted on their chest muscles.

If he was correct, it reasoned that the shooters consisted of one white man and four Indians. The situation could get interesting if there were others hiding nearby, but that didn't matter right now. The most important thing was to eliminate the immediate threat to his men.

Using cedars, scrub oaks, and blackjacks as cover, he kept hidden until he was directly behind the men. He smiled when he had a good view of them. They were almost side by side, firing at his men. It would be much easier to kill them this way, than if they had been scattered about.

He waited until they had fired a volley of shots, and when they began to reload, he made his move and ran across the clearing toward them. One of the Indians looked up but took a lead ball to the chest, squelching the life from him before he could bring his gun up. Sawyer kept firing with both guns until all four men lay on the ground. Three weren't moving, but one was still alive and moaning in agony.

Sawyer kept pulling the hammer back and squeezing the trigger, even though both guns were empty. As he holstered his pistols and reached for his shoulder gun, he was hit with something heavy from behind and knocked to the ground.

Chapter Twenty-One

The hard lick across the tops of his shoulders caused so much intense pain that it almost put his lights out. Enough muscle memory was embedded in his body to trigger an immediate roll to his right as soon as he hit the dirt. An Indian dressed in buckskins came at him with a club raised above his head, ready to strike again.

Although his eyes weren't quite focused because of spots that clouded his vision, Sawyer's instincts caused him to roll a second time just as the savage swung the club, and it hit the ground where Sawyer had just been lying. A swift kick to the Indian's knee, and the man yelled out in pain and dropped to the ground. That gave Sawyer the opportunity to set up and strike the savage on the chin with his powerful left fist. He watched the man lay still as he gathered his wits.

Sawyer stood up and tried to shake off the pain from the blow to his upper shoulders. He cupped his hands around his mouth and called out to his men, "Fellers, come over here, but watch for anyone who might be hiding."

He was reloading his guns when Luke and the others arrived. "Boss, it looks like you had a little party here. Is that one by your feet still alive?" Luke pointed his gun at the unconscious man.

"Yep, he tried to waylay me with that club. I reckon he was hiding back in those trees. He came out and hit me from behind on my upper shoulders and was getting ready to hit me a second time when I kicked his legs out from under him and hit him in the jaw. If one of you will tie his hands behind his back, I'll get some answers out of him shortly," said Sawyer as he slid one pistol back into its holster and began to reload the second.

Austin walked to the men's horses and came back with a length of rope. He knelt and took hold of the Indian's outstretched arm. As Austin tried to get the renegade's arm behind his back, the man rolled over and suddenly sat up. He lashed out with his left hand, which held a knife, and cut Austin on the thigh. Quick as lightning, Sawyer brought his reloaded pistol up and fired one shot into the man's chest before he could do any more harm.

"How bad are you cut?" asked Sawyer.

"I don't think it's very deep, but I can't tell until I drop my britches."

"Tie your handkerchief around your leg to stop the bleeding," said Luke. "I have a needle and thread in my saddlebag back at camp. I may have to sew up that cut."

"There's a saddled mount in with the Indian ponies," said Sawyer, pointing in the direction of the horses. "Turn the ponies loose but bring the one with the saddle on it with us."

"I'll get them," said Jesse.

Luke and Barney took hold of Austin's arms and

helped him back to camp. The knife cut was shallow and didn't need stitches, and Luke wrapped it well to stop the bleeding.

Sawyer searched the four dead men but didn't find anything useful on them, so he caught up with the rest of the group to check on Austin. "How bad are you cut?" he asked.

"It's not as bad as we first thought. Luke has it bandaged, so the bleeding should stop."

"You stay put for a little while. Luke and I will ride the creek and find a place to cross where you won't have to get that wound wet."

"I can ride, it doesn't hurt," said Austin.

"I don't want it to get infected going through that dirty water. We'll find a good location and then head on out." Sawyer motioned to Luke. "Let's check out the road crossing first. If it's too deep, we can ride west and see if those outlaws came across at a different location."

"Sounds good to me," said Luke, and he mounted up.

The creek bank was sloped so wagons and horses could easily ford. Sawyer started out, and the water came to slightly above his horse's knees. Luke waited until Sawyer returned before he said, "I thought it would be deeper."

Sawyer pointed upstream. "There's a rock dam over there holding back the water. Let's go get the others and cross to the other side. I'm afraid yesterday's rains will cause the creek to swell later today, and we need to ride now to beat the rising water."

Sawyer and Jesse helped with the spare horses to give Austin a break from tending to them. He needed to let his leg heal, and that would take longer if the wound opened up while trying to lead the horses.

Two hours after leaving Black Bear Creek, Jesse rode alongside Sawyer. "We should see Alfred's trading store soon if it's still there. I reckon you know that the army runs people off from these lands if they stay too long."

"I've heard that," said Sawyer. "I wonder why the army has let Alfred keep the store here for so long. Do you reckon he pays off the commanding officer who oversees these parts?"

"That could be," said Jesse.

"If the store is that close, you men follow a southwest direction or maybe go west. From what I was told, the cattle should be west of Alfred's," said Sawyer.

Luke stopped and removed his hat to wipe his forehead. "Boss, ain't you coming with us?"

"I'll catch up with you shortly. I'm going to ride to the store and see if Alfred knows where my friends are. If you find the cattle, wait on me before you start a party," said Sawyer.

"You watch your back while you're there. Alfred can be a mean old cuss at times, and he won't think twice about shooting someone from behind," said Jesse.

Sawyer nodded and turned Raven in the direction of the store. He watched as his men and the spare horses headed off west.

The store sat atop a hill overlooking the Cimarron River to the south. Sawyer stood beside his horse and used the spyglass, watching the store for activity. In the five minutes he waited and watched, no one ventured outside, and no customers came by. Which wasn't uncommon, but the thing that spurred his attention was that no smoke came from the stovepipe. Typically, most trading posts had hot food ready for weary travelers.

He took his time and rode in a wide circle around the area before heading to the building. Jesse's words about the army running off squatters from the unassigned lands kept returning to him. That could be why the place looked deserted.

When he stopped in front of the store, he turned his horse sideways to the door and dismounted on the offside, in case trouble came to meet him from within the store. Once on the ground, he rubbed Raven's neck and told him to wait. Sawyer felt an uneasiness in the pit of his stomach as he started for the closed door.

He removed the gun from his hip and stood to the side of the doorframe before reaching out to lift the latch and push the door open.

Nothing happened, so he stayed where he was for a moment before leaning around the opening to look inside. When he saw the scene indoors, he jerked back his head and covered his mouth with his hand.

On the floor was a dead man who had been stripped of his clothes and scalped. To the right of him lay a woman who had also been violated the same way. Now that the door was open, the smell began to escape the small building. One more quick look confirmed they had been dead for days since both bodies were decomposing.

He held his breath, reached for the door, and closed it before walking away.

After mounting up on Raven, Sawyer sat in the saddle thinking about what must have happened in the store. Evidently, renegades had come in and got what they wanted, then killed Alfred and the woman. He could scout and pick up the trail they'd left behind—it would be easy to track them if they carried extra weight on their horses. West would be the likely direction they took, if it was the same group that was after his cattle.

Sawyer searched for signs such as horse tracks, broken twigs on the ground, or broken tree limbs, but found nothing. What if they had left their horses in the brush and walked in on foot? He started to broaden his search, and sure enough, he found horse droppings where ten or more horses had been tied in a stand of trees. He followed the faint trail west until he came to an abandoned campsite, where it looked like they'd spent at least one day. The remains of chicken bones and a few empty jars of preserved vegetables lay near a cold campfire.

Sawyer had a hard time tracking from there. Surely there were more signs to follow from when they had left their camp, but rain and wind had wiped out any tracks, and it would be a waste of his time if he tried searching any longer. It was time to locate Luke and his men to see if they had located anything.

He figured he would intersect with them if he rode due west, or at least he'd come across their tracks. Their trail should be easy enough to find, since they had ten shod horses. Raven was ready to get going, so they crossed the prairie.

The landscape was scattered with cedar and scrub oaks, and they were crossing a gully when he saw the tracks of two unshod horses in the soft soil. Out of curiosity, he followed them. Once the ravine widened out and the banks were shorter, the horse prints took an animal trail up the banks and headed west.

Sawyer had ridden close to one hundred yards

when he came upon his crew's path. He rode through their trail and found the path of the Indian ponies again. These tracks would probably lead him right to the renegade's main camp.

A mile from where the ponies' route had crossed over his crew's trail, he noticed that their tracks changed from running to walking, now heading south. This change meant they might be close to his men, which concerned him enough that he drew one of his guns to hold in his right hand.

He followed the unshod ponies until he got a queasy feeling in his stomach like he was about to be attacked. That feeling wasn't new to the ex-soldier. He had felt it many times during the war, and the old friend had saved his hide more than once.

He dismounted but didn't tie up his horse. If he needed Raven, he just had to whistle, and the horse would come to him. Sawyer made his way around a crop of cedars and in fifty feet, spotted two paint horses tied to a sapling.

Chapter Twenty-Two

Sawyer skirted east around the horses in hopes they wouldn't nicker and warn their riders. After going another fifty yards, he heard men talking south of his location. It was either his men or someone else, and he had to know for sure.

It was time to lie on his stomach and crawl toward the sound. Crawling on his belly was not his favorite way of sneaking up on someone, but sometimes it was necessary, and this was one of those times. He didn't have to go far though, and soon saw the two Indians who owned the horses he'd been following. Both were dressed in buckskin britches and carried new single-shot rifles.

Sawyer dismounted and looked through his spyglass to see what they were up to. To his surprise they were only watching instead of getting ready to attack whoever they were spying on. If the two were indeed watching his men, it was possible they might not want to shoot with just two muzzle-loading rifles against four armed cowboys who had them outnumbered and outgunned.

Sawyer was about to back away when one of the savages put his rifle to his shoulder and pulled back the hammer. Sawyer brought his pistol up and fired, hitting the man, and watched him fall to the ground. He fired a second shot that missed the second Indian, who turned and ran. His third shot missed again, and the man disappeared into the trees and brush. Sawyer ran to the man he'd killed and kicked the rifle out of his hand.

He heard someone holler out, "Who's out there?"

"It's Sawyer McCade."

"Sawyer, hold your fire. It's Luke and your crew. We're coming to you."

It was useless trying to find the one who'd run away. The Indians knew the terrain and could hide in the underbrush undetected for hours.

Luke was the only one who came to Sawyer. "What happened, boss?" he asked.

"This feller and one more were watching y'all. He brought his gun up to shoot, and I got him before he could pull the trigger. I missed the other one, and he took off west. Their two horses are tied up about fifty yards to the east. I should go turn them loose," said Sawyer.

"I'll tag along in case there's more trouble," said Luke.

Sawyer reloaded his pistol and walked in the direction of where he had seen the ponies. Luke followed. But to their surprise, when they got to the spot, both horses were gone.

"Well, I'll be," said Sawyer. "He snuck back around without me hearing a thing and took the horses. There was a time I would have heard him do that. I must be getting rusty."

"We should probably get back to the others. Where did you leave your horse?" asked Luke.

Sawyer whistled, and they heard a commotion nearby. A second later, Raven came out of the brush. "Come on, big feller, follow me," said Sawyer to his horse.

"You have that animal trained mighty good," said Luke. "I ain't never had a horse smart enough to do that."

The other men were in a small clearing, standing beside their horses with their guns drawn when Sawyer and Luke came out of the brush to join them.

Jesse came forward. "Did you happen to see old Alfred's daughter while you were at the store?"

"Yeah, I saw her. The renegades beat me there and have ransacked the place, taking what they wanted. They murdered the man and his daughter, and I can only speculate what else might have happened. I'm sorry to have to tell you this, but all of you need to understand these men are as bad as they come. From here on out, we must all be alert for the faintest movement or sound. They could be hiding anywhere, now that one of them got away and warned the others."

Luke said, "We should put lead ropes on the spare horses so we can maneuver through this brush a little easier."

Once they'd secured all the horses, the five men headed out. Each one had a spare pony close to his side as they made their way through gullies, small streams, and brush. An hour later, Luke held up his arm, turned in the saddle, and motioned to the others with his index finger to his lips.

Sawyer became alert and scanned the territory from right to left, expecting trouble. Then he heard it. It was the sound of bawling cattle off in the distance to the southwest.

"Boss, did you hear that?" asked Luke.

"Yeah, I heard it. Jesse, take my spare horse. I'll follow the sound, and you men can come behind me."

Sawyer urged Raven to move out faster, but not so fast that they couldn't keep a close lookout for the enemy. After another mile he stopped again to listen. Sure enough, the sound was much closer. He walked his horse to the top of a short hill, and there below, scattered over at least fifty acres, was a herd of Texas longhorns.

He let his horse walk in the direction of the cattle while he held his pistol in his right hand. His nervous eyes kept surveying the landscape, looking for his men or the renegades. There didn't seem to be any signs of human life, like campfire smoke or horse nickers.

Where could his men be hiding? Then he remembered the spyglass that he had taken off the gunrunners. With the scope held to his eye, he scanned the brush slowly and saw something that caught his attention— the barrels of three rifles lying across a fallen tree trunk, but there was no one with them. Upon further observation, he detected a gully directly behind the rifles.

At that point, he guided Raven toward the gully, but stayed ready for battle in case it wasn't his friends hiding there. He called out when he was within fifty feet of the three rifle barrels. "Hello in the gully. It's Sawyer McCade."

There was no acknowledgment, so he rode closer, and at the gully's edge, his horse chose a path down the bank and stopped at the bottom. "Hello, it's Sawyer McCade."

He kept going. Just past the three rifles, the soft soil at the bottom of the gully revealed numerous boot tracks. Thirty feet up ahead, another ravine intersected with the one he was in. Approaching with caution, he dismounted and walked the last six feet and peered up the other gully. There was Cowboy and Hooter with rifles aimed at the ravine's entrance. "Hold your fire. It's me, Sawyer."

"Sawyer, is that really you?" called out Cowboy.

"Yep, it's me in the flesh, and I brought help," said Sawyer.

"Well, come on in, we ain't going to shoot you. We ran out of ammo three days ago," said Cowboy. "We left those rifles out there to make the scum think we were ready for them if they came down the gully."

"We should go fetch the weapons, since I have ammunition. Where's the rest of the crew?" asked Sawyer.

"We have a little camp on up the wash. Harold and Ronnie, along with three more men we hired, are laid up in camp wounded. Our cook and one of the wranglers got killed on the first day the Indians attacked us," said Hooter.

"You fellers go on back to camp and get comfortable until I get there. I have four more cowboys with me. They have provisions, ammo, and horses with them. I'll ride out of this gully so they can see me," said Sawyer.

"You watch yourself. Those savages are still out there, just waiting to fill us with slugs," said Cowboy.

"Follow me to my horse and I'll give you some ammo in case we get attacked," said Sawyer.

He gave the two men most of his spare ammunition from his saddlebags. Cowboy and Hooter began to reload their pistols as Sawyer rode back the way he had come. He'd just returned to the top of the hill where he'd first seen the cattle, when gunfire sounded ahead. He touched the spurs to Raven's sides and pulled his pistol and leaned over as close to his horse's neck as possible, ready for a fight.

Chapter Twenty-Three

The shooting eased up until only a single shot could be heard every once in a while. Sawyer slowed his horse to a stop and listened, and a few seconds later, he heard dry brush rustle and crack, then the pounding hooves coming his way. At first, he thought it might be a few stray cattle that had stampeded when the shooting started. Instead, Luke and his men came riding out of the brush as fast as they could, leading the spare horses and pack animals.

Sawyer started to join them but stopped and motioned with his left arm for the men to continue without him. He dropped the bridle reins over his saddle horn and pulled the gun on his left hip.

Hidden behind a large cedar, the lone gunman waited for his prey to arrive. He couldn't see anything but heard the sound of riders crashing through the brush. But he only had to wait for a few seconds before five armed renegades thundered out of the cedars and scrub oak with guns drawn, chasing after Luke and his crew. The bandit in the front was a white man who had on chaps made from buffalo hides.

Sawyer waited until they were almost even with the tree he was using for cover before he made his move. He touched his spurs to Raven, and the horse started forward with a mighty lunge. When the first man, who wore the hairy chaps, saw him, Sawyer fired with both pistols and the impact of the lead balls lifted the rider out of the saddle and onto the ground, where the horses that followed ran over him.

The evil men all looked with surprise on their faces by the rider coming at them out of nowhere with his guns firing. Two of the men were hit by the lead balls and fell off the backs of their horses dead within the first few seconds. The remaining riders' horses spooked and reared up, and then one began to buck, kicking up his hind legs.

As Raven ran through the turmoil, he crashed into another horse and rider. The frightened horse had reared up and was slashing the air with his front legs when they connected with the big black. The force of the blow caused the rearing horse to spin around to his right and let out a loud groan before he lost his balance and landed on his side. The rider was scrambling to get free of the downed animal, which allowed Sawyer to fire an almost point-blank shot into the man's chest.

Sawyer wheeled Raven around to re-engage the fight, and while doing so, he holstered his empty guns and drew the .36-caliber pistol he carried behind his back. But he didn't need to shoot again—the two riders who hadn't been shot gained control of their mounts and took off at a dead run back through the brush and trees.

Cautiously, Sawyer dismounted and checked each of the three men that he had shot. Two were deceased and one was still alive. "Where's your camp and how many men are there?" Sawyer asked him.

"I ain't telling you anything."

Sawyer looked at the blood oozing from the man's stomach wound and thought the man was gutshot, but he wanted to be sure, so he tore the man's shirt open to see where the lead ball had entered his body. Sure enough, he was dying an agonizing death. Sawyer picked up a short stick that lay in the dirt and showed it to the man. "You see this? I'm going to put it in that hole in your stomach and hollow it out so I can pull out your guts."

He sat down on the hurt man's chest so he couldn't move and drew a circle in the air above the hole with the stick before inserting it about half an inch.

The man kicked his legs and tried to buck Sawyer off. "Oh crap, stop! I'll talk!" he said as he moaned in pain and thrashed on the ground. The man's face turned pale, and beads of sweat popped out on his forehead and upper lip. His breathing came in short, quick breaths, and his eyes, which had been bright just moments before, began to glass over and roll back into their sockets.

Sawyer recognized that the feller was on the brink of death, and he needed to get the answers he wanted quickly before the outlaw expired. Sawyer took hold of the man's shoulders and gave him a shake. "Don't you dare die on me. Where's your camp located and how many men are there?"

The man looked at him. "Go to hell." He shivered

and stiffened as he took in his last breaths of air and died.

Sawyer frowned in disgust as he rummaged through the dead men's pockets. Unfortunately, he didn't find anything of value or any indication of who they were. Three of them were white, and two were Indian. The white men all sported beards and long hair. The man who had been in the lead position wore a two-gun holster rig and had an Arkansas toothpick in a sling that hung across his chest. The other two men wore matching brown shirts, and the Indians wore worn army-blue pants and no shirts.

Sawyer gathered their guns, tied the horses together, and took the animals with him. From the top of the hill, he could see Luke and his crew drawing close to the gully where he'd found his friends.

Sawyer fired once into the air as a warning shot to let his men know that he was coming. Luke and his men stopped and waited until Sawyer caught up with them.

"Boss, I take it you killed those men that were after us?" asked Luke.

"Two of them got away," said Sawyer. "I found my Texas friends down this gully, a ways to the east. Let me take the lead, and we'll go to their camp. Some of them are hurt and may need help."

"We'll be right behind you," said Luke.

Sawyer started down the bank of the gully, and one of the outlaw's horses reared up and tried to pull away. The frightened animal almost broke free from the others until Jesse grabbed its bridle and kept his horse alongside the anxious animal until they were at the bottom of the ravine.

"Another gully intersects with this one up ahead. Their camp is somewhere up there," Sawyer told them.

When Sawyer and his crew rode up, Cowboy had already lit wood to make a fire since they were wanting coffee and something to eat.

The camp was a low spot, about twenty feet wide and thirty feet long, that had been eroded by rain and wind along the narrow gully. They had no bedding or provisions that Sawyer could see. "Cowboy, where's your horses and gear?"

"Those sneaky thieves snuck up on our camp, cut the cook's throat, and took our chuckwagon. The next day they attacked us right after we saddled up, and that was when they shot Harold and stole half of our horses. The next day Ronnie rode out and found a herd heading to Cowtown and ask a rider to get a message to you. On his way back, they chased after him and that's when he was wounded. We found this place and have been trying to defend ourselves ever since," said Cowboy.

Sawyer walked over to Ronnie and Harold, who were lying on the ground close to the east wall of the ravine.

"Hello men, I'm going to take a look at your wounds and try to help you," said Sawyer.

"It's really good to see you, old friend," said Ronnie. "We were beginning to think this would be the end of us."

"Yeah, you and your men are a welcome sight," said Harold.

"Looks like we got here just in time," said Sawyer. "I'll try to be careful and not hurt you while I examine your injuries."

Harold said, "You do whatever you need to do. We're happy you're here."

Ronnie had a dirty rag tied around his left thigh, and a nasty-looking gash ran along the side of Harold's head. Dried blood mixed with dirt covered the wound as well as the side of his face and neck.

Sawyer squatted between his two injured friends and pushed Harold's hair out of the way so he could look at his head. The gash looked to be infected and needed to be cleaned so Sawyer could get a better idea of his friend's condition.

Then he removed the rag on Ronnie's leg. The area around the wound was red and inflamed. He touched his finger to the tender flesh, and Ronnie cringed in pain. "I'm going to heat up some water to clean your wounds, and then I'll put some medicine on with fresh bandages. You fellers stay put while I check on the other wounded cowboys."

"Sawyer, you get us doctored up so we can fight alongside you and get a little payback for what that scum out there did," said Ronnie.

Sawyer nodded and went to the other hurt men. Two fires were going by the time he finished his examinations, heating up pans of water and the coffee pot.

Sawyer walked a short distance away from the fires and stood looking to the west.

Luke walked up beside him. "Boss, I don't know much about war or fighting Indians, but I think we should move camp to a location where we can defend ourselves better. This gully seems like a death trap to me."

"You're absolutely right about that," said Sawyer turning to face his foreman. "Tell Jesse and Austin to work on the injured while you and Barney remove the lead shot from Ronnie's leg and that other feller's shoulder. Cowboy and Hooter can make coffee and rustle up some grub for everyone."

"Sure thing. Are you going to scout us out another campsite that's easier to defend?" asked Luke.

"Yeah, I am," said Sawyer. "The way I figure, those two men who got away will be back soon with more men to seek revenge. Go ahead and assign one man to guard watch until I return."

Cowboy overheard the conversation and spoke up. "Those scum may not come back until tomorrow, they usually come but once a day. Some of them shoot at us while others drive thirty or forty cows off. I don't know where they take them or what they do with them, but their camp can't be far off."

"If they've been taking that many head, I'm sure I can pick up their trail, and we can follow them," said Sawyer. "But right now, we need to find a better campsite to defend ourselves and doctor the wounded. Let's get everyone healed up, since we'll need all the help we can get to find my cattle and drive them home."

"You go ahead and secure us a protected camp, and we'll take care of things here," said Luke.

"I saw a place about a half mile away when I came down the hill from the north that may work for us. I'll go scout it out and if I like it, I'll come back and we can move camp," said Sawyer.

Chapter Twenty-Four

Sawyer rode out of the gully and made a wide circle around where his men were camped, and came across the tracks of the renegades and his cattle. They were headed westward and evidently used the same path daily. The grass had been trampled down to almost nothing, and it was easy to make out the route.

Eighty yards south of the cattle trail was the beginning of a stand of larger trees that he had seen earlier. Riding into the timber paid off when his horse walked into a small clearing that was twenty feet wide and forty feet long. Sawyer left Raven ground-tied to graze while he walked back in the direction from which he had come so he could get a picture in his mind how to secure the new camp. A couple of good sentries could easily defend this location until the rest of the men were well enough to engage in a battle.

He returned to the clearing and noticed five big willow trees on the side of the forest and immediately knew why they were there. Enough water was coming out of the ground in that spot to sustain their growth.

He walked to the trees, picked up a stick, and began digging in the soft earth. Water seeped from the ground. After fifteen minutes, he'd dug a hole that had filled with enough water for his horse to drink when they were ready to leave.

The shape of the new camp provided ample room to hang tarps from the trees and make lean-tos for shelter. The trees would also help to disperse smoke from their fires. He laughed. He was thinking like an army man again—sentries to stand guard, hiding the campfire, an area of defense. Indeed, this would be a good place for a base camp.

He climbed back into the saddle, and Abigail's beautiful face came to his thoughts. With his eyes closed, he thought about her and what he wanted for their future. What had she been doing while he was gone? How was his sister doing? Was Abigail helping Nancy at the house? The upcoming life with Abigail and the ranch partnership with his sister was important to him, but he had to shake those questions and images from his mind. Occupying his mind with reflections of home could get him shot or wounded.

It would take some work to get the camp ready, but if they pulled together, they could do it. Maybe they cut down a few trees and placed them strategically, they'd be able defend a first volley if the renegades attacked.

When Sawyer got back to camp, Austin had a pot of food staying warm by the fire and a cup of coffee waiting for him. He dismounted, removed his tin cup from his saddlebag, and found a place to sit.

"Boss, did you find us a good camp location?" asked Luke.

"I did, and it's close to here. We'll have water and

shelter. Someone go get Cowboy, and we'll pack up and head that way."

"I'll go get him," said Hooter.

Sawyer finished his midday meal, although it was the afternoon, and called out to the men. "If everyone will gather around, I'll go over the plan on moving to our new campsite."

He waited for everyone to settle by the fire before he explained his plan. "Ronnie and Harold can ride the two outlaw horses with saddles. Cowboy and Hooter can ride bareback on two of the other horses. The other three injured men can use Jesse, Austin, and Barney's saddle horses."

Hooter interrupted Sawyer and said, "That feller with the red beard is Benjamin. The other two are Rowdy and Mathew."

"Thanks, Hooter, I had forgotten to introduce them to everyone who came in with me. Now if y'all will get loaded up, we can head on out. Jesse, I want you to ride about fifty yards off to the north and keep a lookout for anyone who may be watching. Cowboy, you do the same on the south side, and I'll stay out in front."

Jesse and Cowboy took off and got in position.

Sawyer led the rest of the cowboys to their new camp location and kept a watchful eye out for trouble. When they were in the clearing and had all the horses unsaddled except for Raven, Sawyer called everyone together again.

"I'm going to scout out the area west of us and see if I can find the renegade's camp." He pointed to the timber to their west and made a sweeping gesture with his arm. "I want all the able-bodied men to cut down small trees and tie them or lay them down to create a barricade so that it'll be difficult for someone to get into the camp. Put the tarpaulins over there along the tree line for shelter in case of rain. I saw a few downed trees that you can pull close to the fire so we can sit on them or use the trunks for cover if we need to defend our position."

"You mentioned we had water. Where is it?" asked Luke.

Sawyer pointed to the willows. "It's over there in those willow trees. Someone may want to make a deeper hole if we have a shovel. I used a stick to give us a basin to dip water from."

"Barney, you, Jesse, and Austin unpack those pack saddles," said Luke. "Cowboy, you and your men string ropes in those trees to hang the tarps. I'll dig out the spring and drag logs over here to sit on."

Sawyer mounted up. "I'll be back for supper. Keep your rifles handy, and if you hear anything, be ready for battle."

"Sawyer, can we have your rope to use here in camp?" asked Hooter.

Sawyer untied the leather strap that held his rope and handed the lasso to his friend. Then he removed his bedroll and pitched it to Hooter. "Put this somewhere. I won't need it with me as I hunt for their hideout."

Hooter started walking over to the edge of the clearing where there was grass to lay the bedroll. Cowboy, who was getting an axe, turned back to Sawyer and said, "You do know that it's not just Indians who attacked us, right? There were probably eight or ten white men with them, and I'm pretty sure the leader was white. He stayed on his horse off in the distance while the others did the killing and stealing."

"What kind of horse does he ride?" asked Sawyer.

"It's a big bay gelding with a star between his eyes."

"I'll watch for him. You take care, I'm heading on out," said Sawyer.

Chapter Twenty-Five

The cattle path was easy to follow, and that worried Sawyer. What were they doing with his cows, and why did they use the same trail daily? Did they have men watching their back trail, daring someone to follow them? Was it a trap? It could be, or they might be so confident in their numbers that they didn't mind if someone came for them. It was hard to say. Sawyer rode away from the cattle path far enough that he barely saw it anymore.

The terrain was still cluttered with cedar and scrub oak. The native grass was as high as a cow's belly, and in other places, it was so sparse that the red soil was clearly visible.

He had been riding for almost an hour when he heard cattle bawling. They were close, and he needed to be extra careful. After another hundred yards, he dismounted at the foot of a small hill and left Raven with the reins dangling around his neck. If anyone tried to mount him, they would find themselves missing hunks of flesh. Raven was a one-person horse.

Taking along his spyglass, he climbed to the top of the hill on his hands and knees. Down below were approximately two hundred and fifty head of his cattle, grazing on grass east of a group of buildings. A barn, five tents, and two sod houses all stood together, creating a small settlement. White men and Indians were spread around the camp, doing various chores while children ran and played at different locations in the yard area. With a hand cupped over the end of the spyglass to avoid the glare from the sun reflecting off the lens, which might give away his location, he scanned the countryside around the buildings. West of the compound was a stream and another smaller herd of maybe a hundred and fifty cattle grazing close to the water.

He was curious about how many people lived at the compound and started trying to count them, but the sun had begun to set in the west and its bright rays hit him in the eyes, making it difficult to see.

It was time to return to camp and tell the others what he found. Raven had gotten his fill of grass, and the rest had done him good. Sawyer let the horse lope back to their camp once they were out of hearing range of the settlement.

It was almost totally dark by the time they made it back. The shelters were up, and trees surrounded the spot where they would eat and sleep.

"Where's my bedroll?" asked Sawyer.

"It's down on the east end," said Luke.

"Thanks."

Sawyer removed Raven's saddle and put it with his bedroll so he could use it to lay his head on that night.

Jesse led Sawyer's horse to join the other animals inside a temporary corral.

"Have a seat and I'll get you a cup of coffee and a plate of food," said Barney.

"Don't mind if I do. I'm tired," said Sawyer as he took the hot coffee from Barney. He ate silently, and the men went about their tasks, but they all came and sat down to talk once he set his plate down.

"I found the thieves' camp about seven miles west-northwest of here. They have an encampment with a big barn, two houses, and several tents. I could see the banks of a river to the west."

Jesse said, "I know the place you're talking about. The Cimarron makes a turn to the north and then goes west again. That old barn has been there a long time."

"I didn't think people could live on the unassigned lands around here," said Sawyer.

"White men can't, but there is a piece of land called the Cherokee Strip through these parts. Cherokee Indians can farm it and live there if they get permission from the government," said Jesse.

"That must be what's happening over at their compound. Maybe those Indians are Cherokee and not Apache after all," said Sawyer.

"Nope, they're Apache. My family lived in southwest Texas until I was twelve and then moved to Clarksville. I saw a lot of Indians as a kid, and I guarantee you they're Apache. And even though their leader looks white, I suspect he may have a little Indian in him too," said Hooter. "You can see for yourself at about eight tomorrow morning, when they come for more cattle."

"Eight, you say? Good. We'll be waiting for them about a mile from here. They have to pass through a spot with an outcropping of rocks on one side, and a hill on the other. We'll catch them in a crossfire and even the numbers out some," said Sawyer.

"What about the wounded? Do you want us to come with you?" asked Ronnie.

"No, not yet. I'll need all of you soon when we attack their compound. When that day comes, I don't want any women or children hurt, is that understood?" asked Sawyer.

All the men nodded in acknowledgment of his orders. "Good. Now I'm going to turn in and get some rest. We have work to do in the morning."

Sawyer crawled into his bedroll and fell off to sleep almost immediately. An old familiar dream filled his mind in his state of slumber. He heard cannon fire and smelled the burned powder from gun barrels. That same old dream where men lay dead and wounded on the ground all around him. Some of them were missing arms or legs, or other body parts. There was death all around. Everything was covered in blood. His clothing was drenched in it, and when he raised his hands, blood dripped from his fingers.

He awoke and shot up into a sitting position, soaked in sweat and breathing hard. War was terrible. And tomorrow he would have to get mean and go to battle with the enemy again. Killing against his will was an emotional journey. He was tired of being responsible for deaths, but it seemed like it was his destiny to keep doing it. He hoped and prayed this would be his last battle and could then live a civilized life with his future wife.

A walk to the spring for a cool drink of water helped calm his thoughts. It had been a few days since he'd had dreams about the war. He thought about his fiancée and couldn't wait to see her again. He tried to keep his mind focused on her as he laid back down and drifted off to sleep.

Chapter Twenty-Six

Seven cowboys saddled their mounts under the cover of darkness with only the glow of their campfire to guide them. They were getting ready to engage the renegades in battle. It was a somber time, as each man knew the dangers of fighting with guns. In a short time, men would die, and some of the casualties might be from their own group. But this morning, the odds were in their favor since the enemy didn't know what they were up to.

After today, Sawyer and his men would have to be on guard, since the element of surprise was gone. Of course, Sawyer already planned to get his cattle back, but first, they had to get through the attack he had planned.

The sun began peeking over the eastern horizon when Sawyer and his army of cowboys moved out. He led the way quickly so he could get his men situated before the Indians came for more cattle.

The men stopped when they found a good place to hide between two knolls. Sawyer sent three men to the south side to spread out among the outcropping of rocks that littered the mound. The other three went to the hill on the north side of the trail to hide among the brush and rocks.

"I work better from the back of my horse, so I'll hide on my own," said Sawyer. "When you see them come into the pass, hold your fire until I get the party started. When I holler and fire my guns, y'all come out of hiding and shoot to kill. We want to surprise them, and I don't want any of them to get away."

The cowboys headed on out to hide their horses and get into position. Sawyer found a concealed location from where he could watch the pass from his saddle and be ready for battle when the time was right. The passage was only about thirty yards wide and opened to the west and east. Sawyer had concealed himself at the east end of the pass and looked to the west, where the enemy would be riding in from. He knew the renegades wouldn't be able to see him with the sun in their eyes as they rode east.

Thirty minutes passed with no sign of company. But Sawyer had the patience of a man who had spent three years as an army scout. He had often spent days watching for the right time to attack. He also knew that the Texas cowboys who had served with him could sit all day, if they had to. Luke and his men were solid and had proved themselves on this trip, and he knew he could count on them.

Just as he was starting to wonder where the renegades were, a voice behind him said, "Keep those hands where I can see them."

Sawyer moved one hand closer to his shoulder holster gun, but froze when he heard the click of a gun hammer being pulled back no more than fifteen feet away.

"I'm Deputy US Marshal Rex Waller. Who might you be?" the man asked in a quiet but stern voice.

"I'm Sawyer McCade from Humboldt, Kansas, and I'm here to get my cows back from the thieving, murdering gang that's holed up west of here."

"I've heard of you, I'm putting my gun away and riding on in," said Rex.

When he was beside Sawyer, he stuck out his gloved hand to shake. "It's nice to meet you, Sawyer. I reckon you and your men are about to surprise those outlaws coming this way."

"Yeah, they stole my cows and killed off a couple of my drovers who were driving the cattle," said Sawyer. "They killed the man who runs the trading post east of here and his daughter."

"I'm sorry to hear that old Alfred and his daughter are dead," said Rex. "I always stopped by there for food when I was in the area."

"I found them yesterday, naked and scalped and it's no telling what else they did to that girl before they killed her. I didn't go inside since they had already been dead a few days and the place stunk really bad."

Rex sat looking off across scrub oaks and brush that grew up from the big bluestem grass for a few seconds, like he was deep in thought. He finally looked at Sawyer and said, "Tell me your plan, and I'll help. I've been after this gang for weeks now. It's hard for one man to do much against Sully and his Indians."

"I didn't know the man's name was Sully, I was told it was Sooty. Can you tell me a little about him?" asked Sawyer.

"Sully is half-Indian and used to track for the Army. He drank a lot and killed an officer, then went on the run. The army hunted for him for about a year and finally gave up. He supposedly hid out with the Apache and they started raiding sodbusters and small ranchers in West Texas. When the law started after him, he and his men came into Indian Territory and recruited more disgruntled Apache off the reservation. The word is they steal cattle from the drives and sell them through an agent to the army for a good price."

"I see," said Sawyer. "I was wondering what he intended to do with my cattle."

"Now you know. So what's your plan? They should be along any minute," said the lawman.

"I've got my men hidden on both sides of the pathway. I'm going to fire the first shots when the outlaws begin to enter the pass. We'll have them in a crossfire, and if it goes as planned, none of them will survive. I fight better on my horse, so when the time is right, I'll start the party and approach them from the front," said Sawyer.

"I fight better on the back of my horse too. When you're ready, I'll be beside you in the attack," said Rex.

Another twenty minutes passed, and Sawyer saw a cloud of dust off to his west about a half mile. The renegades were coming, and it was time to prepare for battle. Raven's bridle reins were already lying across his neck; Sawyer planned to use his legs to guide his horse into the fight instead. He looked at the deputy and nodded.

With a pistol in each hand, Sawyer talked softly to his horse, and when the Indians entered the pass, he took a deep breath and was ready to engage the enemy.

He let out a war cry and touched his heels to Raven's sides. Both men took off and headed straight for the Indians, who rode in a line across the path. Both pistols came up and Sawyer fired, knocking one man off his horse. He heard the lawman's gun firing beside him and saw some of the renegades get hit.

Six bodies were on the ground by the time he had emptied both guns.

Sawyer holstered the empty weapons and drew his shoulder holster pistol. There were only two riders left out of the original eight, and they were trying to turn their mounts around to retreat when he and Rex rode up on them and shot them both.

Sawyer sat on his horse, keeping an eye on the area west of the pass while he reloaded his weapons. Rex dismounted and turned over the last two dead men he and Sawyer had killed so he could see their faces. The smell of spent gunpowder was heavy in the air as Sawyer's men came out from the hiding places.

Jesse and Cowboy checked to see if the Indians that were hit in the crossfire were all dead.

Luke walked over to Sawyer. "What do you want to do with the dead bodies?"

"See if the men can catch their ponies. We'll tie the corpses onto their mounts and head them home. That'll be a message to Sully and his men that we're here waiting for them," said Sawyer.

"So the leader is called Sully, not Sooty like Bertha said?" asked Luke.

"Yeah, that feller over there looking at the corpses is a US Marshal who's after him."

"Sending the bodies back may not be a good idea.

He might bring a lot of reinforcements back to kill us," said Luke.

Rex came over and introduced himself to Luke. "I'm Deputy Rex Waller. I don't see Sully here with these men. He most likely stayed in camp this trip."

Hooter came over to join the conversation. "The boss man never takes part in the rustling. He'll come with them sometimes, but always sits on his horse away from the action."

"That would be Sully all right. He likes to let his men do all the hard work and if it doesn't go as planned, he's the first one to turn tail and run," said Rex.

"I'm going to ride over by their camp and see if I can tell what they intend to do next. You're welcome to come along if you want," Sawyer said to Rex.

"I certainly will," said the lawman.

Sawyer turned to Luke. "After you send the dead off on their horses, y'all get back into position and wait for me. Be prepared to shoot if you see me coming at a dead run."

"Okay. You be careful, and we'll be ready if they come," said Luke, who walked off to give orders to the other men.

Sawyer and Deputy Rex rode west toward the renegade encampment. They were careful to stay off the main trail in case the Indians had heard the shooting and were on their way to investigate.

Sawyer took Rex to the same location where he had spied from the day before. They hurried to the top of the hill and watched the activity below at the compound. Kids were playing in the yard, and two women hung up clothes on a clothesline in back of the houses.

Sawyer asked Rex, "If this land is owned by the Cherokee, why is there Apache here? And who has the rights to this land?"

"The Cherokee Strip belongs to the tribe, and they got it thanks to a surveyor's mistake. Most likely there's a Cherokee man living in one of the houses down there, and he's the rightful owner of this land. Sully and his renegades probably moved in on him, and he can't get rid of them," said Rex.

"I'm curious to know how many more fighters are down there. The odds are still high that we're outnumbered, but not as high as they were. I also want to see what Sully looks like," said Sawyer.

"Let me see if I can locate him," said Rex. He reached over and picked up the looking glass to watch for a while.

Hopefully, the Indian horses would soon return to the camp with the bodies tied to them, and Sawyer would get some answers to his questions.

Forty-five minutes after they arrived to spy, Sawyer heard horse hooves approaching and three of his men rode up, herding the Indian horses back toward Sully's camp. Sawyer and Rex hurried down the hill and waved their hats to get the men's attention. All three cowboys stopped, but the Indian ponies continued on their way home.

"Let's go up that hill and watch what happens," said Sawyer.

Sawyer, Rex, and the three cowboys lay on their stomachs at the top of the hill when they saw one of the children playing in the yard run to the front of the barn and ring a bell attached to a post. Immediately, seven

Indians rush out of the structure, and six white men came out of several of the tents.

The men from the barn stopped the horses and a White man and woman emerged from one of the houses. The man went to the Indians, who were cutting the dead bodies off the mounts. He pointed his finger at the corpses, and it looked like he was yelling at the men.

Cowboy whispered just loud enough for Sawyer and the others to hear, "That's the one who sits off to the side and watches on his horse. I think he's the one in charge."

They watched as the man walked from corpse to corpse, grabbing a handful of hair to lift up their heads. Sawyer could tell he was giving orders by the way he made gestures to his men.

The Indians were still busy removing their dead from the ponies when a man and woman came out of the second house. He used a crutch to get around and looked much older than any of the others. He had long gray hair and was quite a bit taller than the Apache warriors.

When all the dead were on the ground, the man in charge shouted and waved his arms in anger. The white men and four of the Indians went to the barn.

Sawyer knew it was time to get off the hill. "Come on, we should go back to the others right now. Those men who ran to the barn will be riding out and heading this way very soon, and we should be ready for them."

They mounted up and returned to the pass where they had staged their ambush. The other men were still in situation for another fight. Ronnie, Harold, and Rowdy were also there, ready to do their part and fight.

Sawyer positioned everyone where he wanted

them, but this time, he placed two men closer to the entrance of the pass so they could stop any riders who tried to retreat.

Another cloud of dust rose up to the west about a mile away. Sawyer told the others, "Get into position, quickly. Based on the amount of dust out there, there's a large group headed our way."

"Yeah, I would say there are more than the few we saw go into the barn," said Rex.

Chapter Twenty-Seven

Sawyer and Rex waited behind the same cedars as before. The outlaws entered the pass from the west and when they had ridden halfway through, Sawyer and the lawman spurred their horses forward and headed at them with their guns ready to fire.

Sawyer was out of range when he fired his first shot, but it was a signal for his men to shoot. A hail of lead descended on the outlaws from both sides of the pathway. Sawyer and Rex came at the gang from the front, so ammo was fired at the renegades from all directions. Three riders turned to retreat and were shot out of their saddles by the two men Sawyer had hiding at the entrance.

The shooting stopped, and Sawyer hollered out to his men to see if any were injured. Jesse had a flesh wound to his side and Austin was missing his hat, that was shot off his head. Rex had a crease on his left arm where a lead ball had broken the skin as it passed by. The remainder of his crew went from man to man that was on the ground, checking if any were alive. One young white man was still breathing. Blood covered the back of his shirt. He was trying to crawl away when Sawyer put a boot in his back and a gun to his head.

"You answer me truthfully, and I might let you live," said Sawyer. He rolled the man onto his back and realized he couldn't have been older than twenty. "Who's your boss?"

The frightened young man paused before saying, "If I tell you what you want to know, will you let me go?"

"Yeah, I'll let you go, but you better not lie to me. Is that understood?"

"He goes by Sully, but his real name is Tommy Rainwater," said the man.

"What's your name?" asked Sawyer.

"It's Billy Westover."

"Why has Rainwater been stealing my cattle and horses?" asked Sawyer.

"He says no White man can come after him since he is on the Cherokee Strip. He plans to take the cattle to Fort Sill and sell them to the army."

"How many men are left at the compound with Tommy?"

"Only three, and they're out west of the barn digging graves for the dead."

"Who's the older man on crutches?" asked Sawyer.

"That would be Willie Tall Deer. He owns the property."

"So what's the connection between Sully and the old man?" asked Sawyer.

"Sully and his men took over the land, and Willie and his woman are like prisoners. He's the one who persuaded the Indians who are with him to leave the reservation. Sully and most of the whites have been riding together for some time," said Billy. "I've told you everything, mister. Can I get on my horse and leave now?"

"Yeah, you can leave, as far as I'm concerned. But if I see you down there when I pay Tommy Rainwater a visit, you're a dead man. Is that clear?"

Rex walked up. "Sawyer said you're free to leave, but I'm Deputy Rex Waller, and you're under arrest for cattle stealing and murder."

"What? He said I was free to go!" said Billy.

"He did say that, and you were free to go until I arrested you. Now turn over on your stomach so I can tie your hands," said Rex.

Billy turned, and as he did, his hand shot out from under his body holding a gun. But Rex had been expecting him to try something, and killed the man before he could get off a round.

"It looks like they're all dead now," said Rex as he started to reload his weapon.

"Looks that way," said Sawyer. "Rex, I'm going after Rainwater before he hightails it out of here. Are you coming with us?"

"I sure am, let's mount up and put a stop to him once and for all," said Rex.

Sawyer looked at Luke and said, "Leave the corpses where they are and tie up what horses you can catch. Then you're going after the cattle at the encampment while I visit Mr. Tommy Rainwater. There should be a herd east of the houses and another smaller herd by the stream west of the barn."

Nine cowboys and one deputy marshal rode for

Rainwater's encampment. Sawyer stopped and spied on the outlaws' headquarters with his spyglass and Tommy was sitting on the porch of one of the houses, looking to the east through his own spyglass. The sun reflected off the glass and Sawyer saw Rainwater get up from his rocking chair and run toward the barn.

Sawyer spurred Raven and rode up beside Rex. "He must see his reign coming to a close because he's running to the barn."

"Let's go get him before he gets away," said Rex.

Sawyer kicked his horse to go faster.

He and Rex were only two hundred yards from the barn and closing fast. A quick glance to his left alerted him that Rex had drawn his rifle from its scabbard in case he had to take a long-distance shot.

Rainwater came flying from the barn mounted on a horse, only to be met thirty feet out by Sawyer and the lawman. The deputy had his rifle in his hand, and Rex fired before Sawyer had time to draw his gun. The outlaw was knocked backward from his horse and turned a somersault when his body bounced off the ground. Sawyer dismounted to make sure the man was dead, and heard Luke give orders to gather the cattle and start them back toward their camp.

Sawyer looked at Rex. "It looks like you got your man, Deputy."

"I couldn't have done it without you and your men. I reckon I'll head on to Alfred's Store and either bury old Alfred or set the building on fire. You take care, Sawyer." Deputy Rex Waller rode east and never looked back.

Sawyer walked to the second house, where the old Indian man stood at the doorway.

"Those cattle are mine and I'm taking them with me," said Sawyer.

The older man nodded and pointed to the other sod house. "My daughter is in there, don't hurt her or my grandkids."

"I won't harm them. Are there any more of that bunch still around here somewhere?" asked Sawyer.

"Three Apache are burying their dead back that way," said the old man, pointing to the river.

Sawyer mounted up and rode west to find the last three renegades. As he passed the barn, he noticed a chuckwagon parked out back and figured it belonged to his friends. They would need it when they headed his cattle home.

Sawyer went to the rear of the barn and saw the gravediggers running as fast as they could to the barn. He palmed his gun and took off to meet them. All three of the men fired at the white rider coming at them but missed their marks since he was out of range of their guns. Sawyer was upon them before they could reload and he commenced to fire. By the time his gun clicked on an empty cylinder, all three lay dead.

He had no compassion for the men and they got what they deserved for the crimes they had committed.

He went back to the compound, and out of curiosity, rode through the open barn doors. No one was present, but five or six saddles sat in a corner, piled on each other. It must have been the gear they'd stolen from Cowboy and his crew.

Sawyer rode out to find Cowboy, who was busy gathering the cattle. "I found all your gear in the barn, and the chuckwagon is out back. Take your men and go get your things. Luke's men and I will get the cows heading east toward camp."

"Okay, I saw the horses grazing, so we'll get them and then get loaded up and meet you there," said Cowboy, heading toward Hooter.

Chapter Twenty-Eight

Sawyer went back to the old man's house before he started herding cattle. "Hello in the house. Come outside, I want to talk to you."

Willie Tall Deer came out onto the porch. "Can I help you with something?" he asked as he put on his hat.

"There's no Apache left on your property," said Sawyer. "Do you own any cattle?"

"I did have five cows and one bull, but those Apache yellow dogs ate them. Now we have nothing."

"I'll leave you five cows and maybe a bull if I have one," said Sawyer.

"Thank you, that's awful kind. By the way, what is your warrior name?"

"I'm Sawyer McCade."

"I'm Willie Tall Deer, and my house is open to you anytime you pass through."

"Thanks, Willie, I best be going now." Sawyer rode off to meet Luke.

"Luke, have the men cut out five cows and a bull to leave here for the old man and his family."

"Yes sir. I'll have them get right on it."

Sawyer took off toward some grazing cattle to the south of the houses. He rode wide of them until he could come up and drive them east to join the rest of the herd that had begun to bunch up.

When he got close enough that he could holler at them, they started walking to join the rest of the herd that was grazing nearby. They'd been on their own for so long, roaming the mesquites and fending for themselves that he expected them to act wild, and be difficult to herd. Instead, he was surprised at how quickly they responded. The cattle drive had taken some of their wild tendencies out of them.

By the time Sawyer and the men he'd brought from Kansas had the cattle ready to head east to join the main herd, Cowboy and his men came around the corner of the barn with the wagon and a small herd of fifteen horses.

"The old man showed us where our spare horses were being kept. It looks like a couple got eaten. I left four ponies with the old man, he was tickled. I'm sending Rowdy on with the wagon and the rest of us will fall in and help get these cows moving," said Cowboy.

Luke went from one rider to the next, giving orders on how he wanted to get the herd moving. When he got to Sawyer, he said, "Boss, you take the lead but swing wide around that rock outcropping where we shot them fellers earlier. I don't want the cows to spook if they start smelling blood."

"I can do that," said Sawyer. "I reckon you want to

put them with the other cows that are grazing near our camp, right?"

"Yeah, but you can peel off and go into camp when we get close. We won't need you once we see the main herd," said Luke. "In fact, anyone who is injured can leave once we get moving. There probably ain't more than three hundred and fifty head here."

"I'll pass the word on to Ronnie and the others as I make my way to the front," said Sawyer.

"Thanks, boss."

Sawyer stopped and told each of the injured men the plan before he rode to the front and got some space between him and the herd.

When he was in position, Luke called out and the men whooped and hollered for the cattle to get moving. Sawyer waited until the ones in the front began to walk toward him before he started off. He turned in the saddle every few minutes to watch for any change in direction or signal from one of the men. The longhorns were still basically wild and could decide not to follow at any time.

Thirty minutes after they were underway, the riders crowded in and urged the livestock to go faster. If they walked, they had a tendency to stop and eat grass. That made the cows behind them want to stop, and it became harder for the men to keep all of them going forward.

Raven walked at a pace that kept him out front enough so the leader of the herd could see him. When they rode past the outcropping of rocks where the corpses of the dead men still lay, buzzards were circling in the sky, and some were already pecking on the bodies. An old saying from Sawyer's army days came to mind: *the buzzards and wild animals have to eat.*

It was late afternoon by the time they had ridden the seven miles from the outlaw encampment to where the main herd grazed on the rich grass north of their campsite. Sawyer veered off to the south toward the clump of trees where the men had set up their base of operation. The injured men followed him, and as soon as they rode in, Mathew put on a fresh pot of coffee by the fire. Sawyer, Ronnie, Harold, Mathew, Rowdy, and Benjamin sat on logs and had a couple of cups, then put more water in the pot for the others who would arrive soon.

After all the cowhands were back in camp and had their fill of coffee, Sawyer stood up to talk. "Men, today is the start of the cattle drive to my ranch. For the rest of the day, I would like for a few of you to pack all our provisions on the wagon but save room for Benjamin and Mathew. I don't think they should be on a horse just yet."

Benjamin spoke up. "I can sure try to ride."

"No, you go in the wagon for a few more days so you can heal more," said Sawyer. "Besides, we'll need someone who's able to drive the wagon and help set up camp at night."

Rowdy raised his hand. "Me, Ben, and Mathew will take care of driving the wagon and we can have supper cooked each night, if that's all right?"

Sawyer looked over at Cowboy. "Is that okay with you, Cowboy?"

"Yep, them three can cook mighty good."

"Luke is in charge of the cattle drive. I've chosen him because he's familiar with the route we have to take. We're going to hold up for a day or so just over the state line at an old corral so we can put sulfur on the cattle. That way we won't bring any Texas ticks with us to my ranch. I don't want my cattle to get infested and become sick with fever."

"You may want to get started on back to Cowtown after we move out tomorrow. I sure would like for the sulfur to be delivered on time," said Luke.

"I plan on leaving when the herd reaches Black Bear Creek. I figure it'll take you six days from here to get to where we are supposed to doctor the cattle. I think I can get to Wichita in two days, and that will give the wagons with the powder four days to travel from Cowtown to the pens," said Sawyer.

"Yeah, right," said Hooter. "We heard about you sending Abigail a telegram a while back. Me and ol' Cowboy think she's waiting on you at your ranch as we speak and you're going into Wichita to send her a little love message."

Sawyer couldn't keep a straight face. He started grinning from ear to ear.

Hooter slapped his leg and pointed his finger at Sawyer. "I knew it! You and Abigail are going to get hitched when you get back with these dogies."

"I sure hope so Hooter. In fact, if she will have me, we may do it before the four of you head back to Texas."

"I'll tell you what, Sawyer McCade," said Cowboy. "Me and the boys would be honored to stay and attend your wedding."

"In that case, all four of you can be my best men," said Sawyer. "I think Abigail would be very proud to have her Texas friends stand with me."

Ronnie said, "She's one fine Texas gal, and I think

she'll be tickled pink for a few hometown boys to attend her wedding."

"That's right," said Harold. "I've known her since I was about twelve."

"That's settled then, y'all will stay until after the wedding," said Sawyer.

The rest of the crew clapped and congratulated their leader.

Sawyer was proud as a peacock by the outpouring of congratulations. He gave everyone a few moments to settle down and then got back to business. "Okay. Now with my love life out of the way, Luke, do you have anything to say?"

"Yeah I do. I want us to go bunch the cattle up tighter, just north of that little valley. I noticed it when we came back. The meadow has a lot of good graze, and I'm almost positive there is a pond over there in the willows. The water and grass will keep them there for the night, and it will be easier to get them moving in the morning if we've grouped them in that spot."

Cowboy stood and said, "You heard Luke, let's get those cows moved so we can eat supper before dark."

The men, including Sawyer, mounted up. He wanted to be part of it so he could learn more about cattle.

Chapter Twenty-Nine

All the able-bodied cowboys started to head out, but Ronnie stopped them before they left camp. "Listen up, most of the herd hasn't been driven in a week or so. They're wild and mean. If you get too close and try to pressure them, it could go terribly bad."

"Ronnie's right," said Luke. "I don't want anyone getting hurt or one of those horns going through a horse. We have to move over a thousand head, and it's going to be difficult the first couple of days. Each of us may have to swap out our horses three or four times a day."

"I suggest you use your rope to slap them on the haunches and keep your distance," said Cowboy. "If you think one is trying to turn toward you, back off and let them have a little space. They'll usually turn back and go with the others."

"Let's spread out along the south side of the herd and push them north. Cowboy, once we get them going, you and your crew can move to the east side and push them closer in. Then my men can move west and drive

173

them toward the middle to tighten up the herd," said Luke.

Sawyer stayed with the drovers on the south side of the herd and rode back and forth, hitting the cows and hollering to make them start heading away from the riders. The riders worked their horses hard for a couple of hours and had to chase a few cows that didn't want to leave. The cowboys who rode drag had a difficult job of keeping the cattle moving forward. By the time the cattle had traveled over a mile, the cowboys had convinced the herd to string out and get in step with the ones in front of them. The men began to ease away from the cattle and let them slow to eat.

Sawyer was proud to finally start the process of getting his cattle home, and that he was learning how to become a cowboy. While patting himself on the back, he happened to miss a young bull turn from the south side of the herd and come at him, ready to fight. The raging bull was within twenty feet when Raven turned to the right and took off as fast as he could. Sawyer almost tumbled off Raven's back and had to grab hold of the horn on his Mexican saddle. One of the other riders came rushing at the bull and slapped him across the face with his rope to get his attention.

The frightened horse and rider stopped when they were out of harm's way. Raven turned back to the herd and snorted at the bull standing off from the rest of the cattle, watching. Sawyer let out about ten feet or so of rope and started toward the excited animal. He touched the sides of Raven with his spurs and lunged at the bull so that he could hit the huge beast with his rope as they went past. He wheeled Raven around for a second pass, but Cowboy and Hooter came over to help.

"Hold up, Sawyer," said Cowboy. "This feller is a nuisance, and the only way to make him behave is if we increase our numbers. Let's get side by side and ride straight at him, showing off our coiled ropes."

The three men rode together until they were within fifteen feet of the bull, who stood his ground, and begin to snort from his nostrils and paw the ground. Cowboy let out his rope and hit him on the nose. The stubborn animal shook his massive head and horns until the second slap of the rope got his attention enough for him to turn and trot back to the herd.

"We should've shot him when we first discovered he had a temper," said Cowboy.

"I vote that the next time he wants to fight, we leave him on the trail," said Hooter. "We've already spent more time making him return to the herd than he's worth."

Sawyer saw Luke and the other wranglers riding toward them. "It looks like Luke is ready to call it a day. Come on, let's head back to camp and eat supper," said Sawyer, and pointed at the campsite.

When they made it back to their spot in the woods, the men took a few minutes to care for their horses and wash the trail dust off their faces.

The tired wranglers sat on fallen logs and ate heartily and when they were finishing up the last of their food, Rowdy and Benjamin came around and topped off everyone's coffee cups.

"Jesse, where do you suggest we cross Black Bear Creek tomorrow?" asked Luke.

Jesse took a sip of coffee and thought for a few seconds. "I think we head northeast in the morning and find that trail we rode in on. We should find it north of

Alfred's Store. Then we can ford in the same place we did the other day."

"I'm not sure we can get the wagon up the far bank at that location," said Sawyer.

"There could be a better wagon passage somewhere close by, since Alfred got supplies from up north," said Jesse. "Maybe you should ride on out in the morning at the same time as the chuckwagon. That way, it can follow you to the creek. Then I would look east of where we were. As for the cattle, we'll make them traverse the stream at the same place we did on the way here."

"I think that's probably the best plan. The cooks can have us an early breakfast. Then they can leave and have a good head start by the time we get the herd moving," said Luke.

"That's fine by me," said Sawyer as he finished his coffee. He took his dish over to the wagon and washed it in a pan of soapy water. The night was still young, and he was not ready for bed yet. "I'm going to walk out to the prairie and look around," he said to the others.

Ronnie was the only one to say anything. "Sawyer, don't you go getting soft on us tonight thinking about Abigail."

Sawyer looked at him, grinned and walked off to be alone.

At the edge of the timber was a fallen tree that made a good place to sit. The wind had begun to blow from the south. Visibility in the darkness was maybe sixty feet, and it was nice to rest watching the tall grass sway in the breeze.

The prairie was so dark that he couldn't see the cattle, but he could hear them clearly. Wanting to get more comfortable, he sat on the ground with his back against the log.

If everything went the way he planned, they should be at his and Nancy's ranch in a week or so.

Thinking of his sister, he wondered if she and Abigail were bonding and getting along. Then he thought about Nancy's baby. She should be due soon, and then he'd be an uncle. Uncle Sawyer had a nice ring about it.

He had entirely different thoughts about Abigail. He was smitten with her and hoped she would want to marry him shortly after his return. He closed his eyes and remembered Sawyer, the killing machine. That man had to cease existing when he returned home. Even though the men he had killed since he'd left home deserved to die, he still felt bad about them. Somewhere they had parents or brothers and sisters. Some may even have had children. Now they were dead, and if they did have someone who loved them, that love was just a memory now.

It was time to stop reflecting of home and dead men. He stood up and went back to camp to find everyone asleep.

Chapter Thirty

The following morning, Rowdy and Mathew fixed a light breakfast of biscuits and gravy. Benjamin worked in the bed of the wagon securing their supplies so they wouldn't shift too much when they traveled.

Mathew walked up to Sawyer, who was rolling his bedroll. "Would it be all right if we hitched four horses to the wagon today? That may save us a lot of time crossing the creek I heard you talking about yesterday."

"You three are in charge of the wagon. Use as many horses as you need," said Sawyer.

"Thanks. We'll be ready to head out in less than thirty minutes," Mathew said, walking away.

After everyone in camp finished eating, the plates were washed, and the wagon moved out. Rowdy and Mathew were on the bench seat while Benjamin sat propped up in the wagon bed.

Sawyer mounted up and rode over to Luke, who was talking to the rest of the cowboys. "If I may interrupt for a moment," he said, lifting a hand. Luke nodded, and Sawyer continued. "I want to tell y'all that

I'm grateful to each of you. I may not see you until you reach the corral, so be careful. I almost messed up yesterday with that spotted bull. If he starts to give you problems, leave him and keep going. Keeping one mean bull is not worth someone getting hurt or losing valuable time."

The men nodded. Cowboy said, "Boss, we appreciate you and the same goes for you. You be careful out there by yourself and keep those guns handy."

Sawyer tipped his hat and rode off after the wagon. He took the lead, and it wasn't long before they were on course to intersect with the trail north of Alfred's Store. Whoever rode point with the herd would be able to see their tracks, and where the ground was hard, Sawyer broke off limbs to mark their trail.

The wagon traveled at a good pace across the prairie heading for Black Bear Creek. Sawyer left them to scout for a place to ford and followed the creek for a half mile until he came to a suitable place. Not only were the banks sloped, but there was a road heading north and south. He had yet to learn where the road went but would soon find out.

Sawyer turned around and went to find the chuckwagon, and about ten minutes later, he saw it coming his way.

"I reckon you found a crossing?" asked Rowdy.

"I sure did. I'll stay with you boys until you get on the other side of the creek and then I'm going on," said Sawyer. "There's a road that travels north also. I don't know where it goes, but I intend to find out. Hopefully it will intersect with the road to Cowtown. I'll leave you a marker if you need to take another route."

"I assume one of the others will direct us tomorrow

on where we need to go since you won't be around," said Rowdy.

"Yeah, Jesse will know, so you may want to stay close to the herd until you get to the Salt Fork Arkansas River," said Sawyer. "But for now, I'll lead you to get across Black Bear Creek and then I'm heading for Cowtown."

"Is that the only river we'll have to ford before we get to the corral you were talking about?" asked Benjamin.

"No, you'll also have to cross the Chikaskia River, but Jesse knows where to cross that one," said Sawyer. "Now let's get the wagon to the other side of this creek so I can head out."

They forded the stream without any difficulty—the red water only came to within a foot of the underside of the wagon bed. Mathew had been wise to use four horses; they had no problem pulling the wagon across the muddy creek and up the far bank.

Sawyer waved goodbye to the men and headed down the road on his own. Bertha's store would be a good place for him to eat and spend the night. He was also curious about what she had done with the place now that she was the owner.

The road turned east a few miles from the Salt Fork Arkansas River. Not being sure about where the road went, he took a chance and rode north. A mile later he discovered the road intersected with the trail they had used when they came down from Kansas. Another three miles and he was at the river crossing where he and Luke's men had forded the stream.

Sawyer decided to wait on the wagon and help them get across the river. It would give him and Raven some rest, and the horse could eat grass. It wasn't long until he heard the wagon, and a few minutes later he saw it. With the help of four horses, the wagon was traveling faster than usual.

Sawyer mounted up and started across the river, but halfway across, he turned back. Raven was walking in deep mud and the water was up to his belly. Sawyer was concerned the wagon might get stuck.

"Y'all take a break while I find a better crossing," said Sawyer when he came out of the water.

"That's fine," said Rowdy. "It'll give us time to get down and stretch our legs and soak some beans in a couple of pots so we can have them for supper."

Sawyer rode south and as he rounded a bend in the river, he encountered a campsite with an older man sitting on the riverbank fishing with a cane pole.

The fisherman stood up and waved. "Howdy stranger, I'd ask you to have a cup, but I ain't got any with me."

"That's quite all right," said Sawyer. "I'm looking for a location to take a wagon across the river. Do you happen to know of such a place?"

The man laid his cane pole on the ground and climbed up the riverbank to talk to Sawyer, still sitting on his horse. Sawyer kept his right hand on his hip gun.

"I know every spot on this river for miles. I live about a half mile west of here and come here to relax and think." He pointed east and said, "Ride on that way a quarter mile or so, and you'll see a crossing where the water is shallow. I like to fish below the shallow spot for perch."

"Thanks, and good luck catching fish today."

Sawyer pulled on Raven's reins and backed him up before turning to go get the men waiting on him.

"I found a better place to cross south of here," said Sawyer when he returned to the wagon. "Follow me and I'll help you ford the stream before I leave out."

"You lead the way and we'll be right behind you," said Rowdy.

The fisherman had been right—it was a good crossing, and the four horses got up the far bank without any problems. Sawyer stayed with the wagon until they were clear of the stream.

"I think you fellers should probably think about making camp soon. We've come a far piece today. Most likely, both the cattle and the men will be plenty bushed after crossing two streams," said Sawyer.

"We were thinking the same thing," said Rowdy. "If we camp close to the river, the men can bed down the herd north of us."

"Sounds good to me," said Sawyer. "I'm going to hightail it out of here and try to make it to Bertha's store tonight."

"I guess we'll see you at the corral then," said Mathew.

Sawyer took off and loped Raven, hoping he could get to the store by dark, but it would be a stretch since he had been riding so slowly, helping the wagon cross the two streams. At least he was somewhat familiar with the trail, and a few minutes before dark, he slowed Raven down at the campsite where they'd found Bertha and the guns.

Chapter Thirty-One

Sawyer let Raven walk the rest of the way to the store so the horse could cool off. The pungent smell of burning wood filled the air, coming in on an east breeze. He didn't think much of it, since Bertha probably had a fire going in the wood stove to prepare her supper.

When he was within twenty yards of the store, Raven nickered. That usually didn't happen unless another horse was nearby, and he caught a sniff of it.

Sawyer spotted the stovepipe sticking through the store roof; no smoke was coming out of it. He dismounted in front of a water trough and let Raven's reins stay across his horse's neck. Something didn't feel right, and Sawyer needed to be ready for trouble.

He went to the door, removed one of his guns, and stepped into the store. Once inside, he took one step to the side of the door, which prevented the setting sun to cast his shadow into the building.

"Hello, anyone here?" he hollered out.

There was no answer, so he eased his way around the interior of the store to the north wall, where a table covered in sewing material could be used as cover in case there was trouble. He kept walking toward the back wall until he could look out the rear window, which was five feet to the left of the back door.

"I'm back here. I'll be right in," Bertha called out.

He saw her walk out of the timber with a man holding her right arm and pointing a gun at her side. Her right eye was blackened, and blood stained the front of her shirt.

When she came through the rear door, the man was not with her and Sawyer put his finger to his lips to try to tell her to not say his name. The man had stayed outside.

"Howdy, ma'am, I was hoping you had food cooked so a weary traveler could eat before heading into the night," said Sawyer. "I have greenbacks to pay for it."

He stepped to his left and peeked out the window. The man with the gun leaned against the outside wall, a foot to the left of the back door. Sawyer took aim at the wall where he thought the man was and fired once, then aimed a few inches closer to the door and fired again.

A scream filled the backyard of the store, and Sawyer ran out the back door so the hurt man couldn't get a bearing on him and shoot. Sawyer shot another round and took the back of the man's head off. Blood and brain matter splattered against the back wall of the store.

Bertha came to the door and pointed at the woods. "There's another one back by the old still."

Sawyer took off running as fast as he could and entered the clearing. A man finished tightening the cinch strap on his saddle near the pile of debris from the old still. He turned and attempted to pull his gun when

Sawyer began to fire. The first ball hit the man with a glancing blow to the side of his nose, tearing out a good portion of his jawbone. The second lead ball hit him in the middle of his chest.

Sawyer had already reloaded the gun when Bertha joined him in the clearing. "Bertha, are you okay?" asked Sawyer.

"Yeah, I'll live. That's the second time you've saved my hide. Those polecats had plans to rob my store and take what they wanted from me. I was glad to see you standing there with your gun drawn."

"How long have they been here?" asked Sawyer.

"They got in about an hour ago. They used to ride with that scum you killed at South Haven and wanted the guns and anything else I had that they could trade to those sorry renegades."

"You don't have to worry about the renegades, they're all dead. But I wonder if there are any more out in the timber who rode with the gunrunners. They were a large group, after all."

Bertha kneeled and started going through the dead man's pockets. She found a wad of money and looked up at Sawyer. "I reckon you just killed the man behind the gun business. This one is loaded with money and the other one only had seven dollars on him."

"Good, maybe you won't have any more trouble from that bunch that rode with Hambone. I stopped by to see if you had something I could eat and if I could bed down here for the night," said Sawyer.

"I tell you what, you drag them pieces of horse dung away from the store, and I'll kill a chicken and fry it up," said Bertha.

"That's a deal," said Sawyer. He took hold of one of

the two horses that were grazing in the clearing and started to the store to drag off the corpses.

Sawyer disposed of the bodies and cared for his horse and the two that now belonged to Bertha plus the ones she already had. He filled the trough in the corral with water from the well and washed up for supper. It was after sunset when he entered the store, and Bertha had lit several lanterns.

The smell of fresh fried chicken filled the building as Sawyer threw a few of the blankets for sale on the floor. He rolled out his bedroll on top of them and now was ready to sleep later.

Bertha fixed them a hearty supper of fried chicken and eggs with hot coffee. When Sawyer laid the last leg bone on his plate, he took a deep breath. "Bertha, that was a mighty fine meal you fixed, and I appreciate you taking the time to cook it for me."

"You just remember to stop by when you're in the area. I'm curious about your life and can tell you've seen your share of killing and wondered how that came to be. Did you have a bad childhood or ride with a gang?"

He paused and looked to the front door trying to find the right words to use.

"You don't have to tell me if it bothers you," said Bertha.

Sawyer picked up his coffee cup and swallowed the last of the warm liquid before he said, "I was a scout for the Confederate army and was trained by William Quantrill's men to kill. I never rode with Quantrill and I didn't partake in any of his raids. Instead, as soon as I was trained, I got assigned to a regiment in Arkansas. When the war was over, I came home to Kansas to find that evil men had murdered my folks and stole their land. They also did the same to a lot of other good people. I used my training and killed every one of those criminals."

Bertha looked at the floor while he talked, listening to every word.

"I became sheriff of Allen County to rid the county of corruption. Again, I had to kill. But I'm tired of killing. I tried to escape it by resigning as sheriff so I could start ranching. Then I heard that my friends, who were on their way up from Texas with my cattle, got bushwacked by renegades. I was pulled back into battle because of that. My future wife is waiting for me at my sister's house, and I'm ready to be done with all this. But I just killed two more men, and I have to ask myself, when will it end?"

"Well, I'm sure it will end when you get home and marry that gal waiting on you," said Bertha.

Sawyer grinned at her. "I hope you're right. Do you want me to help you clean up?"

"No, but you can check on the horses and close the chicken house. I'll take care of the kitchen. What time do you want to get going in the morning?"

"I'd like to be on the road shortly after daylight," said Sawyer.

"I'll have the coffee on and fix you something to eat before you go."

"Thanks, Bertha." He got up and went outside to tend to the animals.

Chapter Thirty-Two

The sun was beginning to peek through the darkness the next morning when Sawyer left Bertha's place with a full stomach and a sack of biscuits and ham for his noon meal on the road. With food and a full canteen, he wouldn't have to stop at South Haven. Time was essential on this trip, since the wagonload of sulfur needed to be at the corral at or before the men arrived with the cattle.

He rode into Wichita in the middle of the afternoon and pulled up to the hitching post at Wichita Feed and Seed. Terrance Rogers greeted him when he walked up to the counter.

"Afternoon, Sawyer, I reckon you're ready for us to deliver that load of sulfur."

"Yes sir, my cattle will arrive at the pens in Crowley County in three days. How long do you think it will take the wagon to get there?" asked Sawyer.

"If we leave at daylight tomorrow morning, I figure we'll be there sometime on the third day. We can also load up the sulfur and put a few miles behind us today, if you want. There's some settlements along the route through the prairie where you can make camp," said Terrance. "Y'all can stop about thirteen miles south of here at Mr. Hay's little settlement, or go on another ten miles and stop at the little community in Sumner County."

"That may work better. If you'll get loaded up, I'll go to the store for some provisions to take with us," said Sawyer.

"I have your bill already figured, so you can go ahead and settle up," said Terrance, handing a piece of paper to Sawyer.

"I certainly can."

Sawyer paid his bill and rode after his supplies. It didn't take him long to buy two flour sacks full of food, and one more skillet, and in thirty minutes, he was ready to meet up with the wagon. As he mounted up, the wagon with Feed and Seed painted on the side boards came down the street. He was surprised at its size; it was built to haul freight and pulled by six strong horses.

Sawyer rode alongside and said to the driver, "I'm Sawyer McCade. I bought us food and coffee for the trip. I'm counting on you to know where we're headed."

"Nice to meet you, Sawyer. I'm Theodore Russell, but you can call me Teddy. I know where we need to go, and we'll pick up the pace as soon as we clear town."

Sawyer glanced at the back of the wagon, loaded with sacks full of the potent chemical. Most of them were covered with a tarpaulin, but the smell was still strong.

"Teddy, that stuff stinks to high heaven. I'll head out in front, so I don't have to breathe in the odor. If there are any ticks left on those cows after we apply this stuff, they might be strong little bloodsuckers," said Sawyer.

Teddy thought that remark was funny and his whole body shook as he laughed.

Sawyer went out in front of the team, and when they were close to Hay's place, he waited for Teddy to catch up. "Do you want to stop or keep going?" Sawyer asked.

"Let's keep going and stop somewhere around Cowskin Creek. That'll give us a good supply of grass and water for the horses, and a good spot to camp. I figure we can keep this pace and be there by dark."

"Fine by me. I'll go ahead and find us a good campsite on the other side of the stream, assuming we can cross before dark," said Sawyer.

They passed a sign that said Haysville and kept going south. After another forty minutes, Sawyer rode up on the creek and saw a spot that was good for crossing where the banks were sloped from numerous trips across the murky water.

He waited on Teddy, and in a few minutes heard him coming, popping his whip on the rumps of the horses. Sawyer moved out of the way, and Teddy headed into the water as fast as he could. The horses strained on the harnesses as they started up the far bank, but they made the grade easily thanks to their momentum.

Sawyer sat watching in wonder. It had never occurred to him to go through the stream so fast. Teddy was quite a wagon driver, was all he could say.

They made camp, and Teddy put hobbles on his horses so they couldn't mosey off. Raven had freedom to graze where he wanted, since he wouldn't wander far from his owner.

Teddy showed off his cooking skills that night for supper. Both men were in their bedrolls, sawing logs shortly after they had filled their bellies.

The following morning, Sawyer was up stoking the fire before daylight. A cool front had blown in during the night, and the north wind chilled his bones. The fire blazed and the coffee water was boiling by the time Teddy rolled out of his bedroll, ready to cook them breakfast.

Sawyer was finishing up the last of his food when Teddy said, "If everything goes well today, we can be at the corral tomorrow morning."

"I sure hope we can make it by then. I want everything in place when the cattle come down the chute. We'll douse them with the sulfur as they come through and then keep them going," said Sawyer.

"If I'm not mistaken, there might be two or three places within the corrals that are narrow enough to apply the powder," said Teddy. "Some US Senator from Kansas City built the pens in anticipation of the railroad coming by, but the war stopped the railroad's progress, and he abandoned the project."

"Do you remember the senator's name?" asked Sawyer.

"Nope, can't say that I do," said Teddy.

Sawyer didn't say anything else about it, but in the back of his mind, he suspected it was the man he had killed a little over two months ago, Senator Bass.

"I'm sure we'll figure out what the best course of action is when we arrive. It's fixing to start burning sunlight, so let's break camp and head on out," said Sawyer.

Teddy picked up the coffee pot, poured the remains on the hot coals, and gathered his bedroll.

After another twenty-five minutes, the two men were back on the road.

Chapter Thirty-Three

Around the time the sun passed by high noon on the following day, they stopped at a settlement and bought some hot food in a tent café. Sawyer had an uneasy feeling as the other customers eating their meal kept a watchful eye on the two strangers. Maybe it was because he was armed with three pistols in plain sight.

When they came out of the tent to get on with their journey, he noticed that the few people on the street kept glancing at them.

Teddy climbed into the spring seat, got the team going, and waved at the men and women who were watching the wagon go by. Sawyer figured they were trying to guess what two men were going to do with the stinking sulfur.

Two miles from the settlement, Teddy turned the team onto a path that led through an area thick with trees and brush. "This here is the railroad right-of-way. They had it cleared, but that's as far as they got with it before it was shut down."

"I'll ride ahead so you don't drive the wagon in a

hole or get it bogged down," said Sawyer. He stayed within eyesight, but far enough in the lead that he didn't have to smell the strong scent of sulfur.

Small saplings had started to grow back in the center of the path from lack of use. The clearing crew had installed wooden crossings wherever a creek or gully existed, and they were still intact, which Sawyer was glad about.

The right-of-way curved to the right, and Sawyer stopped and waited until the wagon caught up before he started around the curve. He was coming out of the bend when five riders emerged from his right out of the timber with guns drawn.

Sawyer was surprised and mad at the same time. He hadn't been expecting riders in a place that seemed so desolate and was angry at himself for not being more prepared.

The odds were in the other men's favor, and it could be deadly for him and Teddy to go up against five armed men who already had their guns drawn. But he wasn't going to show his fear. This was the time to play it calm and see what they wanted.

"Howdy, fellers. I'm Sawyer McCade from Allen County. What can I do for you?"

"I'm Randolph McBride, and I want to know your intentions with all that sulfur." The man pointed to the wagon, which had come to a stop several yards back from the armed riders.

Sawyer wanted to tell McBride that it was none of his business, but thought better of it since he was looking at five guns pointed at him. "We're on our way to the old loading pens. I have a small herd of Texas cattle coming through, and we're going to douse them with sulfur, so they won't bring any ticks into Kansas."

Randolph sat staring at the tall cowboy for a few seconds. "I have cattle east of here, and I don't want any Texas ticks infesting my herd. I've never heard of putting sulfur on animals to eliminate critters."

"I've been told it will make them fall off the cattle and die. I'll soon find out when my herd arrives," said Sawyer. "I'd appreciate it if you had your men point those guns somewhere else. I get mighty uncomfortable when someone is threatening to shoot me."

"Put your guns away, men," said Randolph. "I've heard you're an honest man, McCade. So I'll take you at your word this time. I don't think you would go to the trouble of hauling that nasty-smelling stuff all this way from Wichita if you didn't think it would work."

"Mr. McBride, I have more cattle on my ranch east of Humboldt and I want to keep them healthy, just like you want to watch out for your herd. Me and my men will make sure every cow and horse gets a dose of sulfur before we leave the corral," said Sawyer.

"I'd appreciate that, young man. By the way, are you the feller that killed all those land grabbers a few months ago?"

Sawyer moved his right hand closer to his pistol. "Yes sir. I'm the man who killed the murderers who shot my folks and stole their land."

"I thought so. You have a nice day, and good luck with the ticks."

The man turned his horse around and his men followed him back through the trees.

Teddy brought the wagon closer and said, "I was

sweating it for a few minutes. I thought we were going to go meet our maker for sure."

"He's a concerned rancher, and I can't say I blame him. I bought the sulfur because I didn't want any of my cattle back home to get infected and die. How much farther is it to the cattle pens?" asked Sawyer.

"It can't be more than a few miles. We can try to make it there tonight, if you want," said Teddy.

"We ain't going to get there by sitting here jawing," said Sawyer. "Move on out and I'll ride point again."

For some strange reason, an image of his sister Nancy Lou popped into Sawyer's mind. He wondered if she was getting close to making him an uncle. Then, his attention went to Abigail and their wedding. When he got back, Sawyer would ask Reverend Toliver to officiate, and he figured the preacher would most likely agree. He didn't know how big of a wedding his love would want, and it didn't matter. He just wanted to marry her and spend the rest of his life with the beautiful Texas woman. And hopefully they'd have children of their own. But he knew he was getting a little ahead of himself—he should probably propose first before planning their future.

Several moments later, he came upon a large clearing of about thirty acres, turned in the saddle, and motioned to Teddy that something was ahead. A few hundred yards in the distance, he could see that the cattle pens and loading chutes were still standing. In fact, they looked to be in great shape. Sawyer and his cowboys would soon find out if the wooden posts and side railings would stand up to the abuse of longhorns charging down the chutes, raking their massive horns on the fences.

Teddy guided the wagon toward the loading ramps while Sawyer rode around the pens, looking for gaps in the fence. When he was satisfied that the fence boards were in fair shape and most of the posts looked solid, he joined Teddy, who was unloading the two sacks of sulfur.

"I reckon you want to divide the sacks out at each ramp, don't you?" asked Teddy.

Sawyer thought for a few seconds. "That may work best, if it's not too much trouble." He dismounted and examined the loading chutes to see if it was possible to lower the ramps to the ground. They were positioned so the cattle could walk up them and load into a railcar. "You reckon we can lower the ramps to the ground so the cattle can come through quick?"

"I'm pretty sure we can lift up the end of the ramp and remove the pole under it and let it drop to the ground," said Teddy, inspecting one of the ramps. He tried to pick up the heavy timbers, but they were too heavy.

"Let's find a pole that we can use as leverage and see if we can raise it that way," said Sawyer.

Teddy walked a few yards away and came back dragging a post about twelve feet long. He placed it under the ramp and gained enough leverage to raise it an inch. Sawyer removed three poles on the underside of the ramp that held it up, so it would lower to the ground when Teddy released the pole he was using. One ramp lowered and two more to go.

Teddy sat down for a short break before he started unloading the sacks again and said, "There might be some tools in the office if you need to fix any loose boards on the fence."

"I'll have a look," said Sawyer, and he walked over to the twelve-by-twelve building that had been built next to the pens. Inside, he found a hammer, nails, and rope. He walked down each chute and fixed the loose boards he came across. He hoped to prevent any cattle from busting through the fence and not getting dusted. That would defeat all the effort he and Teddy were doing.

Sawyer was still working on the cattle pens when Teddy took the empty wagon and parked it beside the office building. The wagon driver carried his bedding inside the building and then came back out and started gathering wood for a campfire.

The tired wagon man was sitting on the office porch with a cup of coffee when Sawyer sat down with his own cup.

"I figured I might as well spend the night and get an early start home in the morning," said Teddy. "The horses will be fresh and ready to run with an empty wagon."

"I can use the company tonight. Plus, you're a mighty good cook," said Sawyer, sipping the hot coffee.

Chapter Thirty-Four

Teddy headed back to Wichita the next morning at the light of day. He told Sawyer he thought he could make the return trip in one day, although it might be dark when he arrived home.

Sawyer went back to repairing the fences and opening gates, and it was around eight o'clock when he saw someone on horseback coming toward the pens from the southwest. It was impossible to recognize the person from such a distance, and the rider kept going around trees and down into low places.

He stopped what he was doing and retrieved his rifle from the office, where he had left his saddle. He checked to make sure it was loaded, then took up a position behind one of the loading chutes and waited for the approaching visitor.

When the rider had come close enough to be recognized, Sawyer jumped up, took off his hat, and waved it in the air so Luke would see him.

"Hello Luke, the herd must be close by," said Sawyer.

"Yeah, I think they're about three miles out. I see you have everything ready for us."

Sawyer pointed to the open gates. "We drive a few at a time into the holding pens and then guide them to the three chutes. Three of the men can douse the cattle with sulfur as they come by. We want to be sure not to force them through too fast though."

"I'll have the chuckwagon come on up here and those three can man the chutes," said Luke.

"That's a good idea. I can also be up there with them in case they need help," said Sawyer.

"Sounds like a plan," said Luke. "I'll bring Rowdy, Mathew, and Benjamin up to speed on the plan."

"Thanks, Luke. Tell Rowdy to park the chuck-wagon behind the office over there." Sawyer pointed to the building.

"Okay. I'm going back to the drive," said Luke, and he headed back the way he had come at a fast lope.

When the chuckwagon arrived, Sawyer helped the men unharness the horses and explained to Rowdy, Benjamin, and Mathew what they needed to do. He also told them they should wear their handkerchiefs over their mouths and noses.

The men took up positions along the chutes so they could dust each animal as it made its way through and out the other end. Once the cattle were out, a couple of riders would move them onto the grass so they could graze.

The wranglers arrived with the cattle just after ten o'clock and began to herd them into the pens and down the loading chutes, where the cowboys spread a handful of sulfur on each animal's back. At first the men tried throwing the chemical dust onto the cows' backs, but it caused everyone to cough and sneeze.

After a few minutes, Sawyer went to each of the three men and demonstrated how they could take a handful of sulfur and gently spread it down the animal's spine as it came down the chute. This way, they could better control the amount of powder in the air.

Every twenty minutes or so, Sawyer relieved one of the dusters so they could get a drink and some fresh air. When he had let all three have a break, he took one too.

It took them seven hours to get the herd of almost twelve hundred head of cattle and twenty-nine horses through the chutes. The sulfur smell was so thick in the air that everyone coughed and sneezed, even with their bandanas over their mouths and noses. The men closest to the chutes rode away from the herd long enough to dust off their clothes and suck in fresh air before they came back to join the rest of the crew taking a break.

While sitting on a stump and gulping water from his canteen, Sawyer said, "I passed through a creek about a half mile north of here yesterday. I suggest we take turns riding there to take a bath. You can change clothes if you have any extras, or wash off with the ones you're wearing," said Sawyer.

"I think that's a grand idea," said Jesse.

"Half of you go on, and then the rest of us will come in behind you in a little while," said Luke.

"Me, Rowdy, Mathew, and Benjamin should go first, since we have the most chemicals on us," said Sawyer.

The three men who had been driving the wagon borrowed horses from some of the cowboys, and they rode to the creek. No one had spare clothes, so they removed their boots and washed their garments, wrung out the water, and laid everything on the brush to dry. All four men got in the water and splashed around until the sulfur dust was gone from their bodies. They had to wear damp clothes back to the cattle pens, but no one minded, since they were clean and free of sulfur dust.

There was still some daylight left when all the men were washed, and Sawyer wanted to move the cattle away from the pens, since that was most likely where the ticks had fallen off. It took some work to get the cattle moving, but they made it another three miles until they found a stream with water and graze for the night.

It was a hot night, and after supper, everyone either sat or lay far enough away from the campfire that they didn't feel the heat, but close enough they could still see by its light. The men told Sawyer about the drive to the pens. They had yet to encounter any trouble along the route. When they asked if he'd had any problems, he kept quiet about the run-in at Bertha's store.

Sawyer asked, "Has anyone ever been east of here?"

"I've been as far as the Arkansas River. We forded it once on a cattle drive and then turned due north," said Jesse.

"We'll have to cross it in two or three days. I hope it's low enough that we don't have to swim it," said Luke.

"Once we're past the Arkansas, I'm familiar with the rest of the route," said Sawyer. "We most likely will go over Walnut Creek and then the Verdigris two or three days after that. Another two days and we'll pass through the Neosho River. My ranch is only a few miles from there."

"So we could have these cows on your range in a week, if everything goes right?" asked Cowboy.

"That's right. And I sure am ready to get home," said Sawyer.

"I'm ready for a soft bed and a few days' rest," said Luke.

The other cowboys nodded their heads in agreement.

Sawyer excused himself and went to his bedroll, lying down so that he could look up at the stars. In just a week's time, he could be in the arms of the love of his life.

He decided that this trip hadn't changed him too much. He had killed a few men, but his attitude and demeanor hadn't changed back to the man he had been in the war, or the man he was when he eradicated his hometown of criminals. That was good, since he wanted to be a loving husband and father. The war had taught him lessons on how to survive, but now that it was over, he had to learn to fit in and be a part of the community where he lived. He decided that the transition would be easy, especially with the support waiting for him at home.

This trip had already lasted for two weeks, and it would be one more before he'd get home. He wondered how his sister was doing and if she was about ready to have her baby. Her belly had been mighty big when he'd left, but she'd kept saying it was still a few weeks before the baby was due. He smiled at the thought of being an uncle and getting to teach and spoil the child.

Chapter Thirty-Five

It took the herd two full days once they'd been treated with the sulfur to reach the Arkansas River. Sawyer had ridden ahead from the pens to find where the cattle could cross. When he returned, he met with his foreman off to the side and away from the herd, so they could talk over the noise of yelling men, bawling cattle, clashing horns, and pounding hooves.

"There's a good crossing about a half mile north, if you want to start turning the cattle in that direction. The river is about a mile and a half away, and if we start pointing them that way, we should be in line with the path across the stream," said Sawyer.

"We'll get them headed in that direction, but I don't want to cross this late in the day," said Luke. "I suggest we let them fill up on water and grass tonight and cross first thing in the morning."

"Fine by me," said Sawyer. "Let's get moving."

It took a little work to get the leaders of the herd going in the direction Sawyer wanted them to go, because the cattle could smell the water and wanted to go straight ahead and fill up in the river instead of veering off. Sawyer rode back and forth along the west side of the herd, trying to force them to turn, when he spotted the speckled bull that had given him a scare a week back. He pulled his gun in case the bull wanted to run at him, but the colossal animal turned with the rest of the herd and went peacefully.

A few minutes later, Ronnie came riding up. "I see that troublesome bull is still with the herd," said Sawyer.

Ronnie started laughing. "The day after he went for you, he charged at me, so I left him alone on the trail. Two days later, he came running by the drag riders and rejoined the herd."

"Well I'll be. I guess he got lonely," said Sawyer. "If he tries to charge anyone again, I'm going to put a lead ball between his eyes."

The cattle moved faster the closer they got to the river. The banks were low and sloped, and the thirsty animals went belly-deep into the water.

The cowboys had to ride into the stream and make the first cattle to arrive leave and start grazing, so the rest of the cows could also get a drink.

By the time the cattle were contentedly eating, the cooks had supper ready, and everyone was glad to eat earlier in the day and have longer to rest.

The cowhands were talking and laughing when suddenly Ralph, one of the extra cowboys from Texas, and Austin went after each other with fists. Austin gave the first punch to the lanky Texan, but Ralph came in and landed three licks, knocking the young man to the ground. Luke got up to jump in and break it up, but Sawyer grabbed his arm.

"Let them fight. We'll stop it if they start to get out of hand," said Sawyer.

Both men took punches to the face and midsection. They began to slow down and grasp for air, and finally, they just stopped. They were exhausted and sucking in big breaths. Austin hunched over with his hands on his hips, and so did Ralph.

"How about we sit down and have another cup of coffee?" Austin asked Ralph.

Ralph spit a mouthful of blood onto the ground and wiped more blood from under his nose with his shirt sleeve. "I reckon that's a good idea." He stuck out his hand, and Austin took it in his and grinned.

Sawyer wasn't sleepy just yet and started a conversation with the men around the campfire. "If any of you fellers want to stay on and work for me and my sister, the job is yours. I have a good cowman who is the ramrod, but he can't do it all by himself."

Hooter said, "As soon as you're wed to Abigail, I'm heading back to Clarksville. I've got land and cattle of my own to tend to."

Cowboy, Ronnie, and Harold said the same; they would head home after the wedding.

Sawyer turned to Luke and his men. "Any of you want a job?"

Luke looked at the others and then he said, "I can't speak for them, but I'm tired of trampling around the country picking up work. It's time for me to settle down and stay in one place. So my answer is a big yes."

"Sawyer, how much does the job pay?" asked Jesse.

"I'll pay forty a month, plus food and shelter," replied Sawyer.

"Count me in," said Jesse.

"Count me in also," said Rowdy.

"The rest of you all know my offer. We still have about a week before we arrive, so think it over. You still have time to join up if you want to," said Sawyer.

The moon was up in the eastern sky, casting its light when Sawyer poured the last of his coffee on the ground. "I'll see you all in the morning. I'm turning in and getting some sleep."

He walked to his bedroll and gear, and put his cup in the saddlebags before lying on the covers.

He lay watching the moon climb higher in the sky and knew that he would be home to his future bride in a few more days. The closer he gets to home, the more excited he becomes. It's really almost over.

The men were awakened by a north wind blowing hard sometime before daylight. Sawyer got up and rearranged his bedding so he could cover up with it. By his estimation, it was around three in the morning. The north breeze was so cold it must have been coming off some snow.

They had to place rocks around the north side of the campfire to keep the fire going long enough to make coffee and cook breakfast once everyone got up.

The cool weather made horses frisky as the cowboys headed out toward the grazing cattle.

Chapter Thirty-Six

The colder temperature made the cattle reluctant to get moving and leave the comfort of the tall grass. They had migrated away from the river about a half mile as they grazed on the lush meadow. The wranglers had a hard time getting them to bunch up and go back east toward the Arkansas. The cowboys kept slapping cows with their ropes and crowding them to leave the tall grass and move on out.

Once the leaders of the herd began moving toward the shallow crossing, Luke told Sawyer, "I'm going to go to the drag and fire off a shot with the hope it scares them enough to run on into the water and up the other side. I'll tell the riders toward the back about the plan."

"Give me a few minutes to spread the word about what you're going to do," said Sawyer, and he spurred his horse toward the outriders.

When Sawyer had told everyone, he waved his hat in the air at Luke.

Luke fired one shot. Jesse, who was riding drag, also fired a shot, and all the cowboys whooped and hollered while chasing after the frightened animals. Horns clashed as the animals ran, wild-eyed and spooked. The leaders of the herd hit the water and splashed loudly as they rambled across the shallow stream. When the animals got across the river and up the far bank, they ran a few hundred yards more and began to eat grass.

Sawyer was on the side of the river that they had come from, working as an outrider. About half the herd had already made it to the other side of the Arkansas when he noticed that the cattle were slowing down as soon as they entered the water. He rode along the riverbank to see what the problem might be. The hooves of the first animals to cross made the soft riverbed a muddy mess, and it looked like now they were getting bogged down by the mire. He tried to turn the herd north to get them out of the muck, but he couldn't do it by himself. He waved his hat in the air again, hoping one of the other cowboys would see him.

Hooter and Ronnie came riding up. "What's wrong?" asked Hooter.

"The cattle are getting stuck in the mud. We need to make them cross north of here, where the ground isn't so soft and trampled," said Sawyer.

"Come on, let's crowd them and see if they will move upstream a little," said Ronnie.

The three men hollered and waved their hats at the cattle, and Harold and Jesse came over to help. Now five men on horses were able to turn the cows just enough so they were crossing on firmer ground.

By the time the last cows were on the far bank, the cowboys made them all continue to move east, away from the river bottom. The men with the chuckwagon had to use some of the extra horses to get the wagon across and brought up the rear of the procession.

The small remuda of spare horses were driven by Barney and Austin, and once they crossed the river, they got back in step with the cattle. The horses were never any trouble since they were used to following the herd.

It took a lot of work to manage the cattle through stands of trees and brush, and across gullies and creeks over the course of the next two days. Fortunately, everything went smoothly, but the days were long, and the trail was rough in some spots.

The men were anxious for the drive to be over with, especially Sawyer. Every night, he lay on his bed thinking about the future. On the third morning, he considered leaving the group and heading home, but he knew the men needed him more than ever because the following day they would cross the Verdigris River, and the next day, the Neosho.

Which meant in two days, he should be home.

They crossed the Verdigris without any problems, but a mile out from the Neosho, the sky turned gray, and storm clouds began to roll in. Thunder and lightning were heading in their direction.

Luke put on his rain slicker and Sawyer decided to do the same. In less than five minutes, the storm was upon them, and streaks of lightning came rushing from the sky and hit the ground not far from the herd. Sawyer watched the cattle pick up their pace as they tried to outrun the storm.

Suddenly, a streak of lightning came dancing down from the clouds with its fire-like fingers and hit a giant oak tree, not more than two hundred yards away, splitting limbs and bark. The frightened cattle took off, running as fast as they could.

Sawyer chased after them, but Cowboy, Luke, and Hooter caught up with him and Cowboy said, "Hold up and let the storm pass. We'll be wasting our time if we try to stop them now."

"I don't want them hurt or to die trying to cross the Neosho River up ahead," said Sawyer.

"It's a moot point trying to stop them now. When they passed me, I could see the wild in their eyes," said Hooter.

"They'll most likely turn when they see the river," said Luke. "They get frightened when the lightning hits so close. That last streak made the hair on my neck stand up."

"Okay, we'll let them go. Let's find the chow wagon and have a cup of coffee until the storm passes," said Sawyer.

They circled back to the wagon, where Rowdy, Mathew, and Benjamin had extended a tarp out from the side of the wagon, creating a shelter. Under the tarp, a small fire heated up two pots full of water.

"Did y'all see them scared cows run by while ago?" asked Luke when he got under the shelter.

"Yep, they were running like turpentined cats," said Mathew. "I reckon they don't like this lightning show."

"I don't blame them," said Benjamin. "I ain't too happy about it myself."

The men drank up the two pots of coffee, and by that time the storm clouds were south of them, still raising a ruckus, but at least farther away now.

Luke was the first one to leave the shelter of the tarp and look up at the clearing sky. "It's time we earn our keep. Let's spread out and find our cows. They should be settled down by now, eating grass somewhere."

Cattle tracks led straight to the river, where the men found the animals on the other side, eating grass. Three dead cows were floating in the river; they had most likely gotten knocked down and trampled in the stampede. Luke assigned four men to rope the animals' necks or legs and drag them out of the water and up the riverbank. He told Sawyer that he didn't want the stream to get contaminated.

Sawyer could tell by the surroundings that they were south of Humboldt by about ten miles. "If we push the cattle a little farther east, we'll reach a road running north and south. I know of a meadow where we can bed them down tonight, and tomorrow we'll be home."

The wagon went on ahead with Sawyer's instructions on where to set up camp. The cattle didn't want to head out; they were tired and still a little frightened from the storm. But the riders gave them no choice, and eventually they got going.

By the time they were on the road walking north and cattle were strung out over a half mile, the sun was setting in the west. The cowhands kept the herd moving until they passed the chuckwagon and the two fires the cooks had set up. Then they backed off the herd so they would slow and start grazing for the night.

That night, after everyone had finished supper and cleaned their plates, Sawyer said, "I think we should break up into threes and ride herd tonight. I'm worried the cattle haven't totally quieted down from the lightning today."

Cowboy, Ronnie, and Harold got up off the ground. "We'll take the first watch," said Cowboy.

Jesse said, "Barney, Austin, and I will take the second watch."

"I guess Hooter, Luke, and I will take the final watch," said Sawyer.

The first set of men took off, and the camp was serenaded by the worst singing they had ever heard from the men riding herd. It's a miracle that the cows didn't scatter in all four directions.

Chapter Thirty-Seven

When the sun started creeping up into the sky on the following morning, Sawyer and the night riders came back to camp. Sawyer had ridden one of the spare horses so Raven could rest and swapped his gear back to his favorite horse before he sat down for breakfast and coffee.

The men ate silently, since none of them had slept a whole night. Sawyer finished off the last of his coffee before he started to talk.

"We'll stay on the road another five miles once we leave here. I'll take over point after we get the cows strung out and moving. We'll have to make a few turns, but it'll be a good path, so we shouldn't have any trouble navigating across gullies or through any forest. When we get to my place, I'll open the gates and hopefully find us some more help to turn the herd into the pasture."

The longhorns took to the road easily that morning, like they knew it was almost over. Sawyer could tell that the trip up from Texas had taken weight off his cattle, but they would gain it back over time.

He sat on his horse and watched the lead bull turn onto the road that would take them to their new home. Sawyer went ahead at a gallop, hoping that Edward and Roy would be at the barn, or at least nearby. When he turned up the lane to the house, Abigail, Edward, and Roy ran toward him. He stopped Raven and jumped from the saddle, taking Abigail into his arms.

"Darling, I'm so glad you're back," she said.

"I'm happy to see you. I've missed you so much," said Sawyer.

He turned to Edward. "Get the gates open, and you and Roy can help me turn the cattle into the pasture."

"I can help also. My horse is tied behind the house," said Abigail.

"I didn't know you had a horse," said Sawyer.

"Yes, I went into Humboldt and purchased one." She ran to get it while Sawyer, Edward, and Roy returned to the road.

In a couple of minutes, Abigail came riding up alongside Sawyer. She smiled at him before saying, "You're also officially Uncle Sawyer. Nancy Lou had her baby a week after you left."

Sawyer just looked at her for a second, then grinned as big as a house. "I like the sound of Uncle Sawyer. Is it a boy or girl?"

"I'm going to let your sister introduce you to the baby," said Abigail. "Oh look, here comes the cattle!"

"You stay with me and do what I do," said Sawyer.

As the lead bull approached, Sawyer and the three riders with him waved their arms and blocked the road. Of course, the cattle could have gone right through them, but instead the animals turned into the open gates.

When the entire herd was in the fenced pasture, Sawyer invited everyone who had ridden up on the drive to come to his house to wash up and care for the horses.

Sawyer found Edward and pulled him aside to ask him a question. "It's still early in the day. If I kill a yearling, can you butcher it so we can cook it over hot coals? I would also appreciate it if Lilly and the girls could fix us some food to go with the steaks."

"I believe we can do that," said Edward.

About that time, the chuckwagon came rattling into the yard, and Sawyer led Edward over to the wagon once it came to a stop. "Men, this is Edward and he's the foreman here on the ranch. I'd like for someone to shoot a yearling, and Edward will butcher it for us. We'll need a pit and a fire to cook the meat for supper tonight. If the three of you help Edward, his wife and daughters will fix us vittles to go with the meat."

Mathew said, "We sure will help out, won't we, boys! We're all ready for some fine food."

The others nodded.

"If you want, we can cook a big pot of beans while we get the pit ready," Mathew added.

"My wife will cook the beans and fixings that we need. You men get that pit ready and then rest up after your journey. Me and my boy will go kill a calf and butcher it out," said Edward.

Sawyer went to Abigail, took her by the hand, and got on one knee. She put her other hand over her mouth, knowing what he was about to do. "Abigail, will you marry me?" he asked.

She pulled her hand from his and put both arms around his neck. "Yes, yes, yes! I will marry you."

The men clapped and whooped, congratulating the two lovers. Cowboy, Hooter, Harold, and Ronnie all came to Abigail and gave her hugs and kisses on the cheek. When they were finished, tears rolled down her cheeks. She said, "Thank you, boys, so much! You'll never know how much I love each of you, and having my hometown friends present on my engagement day is special."

Sawyer pulled her to him and kissed the top of her head. She looked up at him and wiped her eyes. "I love you, Sawyer McCade, and it will be an honor to be your wife."

"The honor is all mine. Let's go see my sister and my new whatever-it-is," he said, then laughed.

He informed his men, "I'll be back soon. The cooks know what I want done for tonight."

Cowboy said, "The boys from Texas and I want to go with you and meet your sister, if you don't mind."

Sawyer looked at Abigail. "Do you think she's well enough for company?"

"Of course she is. Sawyer, she had a baby, not surgery," said Abigail. She turned to Cowboy. "Gather up the men and let's get going."

The friends from Texas and Abigail waited outside Nancy Lou's house while Sawyer went inside to see his sister first.

Nancy sat in a rocking chair in her living room, with the baby cradled in her arms. "Hello, Uncle Sawyer, come and meet your nephew," said Nancy with tears of joy. She undid the blanket that covered the boy, and Sawyer kneeled, reached out, and gently touched the child on his cheek. The baby smiled and squirmed in his mother's arms.

Sawyer looked into his sister's eyes and said, "He's so beautiful. What's his name?"

"It's Cade Richard Straight. I named him after our family and his daddy. Sit down over there and you can hold him."

Nancy got up and put the baby in Sawyer's arms. "Be careful with his head, his little neck still needs support." She took a step back and said, "You look very natural holding a baby. Maybe you and Abigail should think about getting married and having children."

"I proposed to her just now, and my friends from Texas will stay long enough to be my best men. By the way, they're outside and want to meet you."

"Really?" she asked. "Why on earth do they want to meet me?"

"You're my sister and they want to meet the person I told them about. Go to the door and tell them to come in," said Sawyer.

"You just hold on for a few minutes. I'll let them come in after I go freshen up."

Sawyer laughed. "They didn't come courting. They are here because I told them how wonderful you are."

"I'll be right back. I need to get changed out of this old flour sack material dress," said Nancy, untying her apron as she hurried to her bedroom.

Chapter Thirty-Eight

Sawyer talked to the baby and little Cade was holding on to his uncle's index finger when Nancy returned to the room. She had changed into a flower print dress, combed her hair, and applied a light smear of rouge on each cheek.

"Sister, you better watch out. Four lonely Texans are outside, and they're all looking for a sweetheart."

"Oh hush." She smiled and asked, "Do I look presentable for your friends, little brother?"

"You sure do. Go to the door and tell everyone to come inside," said Sawyer.

Nancy opened the screen door and walked out onto the porch to announce that everyone could come in. Abigail was first and then Ronnie, Hooter, Harold, and finally Cowboy followed up the steps and onto the porch, where they all made their greetings.

Cowboy and Nancy remained on the porch while the others went inside.

Sawyer got up out of his chair and gave the baby to

Abigail. He walked to the open door and stood watching Nancy and Cowboy.

Cowboy removed his hat with his left hand and stuck out his right hand. "Ma'am, I'm known as Cowboy, but my Christian name is Houston Crawford. You can call me Cowboy if you like." He was still holding onto her hand while he talked. "I've heard so much about you from Sawyer that I wanted to meet you."

"I've heard Sawyer speak of you also," said Nancy, pulling her hand from his.

When Cowboy realized that Sawyer was standing by the door, he said, "I reckon we should go inside with the others."

Sawyer took hold of Nancy's arm as she came through the door. He leaned over and said, "You would be smart to invite him over tomorrow evening for supper."

She looked at her brother and smiled. "Brother, I'm twenty-six years old and I'm capable of finding myself a man. Houston is a very handsome feller, so I might invite him over, not that it's any of your business."

Sawyer burst out laughing and hugged his sister. Then he whispered in her ear, "Cowboy is also twenty-six, in case you're wondering."

Sawyer and his friends stayed with Nancy, talking, laughing, and having a good time until the baby started to get cross. Abigail stood up and said, "Come on, everyone, we should go so Nancy can feed the baby and put him in his crib."

All the men except Cowboy said their goodbyes and went outside. Cowboy asked, "Would it be all right if I went to the kitchen for a drink of water?"

Sawyer was about to say something when Nancy said, "Of course you can. It's right through that door. Let me say goodbye to Sawyer and Abigail, and I'll show you where the bucket is."

Sawyer laughed as he hugged his sister. She hit him on the arm and said, "You get on out of here. Houston will be along in a little while."

They weren't even off the porch yet when Abigail said, "You mark my word, she and Cowboy are sweet on each other."

Sawyer only said something once he'd untied her horse and was handing her the bridle reins. "I think Nancy Lou is ready to find herself a man. She's a grown woman with a child to raise, and I'm happy that she sees something in Cowboy. He's a good man."

"Are we going to wait on him or leave him here with her?" asked Abigail.

"Leave him here so they can get acquainted with each other," said Sawyer, and they followed the rest of his friends back to his house.

When they were on the main road, Sawyer looked over at Abigail. "What kind of wedding do you want?"

She stopped her horse and grinned at her man. "I don't want a big to-do, since I only know a few people here. Nancy told me that you have a friend who is a preacher, so I think a lovely little ceremony at his church would be nice. I can have Nancy and the two Monks girls be my attendants."

"Today is not the right time to ride into Humboldt to talk to Preacher Toliver, but I think we can go in the morning," said Sawyer. "We can also go shopping for new clothes to get married in."

"Sawyer, that's a wonderful idea, I've never had any

fancy clothes in my life, and I would love to have a pretty new dress to marry you in."

"I ain't got a suit, but I have a dress jacket I bought a couple of months ago," said Sawyer. "If it's all right with you, I'll wear that coat but buy new britches, and a new shirt and string tie."

"That's fine by me," said Abigail. "There is one other thing that I'd like to do. Could we buy the Monks girls new dresses and shoes for standing with me? Those are good, hard-working young ladies, and I want them to have some new clothes."

"Then do it," said Sawyer. "Let's get home so I can put the horses in the pen before supper. We should ask Lilly and Edward if the girls can be in the wedding and go to town with us tomorrow for their dresses."

"I hadn't thought about asking Lilly and Edward for permission. That would have been embarrassing to bypass them."

They were still a few hundred feet from the house when Sawyer looked at Abigail and said, "Do you smell food?"

"I sure do. I don't know about you, but I'm starved. We better get on home so you can wash up and put on some clean clothes before supper."

Chapter Thirty-Nine

Sawyer came out of his house with a shaved face and wearing clean clothes for the first time in a long while and stood on his porch to take in the sight before him. The cowboys had brought tables and chairs out of the house and set them up in the yard. The Monks girls, Malinda and Beverly, had placed plates and silverware on the tables. Rowdy and Benjamin were busy basting the steaks cooking over the hot coals. This was teamwork at its best, and he was proud of his friends and how they had all pitched in to help.

"Excuse me, Mr. Sawyer," said a man's voice behind him. He moved to the side so young Roy Monks could take a pot of green beans to the table. Just the smell of the steaks and potatoes cooking gave Sawyer an appetite, and he was ready for a delicious meal.

Nancy Lou's carriage was coming up the lane to his house. Cowboy sat in the front, driving the buggy, and Nancy was in the back seat holding little Cade.

The sights and sounds of the celebration was enough to bring tears to a hard man's eyes. This was something to behold, and he was so glad to be a part of it. All the worry and anxiety he'd had when he'd left to rescue his friends and his cattle was gone. He had prepared himself to rise to the occasion and be the kind of man he'd been when fighting in the war, but the men with him had shielded him from reverting back to the cold-blooded man he used to be. Luke and his men had come through at the very beginning, when they'd encountered the gunrunners. Sawyer didn't have to worry about them having his back after that.

Abigail exited the house and stood beside the man she was about to make a life with. "Darling, I've been thinking that if the preacher is available on Saturday, we should get married at the church and have a cake and punch reception on the church lawn."

He laughed. "I don't even know what day this is."

"Today is Wednesday, silly."

"Let's go into the house and ask Lilly about the girls going to town with us tomorrow and make sure they can attend the wedding. If that goes as planned, we can announce our wedding after supper tonight," said Sawyer.

Sawyer and Abigail arranged with the Monks to take the girls into town the next day. Lilly was so excited that her daughters would be in the ceremony that she cried joyfully and hugged both Sawyer and Abigail.

Someone rang the dinner bell. "I guess we better go outside and join the others while there is still food on the table," said Abigail.

Sawyer stopped to reflect on his and his men's accomplishments over the past few weeks. He was grateful for how they'd all pitched in and for all the work they had done. This was a celebration of not only getting his friends and cattle home, but also for Nancy and little Cade.

Sawyer had Abigail with him now and forever and it was only fitting to cook some delicious steaks to enjoy with all the other food to commemorate a special day.

Sawyer ate until he couldn't hold another bite, pushed his plate away, and took in a deep breath of air. As he sat with his arms folded across his full stomach, Malinda came up to him.

"Mr. Sawyer, would you like a cup of coffee to help settle your food?"

"I sure would, and after you fill my cup, I want you to go ring the dinner bell so I can get everyone's attention."

"I certainly will." She filled his cup, made a beeline to the dinner bell, and rang it several times. Sawyer stood up, and the yard got quiet, waiting for him to speak.

"Everyone, it's an honor and joy to see you all here today, eating some fine food and having a good time. I'm grateful to my friends and partners from Texas for bringing our beautiful longhorns on a long, tiring cattle drive. I'm also thankful to my new friends who put themselves into harm's way to rescue our friends from murderers. We had a few close calls but made it through just fine."

Sawyer took a sip of his coffee. "Everyone has met my future bride, but I will ask her to come and stand with me." The men clapped as Abigail got up, blushing, and went to Sawyer.

"Abigail and I are getting married this coming Saturday at the Baptist Church in Humboldt at two in the afternoon. My friends from Texas will stand with me as my best men."

Abigail spoke next. "Nancy, Malinda, and Beverly will stand with me as bridesmaids."

The two Monks girls screamed out in joy and surprise. Abigail hadn't told them before now that they could be part of the wedding.

"Now listen up, this ain't going to be some big fancy to-do. After the ceremony, we'll have cake and punch on the church lawn, and then my man and I are going to the hotel for a few days," said Abigail.

Sawyer applauded and everyone else started up again too. His face beamed with joy and excitement as he cheered along with the others.

Abigail seemed embarrassed at the attention, but also laughed along with everyone and said, "I better not have anyone drunk at my wedding or I may get real mean, and some of you boys know how mean I can get."

Again, the Texas cowboys whooped and clapped.

Everyone pitched in to help clean off the tables and then continued to sit outside in the mild weather and hold conversations. Hooter started talking about the war and began to tell the story about the time when they'd gone to a farmhouse and Sawyer gunned down five Union guerrilla fighters by himself, but Sawyer stopped him.

"Hooter, no one here wants to hear about that, especially not me. That's in the past, and I, for one, would rather the stories die with the men we lost in battle."

His Army friends became quiet and nodded their heads in agreement.

Hooter said, "You're absolutely right, Sawyer, but I

want everyone here to know that if it wasn't for you, we wouldn't be here tonight having a good time."

Sawyer didn't say anything. Abigail took his hand and squeezed it, letting him know she understood.

Nancy, who was sitting across from Cowboy at the table, got up and said, "Houston, would you please take Cade and me home? It's past his bedtime. Then you can bring the carriage back here so Sawyer and Abigail can use it tomorrow."

The rest of the men roared with laughter and teased Cowboy about Nancy calling him Houston, like she was sweet on him.

He grinned, walked around the table, and stuck out his arm for Nancy to take as they went to the carriage.

Chapter Forty

The following morning, Sawyer and Abigail sat in the front seat of the carriage while Malinda and Beverly sat in the back seat. The girls hummed a tune as the buggy went down the road to Humboldt.

Abigail said to Sawyer, "I think you should let us off at the dress shop first so me and the girls can shop for what we need. I'm also buying Nancy a dress; she gave me her measurements before we left the house. That will give you time to buy whatever you want at the men's clothing store. After that, we can see the preacher and hire someone to bake us a wedding cake."

"That's fine by me," said Sawyer. "I may get a haircut also. My hair is beginning to look a little wild again."

Sawyer pulled up in front of the ladies' dress shop and jumped out of the carriage to help Abigail and the girls to the ground. Abigail kissed him on the cheek. "You take care of your business and when you're finished, we'll either be here or up the street at that café that advertises pies and cakes." She pointed to a sign nailed to a porch post a few businesses up the street.

"I'll be finished in time to join you at the café," said Sawyer.

The girls were giggling when Abigail said, "You run on along and let us get busy." She again kissed Sawyer on the cheek. He wasn't used to such treatment and turned a little red from excitement.

Sawyer started back to the carriage but stopped and said, "I think I'll leave the buggy here so you can put whatever you buy in it, and I'll walk to where I need to go."

"That's a grand idea," said Abigail. She and the girls departed toward the door of the dress shop.

Sawyer strolled along the street to the men's clothing store. As he was about to pass by the door to the hotel lobby, it opened, and a woman came out onto the boardwalk, almost colliding with him.

"Excuse me, ma'am, I didn't see you there," said Sawyer.

"Oh no, it was my fault. I should be more careful." She stuck out her hand. "I'm Agatha Barnes, who might you be."

Sawyer shook her hand. "It's nice to make your acquaintance, ma'am, I'm Sawyer McCade." At the sound of his name, she squeezed his hand slightly, and her cheeks turned rigid like she had clamped her jaws shut. Her right eye twitched faintly.

Then she smiled a big toothy grin and removed her hand from his. "The pleasure is all mine. I hope I see you around town sometime." She started off in the opposite direction he was headed.

He stood for a moment wondering why he had a bad feeling in his gut about this woman.

Sawyer continued to the store and made his purchases before going to the barbershop for a haircut. He knew better than to go there first, since that was where the older men in town congregated to talk and spread gossip each morning. It so happened that he could get in the chair as soon as he arrived, and fortunately there wasn't much talking from the barber that day. Sawyer didn't like gossip much.

With a fresh haircut and some new clothes bundled up in his arms, he returned to the parked carriage and put his things in the back luggage bin. He shunned going into the dress shop since the lady who ran the place was a busybody and always asked him too many questions whenever she saw him. Hopefully, she'd gotten all the information she wanted about the engagement and wedding from Abigail today.

As soon as he entered the shop, a gray-haired lady approached him. "Hello Sawyer, your future bride has already left, and I must say she is quite a catch. Where did you meet her?"

"Thank you, Mrs. Walker, and I agree she is quite a catch, but so am I. I'll be seeing you."

Sawyer left her standing there with a surprised look on her face. He smiled as he left the store, knowing the remark about being a great catch startled her. She would have something to gossip about with the other ladies in town for a few days.

Abigail and the girls were in the café, standing with a heavyset woman who was jawing not only with her mouth but also with her hands. Both of her limbs moved constantly as she talked. Sawyer pulled out a chair and sat down. "Hello Gertie, are you getting my bride what she wants?" he asked.

"Sawyer McCade, you know darn well I am. Just be quiet and let Abigail and me finish our business."

Abigail and the girls laughed when Sawyer made a face and crossed his arms while nodding in agreement.

When they had decided on what Gertie would bake for the wedding, Sawyer asked, "What are you serving for dinner today?"

"Fried chicken, beans, taters, and cornbread. Do y'all want me to get you some plates?"

"No, we'll see Reverend Toliver first and then come back to dine," said Sawyer. "You be sure to save us some food."

"There'll be plenty to eat, and I have freshly baked apple pie."

Sawyer watched the Monks girls' eyes light up at the mention of apple pie for dinner. "We'll be back, and thanks for taking care of our wedding cake," said Sawyer.

Once they were outside, Sawyer said, "We'll ride in the buggy to the church. I don't want to leave my things on the street too long, someone might steal my clothes."

"After we talk to the preacher, do you have someplace else you want to go, or can we go back to the café?" asked Abigail.

"I don't have any place to go, so I guess the plan is to eat unless you have something else in mind," said Sawyer.

"Me and the girls have to go back to the dress shop to try on our dresses again. The seamstresses are doing the alterations now, and they should be finished after dinner."

"That's fine. I'm a patient man," said Sawyer.

Reverend Toliver was sitting in his easy chair under a shade tree reading his Bible when the buggy pulled into his yard. He got up and laid the Good Book in his chair before walking over to greet Sawyer.

"Hello Brother Toliver, it's a nice day to read from the Word," said Sawyer.

"Now Sawyer, you didn't come here to chew the fat about me studying the scriptures. What can I do for you?"

Sawyer reached out his hand to Abigail. "This is Abigail, my future wife. We want to get married Saturday here at the church and would love for you to perform the ceremony."

"Well, I'll be doggone. Sawyer McCade is going to get married," said the preacher. "Congratulations, and I would be honored to marry the two of you. What time Saturday are we doing this?"

"How does two o'clock sound to you?" asked Abigail.

"Excellent time. Do you want my wife to play the wedding march on the piano for you?" he asked.

"That would be wonderful," said Abigail, smiling.

"Are you expecting a big crowd for the service?" asked the preacher.

"No, it will be a few friends, is all," said Sawyer.

"Okay, I'll see you on Saturday," said Reverend Toliver.

"Thank you, Brother Toliver," said Abigail, waving goodbye.

Sawyer slapped the reins to the horse's rump and turned him back toward Main Street so they could go eat.

Chapter Forty-One

Sawyer parked the carriage across the street from the café so the horse could rest in the shade of an elm tree. The engaged couple held hands and Malinda and Beverly acted like young ladies, giggling and skipping as they walked across the street. About the same time Sawyer and Abigail stepped onto the boardwalk, the woman he had met that morning in front of the hotel walked by. Now she wore a fancy shirt with ruffled sleeves, and the tail tucked into a pair of riding britches. Her hair was pulled to the back of her head in a ponytail, with gray roots visible. He hadn't noticed her age that morning, but she was older than he originally thought. She looked to be about forty, judging by the wrinkles beneath her eyes and around her mouth.

"Hello, Mr. McCade. Is this your wife?" she asked.

"Not yet, but she will be this coming Saturday," said Sawyer.

The woman stuck out her hand to Abigail and gave her a slight grin that Sawyer thought looked fake. "I'm Agatha, and you are?"

"I'm Abigail, and it's nice to meet you, Agatha," said Abigail with a big smile.

"The pleasure is all mine, dear. I'll be seeing you, and congratulations on getting married."

Sawyer watched Agatha walk down the street, and as she turned into a store, she paused and looked his way before going in. Her right eye twitched again, and it looked as if she was giving him a scrawl by the expression on her face. He couldn't quite put his finger on it, but that woman was up to something.

Sawyer and the ladies went inside the café and sat down. Abigail looked at Sawyer and asked, "Do you know that woman?"

"No. She almost ran into me coming out of the hotel this morning though. Why do you ask?"

"I don't know, but there's something peculiar about her demeanor, and I didn't like the way she looked at you. If she is up to no good concerning my man, I'll show her what a five-foot-six Texas girl can do when she's mad," said Abigail.

Sawyer looked at his fiancée for a second before he said, "I had the same feeling when I met her this morning. When I told her my name, her right eye seemed to twitch. I noticed that she did it again right before she went into the store."

"We should watch out for her, that smile and handshake didn't seem friendly. In fact, it felt malicious," said Abigail.

"You may be right. Let's enjoy our food and hopefully we'll never see her again," said Sawyer.

After their meal and a slice of apple pie each, the four of them went outside. "The girls and I will walk to the dress shop," said Abigail. "We shouldn't be long in there this time."

"You take all the time you need. I'm going to the bank to get money to pay for the cattle and those extra hands I hired to help get the herd back. I'll bring the buggy to the dress shop when I get finished," said Sawyer.

With his pockets filled with money, Sawyer drove the buggy back to the dress shop and waited until Abigail and the girls came out carrying dresses and a few bags. He helped them stow their things and when everyone was seated, they rode up the street a few blocks where Sawyer stopped the horse in front of a fancy store that sold dishes, jewelry, and dress clothing.

"Let's go in and buy you a wedding ring," said Sawyer.

"Oh darling, you don't have to do that," said Abigail.

"Oh darling, yes I do. I want every man in Kansas to know that you're spoken for, so I don't have to shoot them," said Sawyer, laughing.

Abigail picked out a beautiful ring and even made Sawyer purchase one for himself. "Honey, I'm not excited about the idea of wearing a ring while working around the ranch," said Sawyer. "I've heard stories about rings getting smashed on fingers and having to cut the ring off."

"Sawyer, these rings are a token of our love for each other, and they signify the undying nature of our commitment. So I want you to have a ring also."

"Since you put it that way, I'm honored to wear a ring."

They completed their purchases and headed home in a cheerful mood.

The two Monks girls were jabber boxes all the way home, acting as if they had never spent the day shopping and eating out.

When the carriage was close to the Monks' house, Abigail asked, "Do you girls want to go home or to Nancy's house?"

"Mrs. Nancy's house will be fine. We can give her a break with Cade and go home when Pa heads that way. You can let us out when we get to the lane and we'll walk to the house," said Malinda.

"Okay. I'm sure glad you had a good time with us today, and I know the two of you will look so beautiful on Saturday," said Abigail.

They gave Abigail a hug and thanked her again for letting them spend the day in town.

No one was at Sawyer's house when they got back. Abigail put her and Sawyer's things inside while he let the horse have water from the trough. After that, he saddled his horse and one for Abigail, then tied them to the back of the carriage.

"Why did you tie the horses to the back?" asked Abigail when she came back outside.

"We need to take the buggy to Nancy's house in case she has to go somewhere with the baby. Those horses are our rides back home," said Sawyer. "I also want to see what everyone is doing. No one is here, and I can tell that some of the cattle have been moved."

On the way to his sister's house, they passed some of the men out in the field with the cattle. He figured they were separating them into different pastures. When he pulled into the yard at Nancy's place,

Edward, Roy, Austin, and Jesse were branding cattle in the corral. Luke, Barney, Cowboy, and Harold were out in the pasture, bringing more cattle toward the holding pen.

Nancy came outside onto the porch. "Sawyer, I need to talk to you and Abigail. If you don't mind, bring Edward with you," said Nancy, and she returned inside.

Abigail looked at Sawyer. "What's that all about?"

"It has something to do with the ranch, I suppose," said Sawyer. "You go on in and I'll get Edward."

When Sawyer and Edward came in and sat down, Nancy and Abigail were waiting for them at the kitchen table. Malinda brought the coffee pot over and poured everyone a cup. She then left the room so the grown-ups could talk.

Nancy said, "Mr. McLaughlin and his crew plowed and planted about one hundred acres of winter wheat on my old place while you were gone, Sawyer. I also purchased hay for the livestock to eat this winter. McLaughlin is having his men put it in all the barns on the four properties."

"That's good, I'm glad you thought about that. I stopped at the bank on my way out of town and got enough money to pay for the longhorns and to pay Luke and his men," said Sawyer.

"Speaking of money, we need to watch what we spend until we can sell some cattle. By my estimations, we have enough to get us through the rest of this year and most of next year," said Nancy. "As far as I know, we shouldn't have any large expenses for a while."

She looked at Edward. "Tell Sawyer what you told me about the cattle."

"I think we need to gather all the longhorn bulls and take them to market. If you want to eventually sell a better breed of cattle, we need to use the Shorthorn and Hereford bulls that are on the ranch to cover the longhorns," said Edward. "By crossbreeding, we can breed off the horns and bulk up the amount of meat on each animal. Those longhorns are mostly hide and bone. We need cows with fat on them."

"I agree with that," said Sawyer. "Do you know how many bulls we have?"

"We've been separating them out, and as of a little while ago, there were eighty-two. We should also round up all the old cows that may not make it through the winter and take them to market along with the bulls," said Edward.

"That's fine by me," said Sawyer. "When do you want to do this?"

"The men have already started cutting out the bulls and old cows. Then they'll bring the other stock here to be branded and castrate a few of the young bulls at the same time. They'll be finished by the end of the week, so we can start driving the livestock where we're selling them at the stockyards north of Iola."

"Okay, let's do that. I probably won't be available to help for a few days starting tomorrow, so you're in charge of getting them to the stockyards and sold," said Sawyer.

Abigail spoke up. "When are the men from Texas leaving to return to Clarksville?"

"I'm not sure, but I'll find out," said Sawyer. "When they leave, we'll still have Luke, Jesse, and Rowdy as permanent hands, along with Edward and Roy. I'm sure we can hire a few men to help."

"I asked Barney and Austin if they would work for a few days, and they said they would. Both of them are planning on heading up to Kansas City. They can aid with getting the cattle to market and then continue on to their destination," said Edward.

"Then I think we have a good plan," said Sawyer. "Is there anything else we need to discuss?"

"I have something to talk to you and Abigail about privately," said Nancy.

"I'll be getting back to work," Edward said, leaving the room.

"Girls, come in here, please," said Nancy.

When both the Monks girls came into the room, Nancy said, "Go get Cade and take him outside for a little while. He needs some sunshine."

"Yes, ma'am," said Malinda.

When they were out the door, Nancy said, "Houston wants to return to Texas and sell his place and his cattle so he can come back here to make a life with Cade and me." She broke down crying and tears ran down her cheeks.

Abigail got up and put her arms around her. "It's okay to cry. You go ahead and let it out," said Abigail.

"Sister, why are you crying? Are you unhappy that he wants to return to Kansas to be with you?" asked Sawyer.

She got up and grabbed a dish towel to wipe away the tears. "Sawyer, I'm happy that a handsome man like Houston wants a widowed woman with a child like me. I really like him and want him to come back, but I won't go through with it if you don't approve."

Sawyer moved to Nancy and took his sister in his embrace. "Cowboy and I went through a couple of nasty skirmishes during the last days of the war. He's one to ride the river with, and I'm okay with having him as my brother-in-law. He won't ever hurt you, and I guarantee he'll protect you and Cade with his life."

She beamed at Sawyer and wiped her eyes. "Brother, you've changed these past five months. You're not the hard man you were when you returned from the war. Back then you would have shot him for even looking at me."

He grinned at her and wiped the tears off her face. "It'll all be fine, and I'll tell Cowboy that I favor him courting my sister."

"Thank you," said Nancy.

Sawyer looked at Abigail. "I'm going to help the men gather those bulls. Are you going to stay here or go home?"

"I'll stay here and wait for you. Be careful out there."

He gave her a kiss and headed out the door.

Chapter Forty-Two

Sawyer got on his horse, walked him to the gate, leaned over and pushed it open, then urged Raven out into the pasture, where the cowboys were separating the bulls and old cows from a herd of about four hundred head.

Luke, Barney, Cowboy, and Harold worked their horses hard to make the bulls leave the cows. Some wanted to turn back, and sometimes it took two wranglers to get the stubborn ones headed in the right direction.

Sawyer cut out a young bull from a group of thirty or so head of cattle and managed to get him away from the cows. Luke rode up to help guide the bull to the spot where the others were being gathered for market. Sawyer rode back into the group and located one more bull—the last one in the small group. The rest of the herd consisted only of cows.

Luke came up to him and said, "You go help Cowboy and Harold take the bulls to another pasture, and Barney and I will start this bunch toward the corral to get branded."

"Yes sir, I can do that," said Sawyer.

They made the bulls turn toward Sawyer's house and walk to a small fenced-off pasture where another thirty head were already waiting.

"Reckon these bulls will stay inside this little pasture?" asked Sawyer.

"They will if they don't smell a cow in heat. There's plenty of water and grass to eat, so if we can keep the cows away, I think they'll be fine," said Harold.

They rode back to where the other men were still branding cattle. Cowboy and Harold relieved Roy and Jesse so they could get some fresh air. They had been smelling burning flesh most of the day.

Luke led Sawyer, Roy, Jesse, and Edward to the last of the longhorn herd, which consisted of only about two hundred cattle. "Men, all we're going to do is separate out the bulls and get them over to join the others. Don't crowd them and keep your distance if they want to fight. We can always double up on one to make him move."

The gathering was going well, and the animals cooperated except for one speckled bull that didn't want to move. Jesse gave the bull time to decide what he wanted to do while Sawyer and Roy rode over to help. Sawyer recognized the bull as the one that had come at him on the drive up from Indian Territory.

"Don't crowd this one. He's liable to charge your horse." Sawyer had no more than gotten the words out of his mouth when the bull started after Roy's horse. Sawyer spurred Raven, took off toward the bull, and put three lead balls in his head. The animal went to the ground, dead.

"I should have done that on the trail," said Sawyer.

"Come on, we got to get in front of these cows and settle them down," said Jesse.

The three cowboys hurried to the front of the cattle, which were wild-eyed and about ready to stampede. The men made the animals turn so they would run in a circle until they got tired.

Luke and some of the others came riding up to see what the shooting had been about, and were able to stay and help with the running cows.

The cattle finally slowed and began to graze again, and Luke and Edward joined Sawyer, who was looking at the bull he had killed.

"I'm guessing old Speckle decided he wanted to fight, and you put his lights out," said Luke.

"Yeah, it was a long time coming. He was always looking for a fight. Do you reckon we can skin him out and use the meat for something?" asked Sawyer.

"Oh, heck yes. I'll get a couple of the men and we'll salvage the good meat to grind up for soup and chili," said Edward.

"I think he was the last bull in this bunch of cows," said Sawyer.

"The boys and I will take these bulls over to join the others and then call it a day. We can start branding and working on the young stuff tomorrow," said Luke.

Sawyer returned to Nancy Lou's house to find Abigail waiting for him.

"Are you all right?" she asked.

"Yep, I'm fine. A mean bull took after Roy, and I killed him. We had problems with him on the trail too. Edward and some of the men are going to salvage what meat they can. Let's get your horse and you can ride to my house with me," said Sawyer.

The ride took a few minutes. Before they turned up the lane, Abigail asked, "Can we go to your folks' place so you can show it to me?"

"Sure, let's just keep riding south."

When they rode up the lane where the house and barn once stood, all that was left now was the water well. He had not seen the place since he'd hired his carpenter to clear off all the burned debris.

Sawyer pointed to the bare ground in front of them. "That's where the house was, and that big clear spot back there was the barn, and over there was a smokehouse. The chicken pen was to the left of the smokehouse."

"Can I see their graves?"

"Yeah, come on."

They pulled up in front of the crosses that had been put up when Nancy and some of the locals buried the bodies months before. He sat staring down at the graves and took a deep breath. Teardrops rolled down his cheek as he looked at Abigail, and then turned his horse and started off. She followed him until they were back on the road to his house.

"Sawyer, hold up, I want to talk," said Abigail. "I realize that it's hard for you to see the graves of your folks. My folks are also gone, and it makes me sad every time I think of them. We both loved our parents dearly, and it hurts, but we have each other to get us through the hard times now. Don't ever be embarrassed or afraid to show your emotions to me, and I promise to do the same to you."

"Thanks Abigail. Yes, it hurts and makes me sad, but it also makes me furious that greedy men would kill innocent people over a little piece of land. But at least I have some fond memories, which I'll share with you as we make our life together. Let's go on home."

When they got to his house, he asked, "Would you fix us something to drink while I care for the horses?"

"Of course I will."

She had a cup of coffee sitting on the table in front of the couch when he came inside. He looked at her and wondered what she was up to, sitting on the couch with a grin on her face and patting the seat beside her. She cleared her throat and motioned for him to sit. He did as instructed, sitting down and picking up the cup for one sip.

"Sawyer, I wanted to see your folks' place today to get some insight about your childhood. Where you grew up and what the farm looked like. I grew up in a house where my pa drank a lot, and sometimes we didn't have much. As soon as I was big enough to work, I got a job and started taking care of myself. My childhood is not something that I'm proud of. I miss my folks, but I want you to know I don't dwell on the past. As for your folks, I know what happened out there. Nancy told me."

He took another sip of coffee. "You know me for who I am now. I was not a nice man when I came home from the war. When I left you in Texas, I didn't know if I would ever see you again or if you would want to see me. I came home and killed a lot of men. Every one of them had it coming, but I'm not God. I killed out of hate, although I don't regret that those men are dead. But I do regret that it had to be me who did it. I've worked hard to stop being the uncaring person that I was back then. Your love is a big reason for me becoming who I am now. I was apprehensive about going into Indian Territory after my friends and cattle

245

because I knew I would have to kill again. I didn't want to be the warrior I used to be and kill men in the manner that I was trained to."

Abigail wiped the tears from her eyes. "I want you to know that I love you for who you are. Now, then, and forever."

He smiled and kissed her. "I love you, Abigail, and can't wait to be your husband."

"Darling, you are already my husband. We just haven't made it official."

Chapter Forty-Three

Sawyer spent most of Friday helping the cowhands cut out the old cows and drive them to a separate pasture so they could be sold with the bulls. By the end of the day, they had separated out one hundred and thirty bulls and ninety-seven cows that they would take to market.

The men talked it over, and the plan was to leave for the stockyards north of Iola on Monday morning. They would stock the chuckwagon on Saturday morning when everyone rode into Humboldt for the wedding.

"I wish I could go with you fellers, but I'm going to be out of commission for a few days," said Sawyer, grinning.

"Me, Ronnie, Hooter, and Harold can't help with this one either," said Cowboy. "We'll be leaving for Texas first thing Sunday morning."

"I can give you boys some pointers on a good route to get there if you want," said Sawyer.

"We'd like to know the route that you took. Maybe

we can talk after supper tonight, since you'll be busy tomorrow night," said Hooter.

Edward said, "We have enough men to drive this herd to the stockyards. I figure we can be there in three or four days, at the most. We should be home next Friday or Saturday."

"Abigail and I will be back from our honeymoon Monday or Tuesday, so we can look after the place," said Sawyer.

Sawyer made a map for his Texas friends so they could get back to Clarksville. Then he went home to Abigail, who had washed and ironed his clothes for the wedding. She had also packed the bags that they would take with them to the hotel.

When he came in, she said, "I have a question. We only have one carriage, and Nancy will need that for her and the baby. Are you and I going to ride our horses into Humboldt tomorrow for the wedding?"

Sawyer stood looking at her and burst out laughing. "I never thought about that. I'll go to the wagon yard and rent us a carriage for Saturday."

"We really need it until we come home from our honeymoon," said Abigail.

"You're right. I'll rent it for a few days. I've also been thinking about where we should stay. Let's go to Iola for our honeymoon," said Sawyer. "It's a bigger place with more to do, and we won't know hardly anyone there."

"That sounds just fine!" said Abigail.

"I can go right now and see if I can get a buggy. I know April, who owns the wagon yard. If she has one, we can rent it."

"I think that's a wonderful idea. While you do that,

I'll get supper cooked in time for when you get home," said Abigail, kissing him goodbye.

Sawyer rented a lightweight two-seater Surrey carriage and one horse for the honeymoon. He also invited April to the wedding.

The ride back from Humboldt was most pleasant. He thought the spring seat in this carriage was even more comfortable than the one in Nancy's. He parked it in the barn and cared for his horse and the rented one before going into the house for supper.

The following morning, he and Abigail kept busy getting ready and loading up their bags of clothes and anything else they thought they might need.

Sawyer hid all his pistols except his shoulder holster rig in a chest at the foot of his bed. "Are you going to wear a gun to church for our wedding?" asked Abigail.

He stood looking at her for a few seconds. "Yes, I am. I love you more than anything and will never let anyone harm you. If something bad happens, I want my weapon with me."

"Fine, I'm okay with it if you are. Remember, I'm from Texas, where everyone wears a gun."

"Don't worry about Preacher Toliver; he knows me well and won't have a problem with it either."

"I think I have everything loaded in the buggy. Are we dressing for the wedding here or at the church?" she asked.

"Let's dress at the church so our clothes won't get wrinkled or dusty," said Sawyer.

The two headed out for town. As they made their way onto the main road, the four groomsmen from Texas were waiting for them. Two rode in front of the buggy and two behind, as escorts.

Cowboy looked back at them. "Ain't no one going to stop this wedding today."

When they arrived at the church, some congregation members were busy setting up tables and chairs on the lawn. Reverend Toliver showed the wedding party where they could get changed and wait until it was time to start the ceremony.

Chapter Forty-Four

Sawyer exited the back room at the church dressed in his wedding clothes and walked into the sanctuary, where his four friends sat on the front church pew. Reverend Toliver was also sitting with them, giving them instructions on where to stand and what to do.

"Hello Sawyer," said the preacher. "Let's all go through the motions to familiarize ourselves with the ceremony. Do you have the ring?"

"I sure do." Sawyer pulled it from his pants pocket and held it up.

"Give it to Cowboy so he can hand it to you when I ask for it."

The preacher walked through the service with the men. When he was finished, he told them to go out the back door and wait until he came after them.

Sawyer kept walking around out back until Ronnie took him by the arm. "You have got to be still, or you ain't going to have any energy for the honeymoon."

Sawyer put his hand on his friend's shoulder. "I fought in a war. I've been shot at, and I've killed men, but none of that prepared me for loving the woman who I'm going to spend the rest of my life with. I'm nervous as a cat in a room full of rocking chairs."

About that time, the preacher opened the door and called them all into the sanctuary. Sawyer stopped when he saw that the church pews were full of townsfolk. He smiled and waved at them before he got into place.

Nancy and the Monks girls came in through the front door and marched down the aisle one behind the other about twenty steps apart. They looked beautiful in their new dresses, with their hair fixed and rouge on their cheeks. When the attendants were in place, Mrs. Toliver played the wedding song on the piano, and Abigail walked down the aisle with a big smile on her face, tears rolling down her cheeks. He could see her hands shaking. Sawyer took a few steps toward her and placed her hand in his as they stood in front of the preacher.

The service went off without any problems, and when it was over, the bride and groom invited everyone to join them for cake on the lawn. To their surprise, three cakes had been provided, and some of the ladies from church were serving the guests.

Sawyer took Abigail by the hand and whispered in her ear, "Come with me. I want to introduce you to everyone."

They spent a good hour letting Abigail meet the town's residents, who had thought enough of Sawyer to attend the wedding. Sheriff Craig and the county commissioner, John McDaniel, had even come from Iola to attend.

The Texas cowboys took Sawyer and Abigail off to the side when the festivities started dying down.

"We're going to head on out this afternoon," said Ronnie. "We need to get Cowboy home so he can sell out and get on back. He's a little scared about talking to you about being sweet on your sister."

Sawyer laughed. "Come here, Cowboy." He put his arm around his friend's neck. "I love every one of you men like brothers. Cowboy, my sister really likes you and wants you in her life, and that's fine by me. I hope someday you and she can share your love like Abigail and I do."

Cowboy wiped a tear from his eye and said, "Thanks, Sawyer. I'll be back as soon as I can. This is my see-you-later to the both of you. If you'll excuse me, I need to go see Nancy Lou now."

"You get going," said Abigail, "and remember that we're expecting you back mighty soon."

Once Cowboy had said goodbye to Nancy, the men gathered up their horses and left. Sawyer and Abigail joined Nancy and watched them ride off. Sawyer put his arm around her. "Sister, he'll be back."

She looked up at him and smiled through her tears. "He proposed to me before he left, and I said yes."

"That's a good thing, and don't you ever wonder about him coming back. Cowboy is as solid as they come. What he says is what he'll do," said Sawyer.

"Lilly is inside the church watching little Cade, so I best go get the baby and head home. I asked her earlier if Malinda and Beverly could come home with me for a couple of days to help with the baby and give me some company. I'm kind of lonely with the two of you gone and Houston leaving," said Nancy, and kissed the newlyweds.

Sawyer and Abigail loaded into the carriage and started to Iola for their honeymoon. As they rode through Humboldt on their way out, people stood on the boardwalk to wave and congratulate them on their wedding. When they rode past the hotel, Agatha Barnes was standing in front of the door with two men. She didn't wave or smile as they passed by. Sawyer glanced at Abigail, but she was busy waving at some folks on the opposite side of the street and didn't see the strange woman.

When the newlyweds checked into the Morrison Hotel in Iola, the clerk had a hotel worker take the carriage to the livery stable. Sawyer also made arrangements with the hotel staff to have their supper delivered to their room.

The newlyweds didn't leave their love nest room until Sunday morning, when they went downstairs for breakfast, although it was almost noon. The weather was nice that day, so they strolled around town window shopping, talking, and enjoying each other's company. "Let's go to the café down the street and get something to drink," said Sawyer.

"I hope we can have a piece of pie; this walking has made me want a snack," said Abigail.

Sawyer thought it was nice to walk along the boardwalk hand in hand, still consumed with each other. He had never imagined the happiness he felt in his heart that day.

While sitting in the café eating pie and drinking coffee, Abigail said, "We should go back to the hotel when we finish here. I think we need to continue with our honeymoon, if you get my drift." Sawyer pushed his plate away, stood up, and extended his hand to his wife. It was time to leave.

Sawyer went to the hotel's front desk on Sunday night and ordered room service so they wouldn't have to go out again that evening. They had learned so much about each other over the last two days, and he didn't want to interrupt their time together just yet.

Chapter Forty-Five

The newlyweds ate breakfast at the café down the street from the Morrison Hotel on Monday morning. While sitting at the table having the last of his coffee, Sawyer asked, "Is there anything special you would like to do today?"

Abigail shook her head. "We should go back to the room for a little while and then pack up. We've been away from our home long enough, don't you think?"

"That sounds good to me," said Sawyer.

Around noon, Sawyer and Abigail came downstairs and had lunch in the dining room. Sawyer went to the front desk after they had eaten and asked, "Would you happen to have someone who could go to the livery stable, get our carriage, and bring it to the hotel? My wife and I will be leaving shortly."

"Certainly, Mr. McCade. And I'll have your bill ready when you leave," said the clerk.

Sawyer went back up to their room, where Abigail had already packed up their belongings. He carried their bags down the stairs and the clerk came from behind the counter. "Let me take those to the carriage, Mr. McCade."

Sawyer paid his bill and left a tip for the man who had gone after the buggy. Abigail came down with her remaining small bag.

"I'll take that, dear," he said, taking the satchel from her.

"Thank you, darling," said Abigail as they left the lobby.

They took the carriage through Iola, but Sawyer and Abigail didn't go through Humboldt on the way home. They took the back roads so he could show his bride the countryside and point out who lived at the various farms along the way. They were almost past Nancy's house when Malinda came running toward them, hollering for them to stop. Sawyer jerked back on the reins and applied the handbrake before getting down to see what was wrong.

"We need you at the house. There's a heifer down trying to have a calf, and it's hung up in her," said the out-of-breath girl.

"Hop in the buggy and we'll all go see if we can help," said Sawyer. He returned to the seat and once Malinda had climbed into the back, he started the carriage up the lane as fast as the horse could go.

When they arrived, Nancy was out in the pasture with one of the shorthorn cows that had come with the property. She was crying, not knowing how to help the cow give birth.

Sawyer ran up, assessed the situation, and said, "Hold her head down while I work on the calf. It looks like one of its front legs is bent, and I have to straighten it."

Sawyer took his shirt off, put his arms inside the cow, and felt along the calf's front legs until he found the one bent at the knee. He pushed on the calf until he could straighten the leg. Then he pulled on the calf by holding a leg in each hand until he could see the head. After slightly adjusting the calf's position, he heaved again, and it came out and landed on the ground. Sawyer grabbed a handful of grass and wiped the afterbirth out of the calf's nose.

The newborn bull calf was breathing and still alive. "You can let her go now. We need to see if she can get up and care for her baby," said Sawyer with afterbirth on his hands and arms.

"I'm sorry, but I was so scared, and I didn't have time to go to the neighbors for help," said Nancy.

"It's fine," said Sawyer, wiping his arms on the grass. "Girls, come give us a hand. We've got to get her up so she can tend to her baby," said Sawyer.

Sawyer, Abigail, Nancy, and the Monks girls pushed, pulled, and lifted until they persuaded the cow to stand and get her balance. The unsteady animal went to her baby and began to clean off the afterbirth with her tongue.

"Sister, you did good. If you hadn't seen her out here in trouble, we would have lost the mama and the baby."

"Thanks, Sawyer," said Nancy, giving him a weak smile.

Abigail came to Nancy and gave her a hug. "You did good."

"Let's go to the house and clean up," said Sawyer.

He washed his hands and arms outside at the pump with lye soap and water before he put his shirt back on.

"I think we've had enough excitement for one day. Abigail and I are going home now."

"I'm sure glad you came when you did. I didn't know what to do," said Nancy.

"You did just fine."

Sawyer and Abigail got back into the carriage and headed home.

No one was at their house when they got there and Sawyer assumed that the men had gone to market with the cattle, but he had forgotten to ask Nancy when they'd left.

Abigail helped him unload their luggage before he took the carriage to the barn and put the horse in the corral. The horse and buggy could be returned to April the following day, if everything was okay at the ranch and he had time to leave.

Abigail had coffee made and was preparing biscuits when he came inside from the barn.

"How does ham and eggs sound for supper?" she asked.

"That's fine with me. I usually eat six eggs."

After the evening meal, they sat outside enjoying the fantastic sunset. The nighttime breeze felt good, and they could hear the sound of country life all around them. Crickets rubbing their front wings together, a coyote howling off in the distance and an owl hooting from a treetop. The newlyweds sat talking about different individuals she had met at the wedding when, out of nowhere, Abigail said, "Sawyer, I want us to socialize with people in town. And I think we may need to invite some couples out to the ranch from time to time."

"I'm not sociable, but I'm getting better at it," said

Sawyer. "There was a time when I was mostly alone and didn't trust anyone, not even the men in my detachment. If you want to ask couples out to visit, then by all means, do it. That may be good therapy for me."

"I don't plan on throwing a party anytime soon. In fact, I might wait until Cowboy returns, and then we can start introducing him to everyone you know."

"Now hold on. That's not our place to parade Cowboy around town. We need to leave that up to him and Nancy Lou. She might get her feelings hurt if we butt in on their business."

"You're right, I should back off and let her do that. You need to put me in my place when I get out of line."

"Come on, let's go inside and get ready for bed," said Sawyer.

"I wish we could go to Nancy's house and see how she's doing. I suspect she's had a rough few days, and I'm a little worried about her," said Abigail.

"What do you mean?" asked Sawyer, bewildered by what she said.

"Sawyer, our wedding brought back memories of her dead husband and their wedding. Then her man, Cowboy, leaves and goes back to Texas. She's at home alone with the baby, and that cow getting down giving birth scared her. She's a little depressed with Cowboy leaving and having to stay home most of the time with the baby."

"I'll saddle our horses, and we'll ride over and check on her. You do realize that she is not alone over there. The Monks girls are there to help with the baby."

"I swear you men are so dense at times. She doesn't have a man to cuddle next to, or a shoulder to cry on. That ordeal today would have been so much better if she'd had someone to hold her and give her comfort. Sometimes, women need the shoulder of a strong man to lay their head on and cry, or a man to share a laugh with. Right now, she has no one but us and those girls."

"I'll go get the horses," said Sawyer.

They surprised Nancy and the Monks girls by coming back. The girls went to bed, but Sawyer and Abigail stayed and talked with Nancy. She told them the men had left on Sunday, taking the cattle to market, and she thought they had about two hundred and ninety head to sell.

The clock on the wall showed it was after ten, and Sawyer said, "We need to head to our house. It's late, and I have to ride into Humboldt tomorrow to take the buggy back. If you need anything from town, make me a list, and I'll get it for you."

"I don't need anything except for you to check at the telegraph office for any messages for me," said Nancy.

"Are you expecting a message from Cowboy?" he asked jokingly.

"Yes I am. Houston is supposed to let me know when he gets to his house. I mean, back to Clarksville. This is going to be his home when he gets back." It was Nancy's turn to laugh.

Sawyer got up. "Bye sister. We're leaving."

Chapter Forty-Six

Abigail wanted to stay at their house so she could wash clothes while Sawyer took the carriage and horse back to April at the wagon yard. He left right after he fed the farm animals and let the chickens out. With Raven tied to the back of the carriage so he had a way home, he left for town.

He didn't pass by anyone on the road all the way into Humboldt that morning. April was chipper when he dropped off the carriage. "Sawyer, the buggy rental was my wedding present to you and the missus."

"Thank you so much, we really appreciated it," said Sawyer. "I'll see you later. I need to go by the telegraph office."

One man that Sawyer didn't know was standing at the counter, and another man was seated near the door waiting his turn when Sawyer entered the small room. He waited until both men left before he said, "Hello, Mr. Hoffman. Do you have any messages for my sister?"

"I sure do. How have you been, Sawyer? I hear that you got married this past Saturday."

"I did get married, and I'm doing really good."

"She has two messages, and I suspect we may have another wedding taking place soon," said the operator.

"We might, but let's keep that between us," said Sawyer. He folded the slips of paper and put them in his pocket. "I'll be seeing you, Mr. Hoffman, and thanks for the messages."

Sawyer went out and whistled, and his horse came trotting up to him. After patting Raven on the neck, he mounted up and headed down Main Street to go home. While riding past what used to be his office when he was sheriff, he saw Craig's horse out front and rode up beside it.

He opened the door to find Craig talking to his deputy who worked in Humboldt. "It looks like you two need some criminals to come to town so you have something to do," said Sawyer.

"Come on in! Grab a cup and fill us in on married life," said Craig.

"No, I just saw your horse and wanted to say hi before heading home. I had to bring the carriage we used for our honeymoon back to April before she thought I'd stolen it," said Sawyer.

Craig got up, shook hands with his old boss, and walked outside with him. "I heard you and Abigail were in Iola on your honeymoon, but I didn't want to disturb you just to say hello."

"We did stay in Iola and had a wonderful time there. It's good seeing you, Sheriff. I better be going. It'll be close to dinner by the time I get home."

"I'll be seeing you, my friend."

Sawyer took off home. This time, he met a few travelers going into Humboldt as he returned to the ranch.

He stopped at Nancy Lou's house to find her rocking the baby to sleep in the living room. She put her finger to her lips so he wouldn't say anything, and took the baby to his crib.

When she returned to the front room, she asked, "Did I have a telegram?"

He handed her two slips of paper. She opened the first one, read it, put it in her apron pocket, and read the second one. She put it in her pocket as well and smiled at Sawyer. "They made it to Clarksville, and he has sold his cattle and land to Hooter and Ronnie. He's heading back here the day after tomorrow, Thursday."

"Well, good, you need him here with you. Nancy, if he stays in the house with you and Cade, it's all right with me. There may be some folks who don't think he is Christian-like, but you need him close to you," said Sawyer.

She hugged his neck. "Thank you, baby brother. I love you."

"I love you too, now let me go. I'm hungry."

"You give Abigail my love."

"I'll see you later."

He mounted up, but instead of going right home, he rode out into the pasture to look at the cow and calf they had worked on the day before. The cow was fine, eating grass, and the calf was lying down to get sun. The cow turned toward Raven when they got too close and snorted before she swung her head to one side, warning them that she would protect her offspring. He backed his horse up and left her to graze.

When he got home, there was no sign of Abigail out in the wash shed, so he figured she was busy inside the house. He took Raven to the barn to remove the saddle and fed him a helping of oats. Sawyer went ahead and used the curry comb on Raven's coat while he ate. Raven liked to be brushed and talked to by his owner and friend.

Sawyer finished up and opened the gate at the back of the barn so Raven could go outside if he wanted to. It was time for dinner, so he walked to the house.

Chapter Forty-Seven

He palmed his gun as soon as he got inside the front door. It looked as if a fight had taken place in the living room where the table in front of the couch was on its side, and one leg was broken and lying two feet away. The rocking chair lay on its back and the seat cushion was by the bedroom door. Sawyer put his back against the wall and walked along the perimeter of the room to the entrance into the kitchen. It was open, and he could see that fighting had taken place in there too. Plates and bowls lay broken and scattered about the room. The skillet that she had been cooking meat in was on the floor, along with three pieces of beef meat. The table had been scooted out of place, and two chairs were overturned.

Sawyer shook with fear that something terrible had happened to Abigail, but he took his time to search the rest of the house. Whoever had been there had stayed in the front room and kitchen. He went to the back door— someone had broken the lock and door jamb to get in.

With the gun ready to shoot, he returned to the

front door and inspected it for damage before going out onto the porch. Keeping against the wall, he made it down the west side of the house until he could see the backyard. Chickens were scattered about the yard, pecking at bugs and pebbles. If someone had been nearby, they wouldn't stay so close to the house, and he suspected that no one was out there waiting for him.

He stayed away from the back steps since he didn't want to disturb any footprints or evidence. Whoever had been there might have left some clues as to who they were and how many were in the party.

Why would anyone want to take Abigail? No one knew her, and she didn't have any enemies that he knew of. Had someone kidnapped her because they wanted money, thinking he was rich? Or could it have been someone who wanted revenge for something he had done in the past?

He stepped onto the back porch and made his way carefully back into the kitchen, watching where he placed his feet as he went. Partial prints of someone's shoes were on the floor where flour had spilled, dusting an area of about three feet by three feet next to the kitchen table. It looked like three different people had walked through the white powder, and one was most likely Abigail since one set of prints was smaller than the other two.

What was she doing when they busted through the door? It looked like she tried to get away; there were a lot more of her prints than men's prints, and at several places it looked like her foot had slid.

He took his time, looking at everything as if it were all clues. Then he saw something else unusual—there were actually two sets of small footprints, as if there had been two women in the room. One set was from shoes with rounded toes, and the other set had pointed toes. The pointed ones were Abigail's. Who could the woman be who wore the round-toe shoes?

So besides Abigail, there had been another woman and two men in his house.

Sawyer went back into the front room, stood in the doorway from the kitchen, and looked the room over from there before he started a closer examination for clues.

After searching the house for twenty minutes, he found no additional clues that could be used to identify the two men and one woman who had taken her.

This was troubling. There had to be something he missed. She couldn't have been taken without one of them leaving more clues. He went back through the other rooms in the house but didn't find anything useful.

In their bedroom, he opened the trunk where he kept his extra guns and buckled the .44-caliber gun on his right hip. He put another .44-caliber in the cross-draw holster on his left side, and the .36-caliber on the back of his belt. The extra powder, balls, and caps were placed in a cloth bag to take with him.

His Henry repeating rifle stood behind the bedroom door, and he took it also, and went out to the front porch. There he left the rifle standing against a chair while searching the yard for boot and horse tracks.

There had been a lot of traffic in the yard lately, what with all the new cattle, and finding worthwhile tracks took a lot of work. In the barn, Abigail's saddle was missing. He looked in the corral and sure enough, her horse was also gone. He found another clue in the corral—a boot print with the heels worn on the outside, as if the man favored the outside of his feet when he walked.

Sawyer followed the boot tracks into the barn and then toward the house. But they didn't go to the house. The tracks turned and went in the direction of three elm trees about sixty feet to the right of the house, close to the fence that separated the yard to the pasture. It was here he found horse tracks that looked like the animals had been standing there for a while, based on the amount of dung on the ground. Whoever rode the horses had tied the reins to tree limbs; the bark had been torn up when the horses lowered their heads to chomp on grass. One set of horse tracks spurred his curiosity, in particular: the shoe of the right front hoof was new, while the other three shoes were worn down. This horse had lost a shoe, and the owner only replaced the missing one instead of paying for a whole new set.

A thorough examination of the area under the trees gave him enough clues to determine that four horses had been tied up there.

The tracks went down the lane to the main road, where the four ponies turned south. The hoofprints were easy to follow for another hundred feet until they mixed in with all the other tracks in the road. At that point, Sawyer couldn't tell which prints belonged to the abductors.

Since they went south, it was likely they had come to his house from that direction too. But why? Humboldt was to the west, and Iola was north. Why would they take Abigail and return the way they had come? There was nothing that way except farms. Nothing made sense.

Sawyer walked the road back to the intersection where the lane from his property connected with the road, then kept going north for another quarter of a mile to the corner that turned west toward Humboldt, but there was no sign of the tracks in that direction. He returned to the intersection and walked a wide circle in the junction, and spotted horse tracks coming out of a stand of trees about two acres in size across the road to the west. Following the tracks through the brush, grass, and trees, he found where the abductors had hidden as they watched the house. There were horse droppings and lots of horse and human tracks.

A thorough examination of the area provided him with enough clues to give him a clear understanding that there had indeed been three people—one woman and two men. One set of horse prints was the one with three old shoes and one new one. The unusual boot tracks that he'd found by the barn from someone who walked on the side of their heels were here too, and the woman's round-toe prints matched the ones he had seen in the house.

They had gone south when they left his house, that was for sure too. He walked back to the barn, saddled up Raven, and started across the pasture to Nancy Lou's house with two canteens, his rifle, and provisions, in case he had to spend the night on the road.

When he rode up and dismounted, she came out on the porch, and as soon as she saw him armed for battle, she put her hand over her mouth and started to cry. "Sawyer, what's happened?" she asked through sobs.

"Someone came to the house while I was gone into Humboldt and took Abigail. As far as I can tell, there are three of them, and they headed south on the road."

He approached Nancy, pulled the shoulder holster rig off, and handed it to his sister. "You take this gun and keep it on you at all times. I'm going after my wife. I swear, the men who took her are as good as dead."

"Sawyer, wait. You must let the law know what's happened so they can help you find her."

"I don't have time to do that right now. The trail will grow cold unless I get on it. You have one of the girls go get their mama to come, and the four of you stay in the house until I get back or Edward and the men return from the stockyards," said Sawyer, and he mounted up to leave.

He could see Nancy talking to the girls as he left the yard and knew they would be safe until he returned.

Chapter Forty-Eight

On the way back to the main road where the criminals had turned south, Sawyer let his emotions get the best of him and he cried from fear, anger, and love for his wife. After allowing himself a moment, he wiped away the tears and said, "McCade, it's time to get mean and put all feelings for mankind behind you until you find your bride."

At the junction two miles south of his place, he picked up the tracks of the horse with the one new shoe. Another quarter of a mile south, the tracks mixed in with all the other tracks and were gone. By continuing on the road, he found the same hoofprint again another three miles south of his land. He thought they had kept going south, but he lost the trail entirely after another quarter of a mile.

Returning to the intersection to investigate some more, he then went east. Every once in a while, for the next half mile, he found tracks that looked like they belonged to the abductors, but then they blended in with all the other marks in the dirt, and he lost them.

Sawyer hunted east until it was almost dark, and then finally turned back west to go to Humboldt. Trying to find tracks in the dark was useless, and this was a good time to notify Sheriff Craig. He loped Raven all the way to the telegraph office.

"Mr. Hoffman, I need to send an urgent telegram to Sheriff Craig Martin in Iola."

Mr. Hoffman noticed the concerned look on Sawyer's face. "Is everything all right, son?"

"I don't think so," said Sawyer.

"Well, write down your message and I'll send it right now."

Sawyer handed him a scrap of paper on which he'd written his telegram, and while the operator tapped the switch, Sawyer asked, "Have you noticed any strangers around town in the last week or so?"

Mr. Hoffman finished sending the message and leaned back in his chair. "A traveling salesman was here for a few days, but he left Monday. I saw some cowboys, but I was told they work for you. I can't think of anyone else."

Sawyer knew it had been a long shot to ask, but it had been worth a try. "I'm going to the café to eat. Will you let me know if Craig replies?"

"I sure will."

Sawyer turned to leave when Mr. Hoffman said, "Wait, there was a woman here with two men last week. I'm pretty sure the two fellers worked for her. I never met any of them, but I saw them on the street a few times."

Sawyer nodded. "Did the woman have reddish hair, and was in her late thirties or early forties?"

"Yep, that's her all right. She usually wore fancy

dresses, but I saw her in britches riding a little gray mare Monday afternoon."

"Thanks, Mr. Hoffman."

Sawyer was starving and walked to the café. So many thoughts consumed his being as he made his way down the boardwalk, and the same questions kept returning to him. Why would Agatha Barnes and her men take Abigail? Who was Agatha Barnes, and what was her motive? Where could they be hiding?

He gulped down his food and rode back home for the night. Sleeping in his own bed was way better than sleeping on the hard, cold ground somewhere.

In the end, his own bed didn't help much. After a night of restless sleep, tossing, turning, and waking up multiple times, he got up before daylight and cleaned up the mess in the kitchen while he made his coffee.

He thought about a plan for that day and he sipped the strong black liquid. The first thing he would do was ride back to Humboldt and send more telegrams. They would go to Judge Delahay and US Prosecutor Crozier in Topeka, Kansas. The two men had a lot of information on organized crime, and the criminals who were the ringleaders. Maybe they had heard of Agatha in connection with some of their cases.

If he could find out who she was, he might be able to determine where she and her men had taken his Abigail. Someone had to know who this woman was. He would also ask the hotel staff if they knew anything about her.

On the ride into town, he thought of a few other things he wanted to find out. Where had she taken her meals? Where had she kept the gray mare? Was her horse the one with the old shoe on its front hoof?

Where had the two men with her stayed in town? He was racking his brain, trying to come up with anything that might help. The longer it took to find his wife, the less the odds were of finding her at all.

The shade was up at the telegraph office, so he stopped and went in.

"Good morning, Sawyer. I have a message from the sheriff," said Mr. Hoffman.

I'll be in Humboldt shortly after daylight.

Craig.

"I need to send two more telegrams," said Sawyer. He wrote down a message and handed it to the operator. "I want this to go to Judge Delahay and US Prosecutor Crozier in Topeka. I'll check back before I leave town to see if they've replied."

"Okay. I'm sorry about your wife," said Mr. Hoffman.

Sawyer nodded and walked out, heading to the hotel, where he left his horse ground-tied out front and went in.

"Sawyer, hold up!"

Sawyer spun around with his hand on the grips of his pistol. The sheriff and one of his deputies were riding down the street.

Once the lawmen had dismounted and the three of them shook hands, Sawyer told them everything he could remember about Abigail's kidnapping and who he thought had taken her.

When he was finished, Craig said, "I'll send Hoss out to keep guard at Nancy Lou's house. The same bunch that took Abigail could try to take Nancy or cause her harm."

"That's a good idea," said Sawyer. "I'm sure she's a little upset and scared for her and the baby."

Sheriff Craig sent Hoss off, and when he and Sawyer were alone, he started talking again. "I'm going back to Iola and will search the courthouse records for any land that might belong to this Agatha Barnes."

"Let's talk to the hotel clerk first and see if he knows more about her than I do," said Sawyer.

"Yeah, that's a good idea," said Craig.

They went inside to find the clerk wiping off the counter.

"Good morning, gentlemen. Do you need rooms?"

"No, we need information on one of your guests," said Sawyer.

"Which guest is that?" asked the clerk.

"The woman who goes by the name Agatha Barnes. What room is she in?"

"She checked out on Monday without telling me where she was going," said the clerk.

"If I remember correctly, your name is Jeremy Long, isn't it?" asked Sawyer.

"Yes sir, it is," replied Jeremy.

"Where did she go to eat while she was here?"

"She ate in the dining room most of the time."

"Did she ever have any guests eat with her, like two men?" asked Sawyer.

"No, not in here. But I did see her talking to two men a couple of times outside—once on the boardwalk, and once in the alleyway behind the hotel. She kept a little gray mare back there."

"Did you overhear any conversations where she called the men by name?"

"No sir, I didn't."

Sawyer continued with his questions. "Do you know where she's from?"

"I did hear her tell another guest that she has a ranch south of Olathe," said Jeremy.

"Do you know where the two men you saw her talking to stayed while they were in town?" asked Sheriff Martin.

"No sir, but the time I saw them out in the alley talking to the woman, their horses were lathered up like they had been ridden hard," said Jeremy.

"Is there anything else you can tell us about the woman or any of them?" asked Sawyer.

"The only thing I can think of is that the first day she checked into the hotel, she asked if I knew where you lived."

Sawyer frowned. "She asked where I lived?"

"Yes sir. I'm sorry, but that's all I remember about her."

Sawyer turned the registration ledger on the counter until it faced him and looked at it closely. "Can you describe the two men?"

"Let me think a moment. They were both about your height or a little shorter. I'd say around six feet tall. The younger of the two was skinny and wearing a tie-down gun. He wore his britches inside the tops of his boots and had on a black shirt. The other feller was heavier. Not fat, but muscled up more. He had a salt-and-pepper beard and wore a hat with the brim turned up in the front."

"Thanks Jeremy, you've been a big help," said Sheriff Martin, and he and Sawyer walked outside.

"Sawyer, I have a bad feeling about this woman. Do you have any clue why she's here?"

"No idea. I met her on the street one day and then she spoke to Abigail and me one day on the boardwalk. that's the only two times I talked to her."

"I think she wanted to know where you live so she could take Abigail," said the sheriff.

"I don't know why anyone would take my wife unless it's for revenge for someone who I killed. For the life of me, I don't know who it could be," said Sawyer.

"What do you want me to do?" asked Craig.

"You go back to Iola and search the land records, and I'll do some more checking around town. I sent a telegram to Judge Delahay and US Prosecutor Crozier in Topeka asking if they knew anything about the Barnes woman. I'd like to hear back from them before I leave," said Sawyer. "If I'm gone when a reply comes back, would you see what they say?"

"I sure will. In fact, I'll stop at the telegraph office and tell Hoffman to let me know, and then I'll head back to Iola," said Craig.

"I'm going to the saloon and see if the men have been in there drinking," said Sawyer.

It was still early, and the saloon wasn't officially open yet. The bartender was setting up bottles behind the bar and washing glasses when Sawyer walked in.

"We ain't open yet," said the man in a gruff voice.

"I'm not here to drink. I'm hunting for information on a couple of men that may have been here a few days ago," said Sawyer.

"You must not hear so good," said the barkeep. "It's early, and I don't feel like talking to you or anyone else, so get out before I throw you out."

Sawyer walked up to the bar top and reached across it with his left hand, grabbing the front of the man's shirt and jerking him forward into his right fist, which collided with the man's nose. Blood flew through the air, landing all over the countertop. Sawyer hit the man three more times before he said, "I want answers now about two men who have been drinking in here. They are both about six feet tall. One has a salt-and-pepper beard, is muscled up, and wears a hat with the brim turned up. The other is skinny and wears a black shirt and a tie-down gun."

Sawyer still had the man by the shirt and pulled him onto the bar top.

"If you'll let me go, I'll tell you what I know," said the man.

Sawyer turned him loose but was ready to start hitting again if he tried anything.

The bloodied man took his bar towel, wiped the mess from his face, and held it to his nose. "You didn't have to bust up my nose."

"Just start talking," said Sawyer.

"The skinny one is Kansas Jones, and the other is Albert. Albert's been here before, about a year or so ago. It's rumored that he hires out his gun. I don't know anything about Kansas. They were here on business with some woman who gives the orders. That's all I know," said the barkeep, putting the towel back to his nose.

"Do you know where they stayed while they were here?" asked Sawyer.

"No, but I don't think it was in town. One night when I asked if they wanted another whiskey, Albert said no, it was getting too late, and they had a long ride ahead of them. Can I go now so I can clean up?" asked the barkeep.

"Yeah, I'll leave you alone. But if you remember anything else, you best tell it to the deputy or I won't be so friendly the next time." Sawyer left the saloon and headed back to the telegraph office to check for messages.

Chapter Forty-Nine

Mr. Hoffman looked up when Sawyer entered the office. "I ain't got a reply yet, Sawyer."

"That's fine, I have another telegram to send." He wrote down the message and handed the paper to Hoffman. "Send this to the same two men in Topeka and to Sheriff Martin. I'll be back later to see if I've gotten an answer."

"Sheriff Martin stopped by and said for me to also let him know if you get a reply from Topeka. Is that all right with you?"

"Of course. He's helping me. You have my permission to share any messages with him," said Sawyer, and he left the building.

He just had to find out who these people were and where the two men stayed. It was time to head back home and stop in on the farms east of his house to see if anyone had seen the two men and woman ride by.

He wasted two hours stopping at each house on the road south of his ranch for the next three miles. No one had seen any riders going south that matched the descriptions of Agatha and her men. Sawyer figured they must have turned off somewhere on one of the other roads and either rode east or west. West would take them back to Humboldt, so he went east.

No recognizable tracks turned up for the first two miles. As he rode by an abandoned house not far off the road, he remembered it as the farm where Rufus and Avery had murdered an old man and left him in the yard for his granddaughter to find. It was worth his time to check the place out and make sure Agatha wasn't using it.

A quick ten-minute search of the house and barn didn't turn anything up, and he left.

Sawyer made it back to Humboldt and stopped in front of the telegraph office just as Mr. Hoffman and Sheriff Martin came out.

"I'm glad you're back," said Craig. "We have lots of information for you. The federal authorities sent you everything on Agatha."

"Let's go inside Mr. Hoffman's office and sit down so you can tell me," said Sawyer. He sat in a cushioned chair by the front window while Craig explained what he'd found out.

"Agatha Barnes owns the Double B Ranch south of Olathe, Kansas. But the interesting thing about her is she is the late Senator Bass's daughter. She got married and moved to Illinois, but when her husband died, she returned to Kansas and Bass set her up with the ranch. He didn't want anyone to know she was his daughter, so they kept their relationship a secret since the law was always meddling in his crooked affairs," said Craig.

"So now she has come here to get revenge on me for killing her evil daddy?" asked Sawyer.

"Yep, that's the way it seems. She has two hard cases with her by the names of Kansas and Albert. Both men are wanted by the law in Kansas City. Now we know who they are and why they took your wife."

"Yeah, but now we have to find where they took her. The barkeep at the saloon said the two men stayed out from town a ways, but he didn't know where," said Sawyer. "I asked my neighbors if they saw them, and no one has."

"Do you reckon they could be holed up on one of the properties that Bass and his cronies stole from the folks around here?" asked Craig.

"That could very well be," said Sawyer. "Nancy will know what properties the original owners didn't get back once all the killing was over. I'll talk to her and see if we can figure it out."

"That's a good idea. I have the ladies in the county clerk's office searching the records for any property Senator Bass owned. I'll ride back to the courthouse now and be back tomorrow," said Craig.

"Okay, thanks for helping me, Sheriff. I'll see you tomorrow."

Sawyer rode to Nancy's house. The deputy who had been sent to protect his sister sat on the porch with a double-barrel shotgun lying across his lap.

"Hello Hoss, did that arm get back to normal after you got shot?" asked Sawyer while he dismounted and dropped the reins to his horse.

"Yes sir, it's as good as new," said Hoss. "Are you going to be here for the rest of the day, or am I supposed to stay?"

"I'll let you know in a little while. You sit tight for now."

"I can do that. It's good to see you again, Sawyer."

"You too, Hoss." Sawyer went to the door.

Nancy was waiting just inside when Sawyer entered the front room. "Have you found out anything about where Abigail was taken?" she asked.

"I found out who took her and why. It was a woman by the name of Agatha Barnes," said Sawyer.

"Who is that? I've never heard of her before."

"You're not going to believe this. She's Senator Bass's daughter, and she's here seeking revenge," said Sawyer.

Nancy shook her finger in her brother's face. "I'm sick and tired of that family trying to destroy us. They have already done enough, and I won't stand by any longer and let it happen." Her face was red and her nostrils flared in anger. Sawyer didn't try to quiet her down. He was afraid that she might attack him like she used to when they were kids.

"I need to know if the Bass crew stole any land that wasn't recovered by relatives of the rightful owners," said Sawyer.

She looked at him with a clenched jaw and wrath in her eyes for a few seconds before she blinked and composed herself. "I remember the place down on the river where Lefty Branch and Lesley Overstreet were found dead. I think you know where I'm talking about?"

"I believe I heard something about that. I'll go down there to see if anyone is at the house," said Sawyer.

"Sawyer, I know darn good and well you know about those two," said Nancy with both hands on her hips. "You get on down there and see if they have Abigail hidden in the house. We've been through enough with that sorry family. If that woman is there, you kill her and anyone she has with her. Did you hear me?" Nancy stepped within inches of his face as she spoke.

"Nancy, I ain't never killed a woman, and I don't intend to today. You need to get a hold of your anger and start thinking straight," said Sawyer, and he walked out the door.

"Hoss, you stay here with her until I get back," said Sawyer, and he mounted up.

Sawyer remembered the way to the house that was close to the river; it was where he had killed the two murderers. Their bodies had been left in the backyard, and a few days later, their corpses had been found and buried by the people Bass stole the land from. No one knew he had been the one to kill them. Nancy suspected it, but to Sawyer's knowledge, she wasn't sure.

The house looked deserted from a distance as he watched from the trees on the east side of the house. Sawyer waited for any sign that someone might be there. There were no lights on, and there were no chickens or other animals in the yard. He rode on in and dismounted. The door gave way when he pushed it, and the inside of the place looked the same as it had the last time he was there, months ago. He had made a dead-end trip. Where in the world did they have his Abigail hidden?

He took off back to Nancy's house in hopes she had thought of another place for him to search.

Chapter Fifty

No one was home when he arrived at his sister's house. This alarmed him to the point that he pulled his gun and eased his way inside. Now where had she gone off to? Hoss was also absent, and it wasn't like him to abandon his post.

Sawyer went out to the barn and the carriage was gone, and so was the deputy's horse. Had they ridden into town?

Sawyer was walking back to the house when he heard the buggy approaching. Nancy was driving the rig up the lane toward the house, but Hoss wasn't with her. She didn't stop until the cart was inside the barn.

Sawyer followed her in and said, "Just what do you think you're doing going off on your own? Where's Hoss? He's supposed to be protecting you."

She looked at him and said, "I left the baby with Lilly Monks. Hoss is there to protect Cade until Edward and the cowhands get back. I'm going with you to make sure that evil hussy doesn't get away." She climbed down from the buggy and spouted at her brother. "You get my horse saddled while I change clothes. You and I are going into town tonight to see if the men are in the saloon."

Sawyer shook his head, shocked by his sister's demeanor, but didn't say a word. He didn't want to fight with Nancy. Her coming with him could create more problems for him—he would have to watch after her as well as himself. But he did what he was told and had her pony waiting when she came out of the house dressed like a man in britches, shirt, boots, and hat. He smiled when he noticed she carried the shoulder holster gun he had left with her in her right hand. "Do you plan on carrying that hog leg in your hand the whole time?" he asked.

"I don't. I'm giving it to you, and you're giving me that holstered gun you have behind your back. That holster fits my belt." She handed him his gun.

He took off the .36-caliber gun and holster and handed it to her. She undid her belt, put it through the belt loop on the holster, and fitted the gear onto her right hip. She pulled the gun from the holster a couple of times and said, "Let's get going. I'm ready for war."

It was dark by the time they arrived at the Lariat Saloon on the south end of Humboldt. They didn't see anyone who fit the descriptions of either of the two men. Sawyer and Nancy were walking to a second saloon when Sheriff Martin approached them on his lathered-up horse.

"Sawyer, I think I know where they're keeping your wife. When I searched through the county records, I discovered an interesting piece of property information. It seems there's a farm east of town that is shown to belong to a family named Elliott," said the sheriff.

"Yeah, that's former Judge Elliott's place," said Sawyer.

"Nope, it's not Judge Elliott's place. It's his sister's place, Joanna Elliott, who is the dead wife of Senator Bass. His wife owned that land so now Agatha owns it, and that's the most likely place for them to hole up with your Abigail," said Sheriff Martin.

"I know the way there," said Sawyer. "Come on Nancy, let's get going."

"Do you want me to come along, or should I stay here in town?" asked the sheriff.

"Craig, I would appreciate it if you would stay in town and let Nancy and I go this alone."

"You two be careful out there. Let me know when it's over so I can send the undertaker to collect the bodies," said Sheriff Martin. He tipped his hat to Nancy, turned his horse around, and rode away.

"Sawyer, what just happened?" she asked with a bewildered expression on her face.

"Craig knows what we're going to do when we find that bunch, and he's turning his back so we don't get in trouble."

"Are we going there tonight? It's almost seven," said Nancy.

"Yeah. It'll take us a couple of hours before we're in position and ready to confront them, and they won't be expecting us at night. I've been there before and know the way. Let's go."

The moon was up and supplied them enough light to see where they were riding. An hour after leaving town, they were close to the house where Judge Elliott lived before he was killed by Senator Bass's men. Sawyer and Nancy left their horses three hundred yards away from the home and went in on foot.

He and Nancy walked slowly and tried to be as quiet as possible, sneaking up to the front of the house. They hid behind shade trees thirty yards away. Sawyer still remembered the layout of the house and whispered to his sister, "I'm going around to the back. Count to twenty-five and then walk up to the front door, stand to the side, and knock. Call out real loud that you're hurt and need help. When the door opens, you fire your gun, and I'll come through the back door on your shot."

"Do you want me to shoot whoever it is that opens the door?" asked Nancy.

"If you do, don't aim to kill, we need them alive in case she's not here. We need to get in quick and rescue Abigail if she's here."

"Okay, but if whoever answers is about to shoot me, then I'm going to put their lights out for good," said Nancy.

"I tell you what we'll do. When I start going to the back of the house, we both count to twenty. Then I'll bust through the back door, and you bang on the front entry. Just make sure you're not standing in front of the door, in case someone shoots at you," said Sawyer.

"That sounds better to me. I'm ready when you are." She pulled her gun from its holster.

Walking slowly and carefully with each step, they made their way to within ten feet of the house. Sawyer tapped his sister on the arm and headed toward the rear of the dwelling. At the count of twenty, he opened the back screen and stepped inside. The place was so dark that he had to feel his way along the chairs at the kitchen table. A second later, he heard Nancy hit the front door with what sounded like something heavy. Then she pounded on the wooden door with her fist. The glow of a match flared up through an open doorway connected to the living area, and he heard someone holler out, "I'm coming out unarmed, don't shoot."

Sawyer waited where he was, standing in the opening that divided the kitchen from the living room. He thought it was odd that someone would say they were unarmed, unless this was a setup. A man in his long johns came out of the front bedroom carrying a kerosene lamp. When the half-dressed man reached for the door latch, Sawyer said, "Don't move another muscle. Put the lamp on that table to your right and keep your hands up."

The tall, slender man did as he was told, and when his hands were empty, he said, "Mister, I'm unarmed, but I've got an important message for you."

"You keep quiet," said Sawyer. "Nancy, come on in, it's clear," he called out to his sister.

She came through the door with her pistol ready to shoot.

Sawyer aimed his gun at the man and said, "Okay, start talking. What's the message?"

"My boss said to tell you that if you want to see the woman alive, you have to come to a place outside Iola at noon tomorrow."

"And where's this place located?" asked Sawyer.

"It's the old Jefferson farm. She said you would figure it out," said the man.

"I don't have to figure it out. You're going to tell me, or I'm going to cut you up and leave you for the rats to feed on," said Sawyer.

"Now wait a minute! I ain't never been there before, I don't know where it is," said the frightened man.

"You're a liar!" shouted Nancy. "Go get a knife and make him talk," she told Sawyer.

She put the barrel of her gun against the man's forehead while Sawyer went into the kitchen and returned with a butcher knife in his hand.

"Mister, I'm telling you the truth. I ain't never been to that place. I'm a cowhand who works on the Double B Ranch. That other feller is Miss Barnes's hired gun, and he's with her. I'm only supposed to give you the message and then return to the ranch."

"How long have they been at the old Jefferson place?" asked Nancy.

"Ever since the day we took her. I came here, and they went to the farm."

"Is your name Kansas?" asked Nancy, still holding her gun on him.

"Yeah, how did you know?"

"Who is with Agatha besides Albert?" asked Sawyer.

"I don't know their names, but they are two brothers. And by what little I heard, they'll be waiting on you when you cross the creek," said Kansas.

Sawyer placed the blade of the knife against Kansas's throat. "What creek?"

Kansas swallowed when the blade touched his Adam's apple. "I don't know. That's all I heard."

Sawyer motioned to Nancy. "If he tries anything, you shoot him. I'm going to get his britches and boots. We'll take him into town for the sheriff to lock up."

Once Kansas was dressed and his hands tied, they helped him onto his horse and headed to Humboldt.

As soon as they left the judge's house and were on the road going west, Nancy asked her brother, "How do you plan on finding out where they're holding Abigail?"

"I'll tell you after we drop him off," said Sawyer.

"You do have a plan, don't you?" she asked.

"I have a plan, but I'm not talking about it in front of him."

Kansas twisted in the saddle so he could look at Sawyer. "Mister, if you let me go, I'll leave here and never come back."

Sawyer didn't reply to the man and kept focused on how he was going to get his beloved wife back.

Nancy heard what he said and replied, "Fool, once we hand you over to the law, you won't be coming back. Kidnapping is a hanging offense."

Chapter Fifty-One

The deputy was asleep in the back room in the jail when Sawyer pushed Kansas into the jailhouse. The prisoner was put in a cell and Sawyer was locking the iron-bar door when the deputy came out into the hallway, rubbing his eyes.

"What're you doing with that feller?" he asked.

"I'm Sawyer McCade, and I arrested this man for kidnapping. His name is Kansas Jones. You can message Sheriff Martin about it when the telegraph office opens in the morning."

"Yes, sir, the sheriff said you might come by. I'll take good care of him for you," said the deputy, still trying to rub the sleep from his eyes.

"You do that," said Sawyer, and left the jail.

Back outside, he said to Nancy, "Let's head on out to Iola. I want to stop and talk to Lawrence Mullins. He'll know where the Jefferson place is."

"Sawyer, we shouldn't call on folks so late at night. We might get shot," said Nancy Lou.

"We'll be fine. Let's go."

It was midnight by the time they got to the Mullins' ranch. They stopped their horses out front but didn't dismount just yet. The family's dogs came to the porch and barked at the late-night intruders.

Sawyer called out, "Hello in the house. It's Sawyer McCade, and I'm in dire need of help."

A lamp illuminated one of the rooms that faced the front yard, and then another one came on in the front room. Larry Mullins opened the door holding a rifle. "Sawyer, is that you?"

"Yeah, it's me and my sister Nancy Lou. We need to talk to you and your pa."

"Come on in, I'll get everyone up. Y'all can have a seat in the living room," said Larry, stepping back into the house.

Sawyer and Nancy were seated when Lawrence and his wife came in. They all shook hands and the couple sat down in matching chairs that were separated by a small table.

"Sawyer, what's this all about?" asked Lawrence. About that time, their four sons came in and also sat down.

Sawyer told them the entire story about Abigail getting kidnapped and taking Kansas to jail. Then he said, "They have her at the old Jefferson place outside Iola, and I have to be there by noon today, or they'll kill her. Do you know where that place is?"

Lawrence sat there, mulling over his answer for a moment. "I know of four or five places around here where folks by that name have lived. Do you have a better description than just the name of Jefferson?" he asked.

"No, I was told to go to the old Jefferson farm outside of Iola," said Sawyer.

"Wait," said Nancy. "Kansas said the brothers will bushwack you when you cross the creek. So I'd assume the farm is on the other side of a creek."

"That's right. Do you know where the creek is?" asked Sawyer.

Larry spoke up. "That would have to be Rock Creek, out east of town."

Lawrence nodded. "Larry, get dressed and saddle up so you can show Sawyer the way. Sawyer, that farm is in between two big bends in the creek. The road crosses Rock Creek, cuts through the farm, and then crosses the creek a second time about a mile east."

Larry got up and started to his room.

Jeffery said, "Do you mind if I go also?"

"There ain't no need for the both of you to go. Larry will lead the way there, and then he'll turn around and come home," said Lawrence. "This is Sawyer's fight, and you boys will only complicate things for him."

"That's right," said Sawyer. "Me and Nancy will do this alone."

Larry came back into the room and Lawrence said, "When y'all get to the Hope farm, Larry, you stop there and return home. Sawyer, you ride on. The road will curve to the right before it crosses the creek. There's a bridge at that crossing. If someone is waiting on you, they will be on the other side of the bridge," said Lawrence.

"Thanks, Lawrence," said Sawyer as he shook the man's hand. He turned to Larry. "I'm ready to go if you are."

"I'll go get my horse and meet you outside," said the young man.

They had covered six or seven miles without any problems when Larry finally stopped.

"This is where I turn around. If I were you, I'd wait until just about daylight before I tried to cross the creek. Those men waiting to waylay you might be tired by then, and with the sun coming up, they may fall off to sleep," said Larry.

"Is there someplace to cross without using that bridge?" asked Sawyer.

"Yeah, I think so. I remember taking some cows across almost due east from here. You might see if the banks are sloped toward the water over there." Larry pointed to the east.

"We'll check it out," said Sawyer. "You head home, and thanks for your help."

"Thanks, Larry," said Nancy. "You get on home. Me and Sawyer will be fine."

"Y'all be careful out there," said Larry, and turned back toward home.

Sawyer and Nancy walked their horses until they found the creek and rode north a short distance until they found a crossing. Sawyer looked down at the water, not wanting to cross in the dark, but knew he had to. Abigail's life depended on him.

They took it slow as they entered the dark creek. Sawyer nudged Raven in a little farther, and the water only came up to the horse's knees. They crossed over and up the far bank.

When Nancy was across, Sawyer said in a whisper, "We're going to ride east a little ways and then turn north. The men at the bridge won't expect us to come in from that direction. If it goes as I plan, I can sneak up on them and cut their throats before anyone at the house knows we're here."

"You lead out and I'll follow," said Nancy.

They did like he said, and when they were far enough east, they turned north and found the road. Sawyer dismounted and went on foot to look for the men's hiding place. Every so often, he stopped and listened for noises that didn't blend in with the natural sounds of the night. Another few feet forward revealed the faint sound of someone snoring. Sawyer left the road and crept through the trees along the creek bank until he heard his prey up ahead. Armed with the skinning knife from his saddlebags, he made his way toward the snoring man. Sure enough, he was able to get right up to him.

Sawyer's left hand came down over the man's mouth and his right hand sliced the sleeping killer's throat. The surprised man tried to move but with a hand over his mouth and one on his chest, he quickly bled out and died.

Sawyer explored that side of the road and didn't find anyone else, so he went far enough up the road to cross over to the other side in case the other man was watching the path. It wasn't long until he heard water hitting fallen leaves. Whoever was up ahead must be relieving himself, and perfect time for Sawyer to make his move.

With catlike steps, he crouched down and crept forward until he saw the dark figure coming his direction. Sawyer stopped and waited until the man was upon him, then he stood up and plunged the knife into the man's abdomen near his heart. The man tried to scream, but nothing came out, and he went to the ground dead.

Sawyer went back to where he had left Nancy with the horses, and when he got close, he identified himself so she wouldn't shoot him.

"Did you take care of the bushwhackers?" she asked.

"I did, and they won't ever shoot anyone again."

Nancy handed him Raven's reins. "Good, they had it coming."

"Let's ride the creek and stay off the road if we can. I would like to come in from the back of the house if possible," said Sawyer.

They gathered up their horses and rode closer to the house. After several minutes, they were able to make out the old Jefferson homesite and a few outbuildings in the darkness. Sawyer left his horse with the bridle still on his neck and tied up Nancy's horse. "I want us to go slow and not make any noise all the way to the side of the barn," he said.

It would be daylight soon, and he wanted to be in place when whoever was in the house came outside to use the outhouse. That would be a good time to eliminate the captors and rescue Abigail if they let her go out.

Sawyer led the way to the side of the barn and Nancy followed behind him. He reached back and touched Nancy's hand. She stood still while he put his ear to the wall of the barn and listened. Someone was asleep in there, and he could hear them snore.

He pointed to the wall and put his palms together on the side of his head to let her know that someone was inside asleep, then he mouthed, "Stay here."

Keeping as quiet as possible, he made his way to the front of the barn, where the door was open about four feet. On catlike feet, he moved inside and stood still, waiting until he was able to see a few shapes. Walking inside the barn was difficult since there were buckets in the way and empty corn sacks that could trip him if he hit one with his foot. His training kicked in, and he went slowly, feeling his way toward the sound of the sleeping man. Just as he had one foot in mid-step, the sleeping man made a noise and turned over.

Sawyer pulled his gun, and when the snoring started again, he placed his hand over the man's mouth and hit him on the head with his pistol. Silence filled the barn. Sawyer reached down and removed the man's belt. Then he tied the unconscious man's hands behind his back, and removed the handkerchief from around his neck and stuffed it into his mouth.

Leaving the man tied where he found him, Sawyer backtracked to Nancy and had her follow him inside the barn.

"You stand inside the door so you can see the backyard, but stay out of sight if someone exits the house. If the guy I have tied up over there comes to, hit him over the head with your gun. I'm going to find a location to attack from."

"Okay, I'll be ready when you make your move," said Nancy.

By now it was beginning to get light, and Sawyer ran to what he figured was the smokehouse. From there, he had a clear view of the back of the main house. He stayed there and waited.

It wasn't long until the back door opened and out came Agatha, still wearing her nightgown. She went into the outhouse, and Sawyer looked at Nancy, motioning with his gun for her to watch Agatha.

Sawyer ran to the back door and entered, finding Abigail tied to a kitchen chair. She moved her eyes to the right, warning him that someone was in the next room. He rushed through the door that connected the kitchen to the living room and came upon the man who he assumed was Albert getting up off the floor from his bedroll. Sawyer fired one time, hitting him on the side of his head. Blood and brain splattered the wall. He ran back to Abigail and was starting to untie her hands when they heard the outhouse door slam. He dashed out the back door with his gun pointed at Agatha, and the running woman stopped in her tracks.

"It's over with. You are definitely your daddy's girl," said Sawyer. "You people never know when you're beat."

"Are you going to kill me like you did my poor helpless father?" screamed Agatha in a fit of rage.

"No he's not," said Nancy, coming out of the barn with her pistol in her hand. "Your family killed our parents and murdered my husband and tried to take my land." Nancy walked up to Agatha and hit her on the side of her face with her left fist. Agatha fell to the ground, but came right back up in a fit of rage. Nancy raised her gun and cocked back the hammer. "My brother doesn't kill women, but I do!"

The first lead ball hit Agatha Barnes in the chest. Her eyes got big as saucers, and she put her hand over the bullet hole. Blood seeped out between her fingers. The second and third shots also hit their marks to her chest, and the woman tumbled to the ground.

Nancy kept pulling the trigger until Sawyer ran to her and took hold of the gun. "Sister, she's dead."

Nancy started crying and hugged her brother. "Is Abigail okay?"

"Yeah, she's inside. Let's go in and untie her," said Sawyer.

Chapter Fifty-Two

Abigail was bent over, untying the rope binding her left leg to the leg of the chair. Sawyer kneeled and helped her get loose. He hugged her to his chest and smoothed her hair. "Darling, are you hurt anywhere?" he asked.

"No, I'll be fine now that you're here. Sawyer, I was so afraid of that crazy obsessed woman."

"I know. But you're safe now, and we're going to get you out of here and go home."

Nancy came over with a wet rag in her hand. "Look at me. I'll wash your face, and then we'll get you presentable for the ride home. Sawyer, you go get the horses. Abigail's is probably in the barn or around here someplace."

Sawyer kissed his wife. "I'll be back in a few minutes. You do whatever you need to, to get ready to ride."

Sawyer went to the barn, and the man he'd hit over the head had rolled off the hay where his bedroll lay and fallen on the hard floor. His arms were still bound with his belt, and he was struggling to get up.

Sawyer looked down at the man. "You lie still and don't try anything. I'm saddling you a horse and taking you to the county sheriff."

The bound man muttered something through the handkerchief in his mouth and lashed out at Sawyer with his booted foot but missed.

Sawyer saddled Abigail's horse and one for the man. Holding the prisoner by the arm, he walked him to the horse. The man got his foot in the stirrup and then Sawyer grabbed the heavyset man around his thighs and lifted until he could sit in the saddle.

Sawyer tied both horses to the back porch post and went after Raven and Nancy's horse.

When the two women came outside and Abigail saw one of her assailants on his horse, she reached over and grabbed Nancy's gun out of its holster, cocked the hammer back, and let it drop. But it fell on an empty chamber, since Nancy hadn't reloaded her weapon. Nancy took her gun back. Tears rolled down Abigail's face. "This piece of horse dung doesn't deserve to live."

"I'm sure he'll hang from the gallows," said Nancy.

Sawyer went to his wife and took her in his arms. "You'll have the opportunity to see him hang if you want. We're taking him to Sheriff Martin, and kidnapping is a hanging offense."

The man started muttering, but no one could understand him since the handkerchief was still in his mouth.

Abigail mounted up and rode alongside the man and struck him in the face with her closed fist. She looked at Sawyer. "I still think we should kill him and leave his body here for the buzzards."

"There's already been more than enough killing. Let's go see the sheriff," said Sawyer.

The people walking along the boardwalk in Iola stopped and watched as Sawyer, leading a horse carrying a man with his hands tied behind his back, and two women rode down the dusty street. They stopped in front of the sheriff's office and Sawyer called out, "Sheriff, I have a prisoner for you."

Sheriff Martin came outside. "Hello, Sawyer. Who you got with you?" He walked to the criminal sitting on his horse.

"I don't rightly know," said Sawyer. "I never asked him his name. He worked for the late Agatha Barnes, along with a man named Albert."

The man started to mutter again and squirmed in the saddle like he wanted to talk.

The sheriff ignored him and continued to talk to Sawyer. "I see, and where might Agatha and Albert be?"

"I was getting to that," said Sawyer. "Right across the bridge on Rock Creek, you'll find two brothers. I don't know their names, but they were employed by Barnes to kill me. Albert and Agatha are at the old Jefferson farm near the creek, and the other man who worked for her is in jail at Humboldt."

"I've already had him brought up here. I'll send some men out to collect the dead," said the lawman. "Abigail, are you all right?"

"I'll be fine as soon as my hubby can get me home," she said.

The man on the horse started mumbling again, and the sheriff said, "You keep quiet. I'm going to get you off that horse and when we're inside, you can talk." Sheriff

Martin grabbed him by the arm, jerked him off the horse, and looked at Sawyer. "Y'all head on out, and I'll take care of our new guest."

Two miles south of Iola, Abigail asked, "Why was that woman so adamant about getting revenge on you that she was willing to die over it?"

"Her father was the mastermind behind the criminal organization that murdered farm folks around Allen County and then stole their land, claiming that they owed money at the bank. When I left you in Clarksville and came back here, they had shot Nancy's husband in cold-blooded murder and were threatening her with violence if she didn't leave her house, so Bass could take it. I was still a soldier in mind and spirit, and I eliminated the entire gang. When Agatha's father, the big boss of the organization, came looking for me, I eliminated him too. But I'm not the same man I was back then, and I want this to be finished and not talked about as we go forward," said Sawyer.

Abigail leaned over in the saddle and took hold of his arm. "You give me another kiss, and then I'll consider what you said about this being over."

Sawyer shook his head and did what she'd told him to do. When they parted, she said, "I knew why you came back here from Clarksville. I fell in love with Sawyer, the soldier, the rancher, and, most importantly, the man. Those men who did those terrible things are all dead, and we'll leave it that way. No more talking about them."

"Thanks, Abigail. I'm tired of seeing people die."

Nancy kept quiet and listened to her brother and his wife. When they had kissed and stopped talking, she said, "Brother, I know what happened in Humboldt when you came back from the war. We're blood and have a few of the same traits. I killed an awful woman today, and I don't regret it one bit. I agree with the two of you, it's over, and I won't ever talk about my actions again."

Sawyer and Abigail both gave her a nod and they all moved out.

The three rode on to Nancy's house. The men who had taken the cattle to market had just come home and were turning their horses into the corral.

Edward came over to them with a smile on his face. "Y'all ain't going to believe this, but we sold the cattle for ten dollars a head."

"That's good. I only gave four dollars a head for some of those longhorns," said Sawyer.

"Miss Nancy, the girls have little Cade inside. I stopped by my house on the way here, and brought the womenfolk here with me," said Edward.

"Oh, thank you so much," said Nancy, and she headed to the house.

"Abigail and I are going home," said Sawyer. "I may not see any of you for a few days."

Chapter Fifty-Three

Three days after Sawyer and Nancy rescued Abigail from Agatha, Cowboy showed up at Sawyer and Abigail's front door with his hat in his hand and wearing new clothes.

"Come on in, Cowboy," said Sawyer when he opened the door.

"If it's all right with you, I'll stay on the porch. Nancy didn't want me to come over here, but I thought it was the proper thing to do."

"Well, can't you say whatever it is sitting down?" asked Sawyer.

Cowboy started pacing, wringing his hat in his hands. "Sawyer, I want to marry Nancy, and I was hoping I could have your blessing since you're her only kin."

Sawyer looked at the man he had fought beside, the man he'd rescued from renegades, the man who was his friend. "Cowboy, you have my blessing, and I'm proud to have you as my brother," he said, giving the man a big bear hug.

"Thanks, Sawyer. You can let me go now."

"Nancy told me this at our wedding," said Sawyer.

"I should have known that she told you. I asked her right before I left for Texas. I came here today because I wanted to get your blessing before we started planning the wedding. Now that I have it, I reckon I better high-tail it back over there and make some plans," said Cowboy.

"I think so," said Sawyer. "I'm sure Nancy is anxious for you to get back."

"So long, Sawyer, and thanks." Cowboy tipped his hat and rode out.

The following day Sawyer, Abigail, and the Monks family were sitting on Nancy's porch when Reverend Toliver and his wife pulled up in his buggy. The cowhands walked from the barn to the house to join the group.

Reverend Toliver married Nancy and Cowboy that day in a private ceremony under the big oak tree in her front yard. Sawyer and Abigail were the best man and bridesmaid. The ranch hands and the Monks family were the only ones to witness the occasion.

Sawyer held on to Abigail as the bride and groom kissed, both of them happy for the newlyweds.

The guests gave Nancy and Cowboy a few seconds before they rushed over to congratulate the couple.

Lilly Monks brought a big double-layer cake from the house, and Malinda brought a pitcher of punch. Beverly served the punch, and everyone in attendance toasted Nancy and Cowboy.

When the cake was all gone, Roy Monks led the horse-drawn carriage from the barn. Sawyer stood up from his chair and quieted everyone down. "Nancy and

Cowboy, we're all proud of the both of you being united in matrimony. Abigail and I have arranged for you to stay in the best rooms at the hotel in Iola as a wedding gift."

"Oh my, Sawyer, what a wonderful gift!"

Malinda and Beverly came out of the house with two traveling bags and set them in the back seat.

"Load up and head on out," said Sawyer. "Lilly and the girls will stay here and care for Cade and the house."

Chapter Fifty-Four

For the next five days following Nancy and Cowboy's wedding, Sawyer and Abigail stayed at their house. He wore a gun all day, and at night he put it under his side of the feather mattress to make her feel safe.

He could see the struggles that Abigail experienced during her terrible ordeal. She kept looking out the windows, making sure no one was outside. She seemed fidgety and was startled easily by any unusual noise.

Sawyer took her with him to the barn whenever he fed the horses. If he had to go out into the pasture to check on a cow, she was with him. He even took her with him to the neighbor's house to buy a few Guineas that would raise a ruckus if an animal or someone came into the yard. The couple even discussed getting a watchdog, to see if that might help her feel safe.

Nancy and Edward came to the house at the beginning of the next week and the Guineas made noise as they came up the lane. Sawyer was waiting for them at the back porch and Abigail stayed in the kitchen. When the two riders came around to the back of the house, he said, "Hello Nancy, hello Edward. Is everything all right?"

"Yes it is," replied Edward.

"How did you know we were coming to see you?" asked Nancy.

"The Guineas warned me that we had company."

"Maybe you should get a dog instead of those nasty chickens," said Nancy.

"Maybe so, but you didn't come here to talk about dogs and chickens, did you?" asked Sawyer.

"No we didn't. We came to discuss ranch business with you and Abigail. May we come inside and sit?"

"Of course, come on in. Would you like a glass of water?"

"I would," said Edward.

"No thank you," said Nancy.

Abigail came into the front room from the kitchen, drying her hands on the apron she wore over her dress. "Hi Nancy, it's so nice to see you. You too, Edward."

Their foreman smiled and Nancy hugged her sister-in-law.

"Sweetie, are you doing okay?" asked Nancy.

"I have my moments. Please have a seat and I'll get us a glass of water," said Abigail. "Sawyer, would you help me, please?"

"We'll be right back," said Sawyer and followed his wife to the kitchen.

Abigail filled the glasses and when she handed two of them to her husband, she mouthed, "What do they want?"

He shook his head and shrugged his shoulders.

They went into the living room and handed a glass to Edward.

"You said we had ranch business to discuss?" asked Sawyer.

Edward took a drink and set his glass on the table in front of the couch. "I recommend that you, I mean the ranch, lease some more grazing land for the cows. We only have two sections with any grass on them, and that's not enough to get the cattle through the winter. The other two sections won't be able to support but a few cows until we can get good grass established on the former farmland."

Sawyer looked at Nancy. "Why ain't Cowboy here discussing this with us?"

"Even though he's my husband and works hard on the ranch, he doesn't feel comfortable being one of the owners until he contributes either land or cattle to the operation. He's looking for land close by to purchase, but that may take a while."

"I understand that he may feel that way but he's family now and should have a say in ranch operations," said Sawyer.

"I'll tell him what you just said," replied Nancy.

Edward went on. "I spoke with Kyle Hamby, who lives two miles south of here. He owns two sections of land but has gotten too old and crippled to work it anymore. It's covered in grass, but the drawback is, there are no fences on his property. Me and Luke rode over the land, and on the south side is a sizable creek that would most likely keep the cattle from going farther south. To the west is open range all the way to the river, which is four miles away. And to the north is his neighbor's land, which is a plowed field. Me and Luke think that his property would give us a lot of land for the cows, and in the long run, we won't have to buy so much hay."

"That's fine by me, if Nancy, Cowboy, and Abigail are okay with it," said Sawyer.

"Me and Cowboy are good with it," said Nancy. "How about you, Abigail?"

"Oh, I'm good with whatever Sawyer says."

"Well then, I'll finalize the lease with Kyle and we can start moving cattle in three days," said Edward.

"Which ones are you planning on taking over there?" asked Sawyer.

"All the longhorns that are on this section where you live. It's the closest to the new graze. and then we'll have more grass for the remaining cows here."

"I'll go with Edward and pay Mr. Hamby," said Nancy.

Sawyer and Abigail sat on the back porch or under a shade tree for the next two days, watching the cowboys gather the cattle and move them closer to the gate by the house.

On that third day, when the drive was to take place, Sawyer went outside to watch the men get started. Roy and Luke had just brought some strays to the main herd of maybe five hundred head when Abigail came outside to join him.

She was dressed in britches, shirt, hat, gloves, and boots. The thing that stood out the most was his .36-caliber gun on her right hip.

"Mrs. McCade, what in blue blazes do you think you're doing?" he asked.

"Let's get our horses. We're going to move some cattle today, Mr. McCade."

Sawyer smiled at his wife, then leaned down and

kissed her. "Well okay. Let's get saddled up before they leave without us."

Sawyer could tell that moving the cattle that day did Abigail a world of good. She rode off and hollered at the cows, and talked to Cowboy and Luke. Later that afternoon, she told Sawyer that she never thought about her ordeal with Agatha the entire day while on the back of her horse.

On the way back home, Luke said, "You do know that we have room, and when spring gets here and the grass is turning green, we can handle another three or four hundred head of cattle."

"I was thinking the same thing," said Sawyer.

Chapter Fifty-Five

Eleven months had passed since Abigail was abducted and rescued. Occasionally, she still had a few frightful nights dealing with nightmares. It took weeks before she finally got to where she could be alone in the house. Sawyer knew the ordeal had stuck with her longer than either of them had anticipated.

They spent a lot of time talking about her fears and what she needed to do so she could put it all behind her. He did his very best to be kind and patient through all her nights of anxiety and distress. He either stayed home or took her with him everywhere he went.

His brother-in-law, Houston—no one called him Cowboy anymore—used the money from the sale of his land and cattle in Texas to buy a section of land adjoining the four that Nancy and Sawyer owned. The ranch operation now-owned-and-operated a ranching business that ran a little over two thousand head of cattle.

In those eleven short months since Nancy and Sawyer started their ranching operation, calves were being born from the mating of Longhorn cows and Shorthorn or Herford bulls. The pastures were divided so that the cowhands could keep the crossbred cattle separate from the pure Longhorns.

Nancy and Houston were expecting their first child, and little Cade was already walking and jabbering.

Sawyer often sat on the porch in the cool evenings. He liked to look out over the land to watch the cattle graze while the calves ran and played. He hardly ever wore a gun anymore; if he did, it was the shoulder holster.

He was proud of the man he had become as a husband and rancher, but that didn't compare to his and Abigail's accomplishments. Abigail's companionship was special to him, and he loved being married to the most beautiful woman he had ever seen. They did everything together and had grown closer than ever since her unfortunate ordeal. Sawyer was a grateful man married to a beautiful woman who was not only his wife but his best friend. She had taught him love, compassion, and humility. Something that he had lacked in his life before he met her.

One particular evening, he was rocking back and forth on the porch in his favorite rocking chair, watching a couple of young bulls butting their heads in a challenge to see which was the strongest. They would plant their hooves on the grass-covered ground and heave with all their might.

Abigail came out the front door to join him. "Sawyer, take your daughter while I finish cleaning the kitchen."

"Of course, dear. She needs to come outside and learn how to be a rancher like her mamma and daddy."

Sawyer cradled the six-week-old Becca, short for Rebecca, in his arms and began to rock, humming a tune.

He looked at her innocent face and then back to the two bulls, who had stopped butting heads and were now back to grazing. Sawyer paused rocking for a second as the proud daddy looked up into the heavens.

"Thank you, God," said Sawyer. He now had a family that would grow in the years ahead. The ranch that he had wanted after the war was now a reality.

A smile spread across his face as he thought back to the long ride home from Arkansas just after the Civil War ended. At the time, he had no idea what he would do or who he might become. But today, sitting on his own porch, holding his beautiful offspring, life after war was a good thing now. He was content, and he and Abigail would live a long and fruitful life together. Sawyer McCade was the happiest man alive at that very moment, and he couldn't imagine any other life other than the one he had.

A Look at:

Card, Kill Them All (Card Jordan 1)

Step into a pulse-pounding western adventure where justice rides on a bullet and vengeance blazes a trail across the untamed frontier.

In 1875, sixteen-year-old Card Jordan returns from his first solo hunting trip to discover a nightmare—his family brutally murdered by a ruthless gang. Scrawled in the dirt beside his mother's body are the words that will forever change his destiny: CARD, KILL THEM ALL.

Fueled by vengeance and armed with his father's Cavalry hat, Card plunges headlong into a relentless western adventure. He must leave his innocence behind and become a force for frontier justice, tracking the killers through the wilds of North Texas and Indian Territory. Along the way, Card endures heartbreak, illness, and the unforgiving challenges of the Old West, sharpening his skills as a gunfighter with every step.

As Card closes in on the gang's vicious leader, Ned Black, his quest for retribution becomes a test of courage, resolve, and the true meaning of justice. Will avenging his family bring him peace—or only more pain?

AVAILABLE NOW

About the Author

Monty was born and raised in Southeastern Oklahoma in the small town of Sawyer, which is nested along the banks of the Kiamichi River. He's owned horses and cattle, riding the former and working the latter. Over the years, he formed a deep connection and respect for the Old West and the courageous folks who braved the wild frontier.

Monty is an avid reader and is particularly enthusiastic when it comes to Western authors and novels. His love of reading sparked his desire to write his first short story. He loves writing about real places and landmarks from the 1800s. In college, he wrote a ten-page paper about his grandmother, born in 1886, who married at fourteen and took in five orphaned nieces and nephews shortly thereafter. Monty's love for history and penchant for storytelling earned him an A+, and he hasn't looked back since.

Now retired, he loves to travel, fish, spend time with his four grandkids, and tell stories. He looks for inspiration for future books wherever he goes, and he is a member of the Western Writers of America Inc.

www.montygarnerauthor.com